Rain on the Dead

Jack Higgins

W F HOWES LTD

This large print edition published in 2016 by
W F Howes Ltd
Unit 5, St George's House, Rearsby Business Park,
Gaddesby Lane, Rearsby, Leicester LE7 4YH

1 3 5 7 9 10 8 6 4 2

First published in the United Kingdom in 2015
by HarperCollins*Publishers*

A CIP catalogue record for this book is available
from the British Library

ISBN 978 1 51003 773 1

Typeset by Palimpsest Book Production Limited,
Falkirk, Stirlingshire

Printed and bound by
Printforce Nederland b.v., Alphen aan den Rijn,
The Netherlands

In fond memory of my dear mother-in-law,
Sarah Palmer

*Rain on the dead
and
wash away their sins*

—IRISH PROVERB

NANTUCKET

CHAPTER 1

The island of Nantucket, Massachusetts – high summer, the western end of the harbour crowded with boats, many tied up at the jetty. Among them was a scarlet-and-white sportfisherman named *Dolphin*. On the flying bridge, a grey-haired man sat at the wheel playing a clarinet, something plaintive and touching. He was around sixty, a white curling beard giving him the look of an old sailor.

The man who joined him from below, wearing swimming trunks, had dark tousled hair and the beard of some medieval bravo. He was fit and muscular, his smile pleasant enough, his only unusual feature two scars on his left chest which any doctor would have recognized as relics from old bullet wounds.

He spoke in Irish. 'Big night, Kelly!'

The other answered in the same. 'You could say that. It'll be dark soon, Tod – if you're going to grab that swim, it'd better be now.'

'I will. Keep your eye out for that kid, Henry, from the harbourmaster's office. He's bringing our passports and the credit card, so don't forget to speak like the Yank your passport says you are.'

He slid down the ladder, vaulted over the rail, and swam away. Kelly heard a call from the dock.

'Mr Jackson, are you there?'

Kelly descended the ladder. 'He's having a swim. I'm his partner, Jeremy Hawkins.'

Henry handed over the two passports. 'There you go, sir, Mr Jackson's credit card is in the envelope and your mooring licence covers you until Friday.'

Kelly took the package. 'Thanks, son.'

'That's great clarinet I just heard. Kind of sounds like Gershwin, though I don't recognize the tune.'

'It's an Irish folk song called "The Lark in the Clear Air". And you're right, I did put a bit of Gershwin in there.'

'I think he would have been pleased, sir. Are you and your friend professional musicians?'

'I was for a while and he does play decent piano, but on the whole we found other things kept getting in the way.'

'Well, that seems like a damn shame to me,' Henry said, and walked away, calling at another boat.

Kelly turned and looked out over the harbour to see how Tod was getting on, and saw him swimming towards a round buoy floating on a chain. Many people were diving or jumping off the boats, some in wet suits, generally having a good time while the light still held.

For his part, Tod stroked the last couple of yards, then grabbed onto the chain, aware of the unmistakable sound of a helicopter descending somewhere in the distance.

He hung there, listening, and two young men erupted from the water, like black seals in their wet suits. They were like twins, darkly handsome, the same wildness apparent in their faces.

The nearest one grabbed the chain and laughed as his brother joined them. 'Mr Jackson, I recognize you from your photo. We're the ones you came to meet. The Master sends his regards and hopes that success in our venture will make us your favorite Chechens. I'm Yanni and this is Khalid.'

He had no accent, which his brother explained in a rather mocking tone. 'Our parents were killed by barbaric Russian soldiers in the Chechen war. The wonderful American Red Cross saved us and our grandparents, and gave us a new life in good old New York.'

'Where thanks to the public school system, we emerged as normal American teenagers,' Yanni said.

'Creating a problem for Westerners who expect Muslims to look and sound like Arabs,' Khalid said.

'So what can Muslims who look like Westerners do?' Yanni added.

'Why, serve Allah as undercover warriors in the great struggle,' his brother said. 'And here we are. We've already checked out the house of our target. It's just off the beach, surrounded by trees – no problem. An easy one, this.'

Tod said, 'Except that every security camera on every property you passed walking along that beach probably has your faces now.'

'So we'll wear ski masks for the hit,' Khalid said. 'Why should it matter as long as the target is dead? That's all that counts.'

They were no longer smiling. Their faces were like death masks, their eyes pinpricks. They were obviously on drugs, which exasperated Tod, though there was no point in mentioning it now.

'I'm going back to that boat.' He indicated the *Dolphin*. 'I'll see you there in forty-five minutes.'

They didn't reply, simply turned and swam away, and so did he.

Hawkins was Tim Kelly, and Jackson, Tod Flynn, both of them Provisional IRA who had served sentences in the Maze Prison in Northern Ireland for many killings. Released during the peace process, they had become mercenaries. The situations in Bosnia, Kosovo, Iraq, and elsewhere offered highly paid security work and sometimes rather more than that, for Flynn had been a top enforcer with the IRA, and reputation was everything in the Death Trade. It brought the cautious phone calls, the offers of the big money that went with them, and the offer for this present job had been very big.

In the cabin belowdecks, he had a large whiskey, feeling strangely cold, and told Kelly about his meeting with the Chechens. Kelly said, 'I knew it was a mistake to get involved with sodding Muslims. What are we going to do?'

'There's not much we can do, but I'll tell you this. I'm putting a pistol in my pocket for when they come, just in case it gets nasty. You should, too,' and he hurried away to his cabin.

He showered and dressed, and as he did so, remembered the first time he'd heard the Master's voice, filled with quiet authority, and a touch of English upper class.

'Would that be Mr Tod Flynn?' the voice had asked.

'Who wants to know?'

'I've just credited your bank account with a hundred thousand dollars. Check for yourself, and I'll be back in fifteen minutes.'

Tod frowned, but called his bank and received the happy news that the money had indeed been deposited from a Swiss bank in Geneva.

When the second call came, he said instantly, 'Who is this?'

'People know me as the Master. That will do for the moment.'

'Al Qaeda,' Tod said. 'Everyone in the business

knows about you guys and the way you operate. Don't you have enough of your own people to call on? What do you want me for?'

'Oh, I'm a great admirer. That finance man in Nigeria you took care of – five hundred yards through an open window of a car doing seventy. Splendid work. I have a list. My favourite was the Russian paratroop general who glanced out of the turret of his tank for a moment during a street battle and you took him at five hundred yards.'

'Four hundred,' Tod said. 'And it was snowing. So what do you want?'

'I have a target, living quietly in a house on the island of Nantucket with a manservant. I'm sending in a couple of Chechen boys to knock him off. All I need from you is to keep an eye on things and pick them up when they're done. You'll be waiting in a boat off the beach and they'll swim out to you.'

'So I'm the getaway driver, is that it?' Tod laughed harshly. 'What's he done, this target?'

'No need for you to know. Let's just say he's an old enemy.'

Tod nodded. 'And what would be in it for me?'

'You've already got one hundred thousand. That's for you and your friend Kelly. I'll give you another hundred afterwards and take care of your expenses.'

As usual, greed won the day. 'Add another fifty thousand,' Tod said. 'Which rounds it to a quarter of a million, and I expect the full advance before we go.'

The man who called himself the Master paused, then said, 'Agreed.'

And Tod, some part of him already regretting it, said, 'Done. When do we meet?'

'That will never happen, my friend. You'll have to be content with my voice on the phone. I'll send you a coded mobile with the tickets.'

Tim Kelly was shocked when Tod told him about the call. 'Holy Mary, do we have to get involved with a bunch of Muslims like Al Qaeda?'

'You'll dance a jig when that money turns up in your bank account,' Tod said. Later, he did wonder why the Master wanted him at all. The mystery man had made all the arrangements and the plan itself was simple enough. It was the height of tourist season, and the two assassins would be just another couple of people strolling along by night, carrying beach bags that would contain a couple of silenced Glocks, more than adequate to handle the situation. When they were done, they could just walk away from the scene of silent slaughter, which wouldn't be discovered until morning, long after they had swum out to sea, each with a phosphorescent signalling ball held in his palm to guide in the waiting *Dolphin*.

It seemed *too* simple, and Tod couldn't think why, still couldn't as he finished dressing now, and then he heard a disturbance above. He hurried through the cabin, went on deck, and found Kelly switching on all the lights against the hurrying dark. The Chechens were there.

'What's going on?' Tod demanded.

'These two bastards are cracked, if you ask me,' Kelly said. 'They were sharing a bottle as they came along the jetty. That young guy from the harbourmaster's office remonstrated with them as they were boarding.' He pointed at Khalid. 'This one told him to fuck off.'

Tod grabbed Khalid by the front of his shirt. 'Stupid bastard, are you crazy? That kind of trouble is the last thing we need.'

Yanni reached in his beach bag and produced a silenced Glock. 'Touch my brother again and I'll kill you.'

Kelly, standing behind them, drew a Walther, but Tod released Khalid, laughing harshly. 'Go on, do it. Kill both of us, why don't you? Then tell me who's going to wait off that beach to pick you up.'

Yanni put the Glock away and smiled falsely. 'Hey, can't you take a joke, Mr Jackson? Khalid was having a laugh. Like boxers going in the ring for a big fight. You get kind of nervous waiting for the action.'

'Then I suggest you go, find the action, and get on with it, and we'll get on with our part of the job.'

Yanni laughed out loud. 'You know something,

you're a real funny man, Mr Jackson. I like you, I really do . . .'

He gave his brother a push and they scrambled up onto the jetty. Khalid took a bottle from his pocket, held it up, then tossed it into the harbour. 'Just kidding, Mr Jackson,' he said, and they walked away.

'Total fruitcakes,' Kelly said in disgust. 'Where the hell did this Master find them? Don't tell me he didn't know they had problems.'

'Never mind that for now. We've got half an hour to spare before we have to cast off and go round the coast to wait for them. I could do with coffee and a sandwich,' Todd said.

He led the way below, and as they reached the kitchen area, the coded mobile phone the Master had given him trembled. He took it out and switched it to speaker. He turned to Kelly, touched a finger to his lips and waited.

'Mr Flynn, I'm afraid something's come up that affects our plans,' the voice said.

'And what would that be?' Tod demanded.

'I've just heard from a source that the target is receiving guests tonight by helicopter.'

'We heard one arriving somewhere in the island not long ago,' Tod told him.

The Master's voice was unemotional. 'Probably the one delivering them.'

'They'll get a shock when they find themselves invaded by two crazy Chechens.'

'It's the Chechens we need to worry about,' the

Master said. 'His guests are General Charles Ferguson – who commands the British Prime Minister's private hit squad – and two of his top people, a Captain Sara Gideon and one Sean Dillon, a notorious IRA gunman who now works for Ferguson.'

'But I know these people, everyone in the Death Trade does.' Flynn was angry now. 'Why the hell would they be here?'

'It's time to tell you who our target is. It's the former President of the United States, Jake Cazalet.'

Tod was shocked. 'You lousy bastard.'

The Master continued. 'You must cancel the operation. I can't do it. Yanni and Khalid have no phone.'

'I see,' Tod said. 'You knew they were wild cards and too untrustworthy to handle your special phone.'

'You must try and stop them. Surely there's still time?'

Tod was so angry he switched off.

Kelly said, 'Christ, what a cockup. Maybe we'll be lucky and catch them walking the beach to Cazalet's house.'

'No, we won't,' Tod told him. 'I don't want anything more to do with this. We'll cast off right now, sail overnight to Long Island, and leave the boat at Quogue. Then we'll head straight to the airport and find the first plane that'll take us back to Dublin.'

'And not even try to pick the boys up?'

'Do you really think there'll be anyone to pick up? Sean Dillon is a bloody living legend of the IRA, as no one knows better than you, and this Sara Gideon lass has a Military Cross for killing Taliban. Not to mention Ferguson himself. No, those Chechens are dead meat. And frankly, I couldn't care less.'

The house stood in trees behind a vast beach reaching out from town. The helicopter had landed some distance away, where Cazalet's Secret Service man, Dalton, waited in a Jeep. He went to greet Ferguson and his people, who walked to meet him.

Ferguson shook hands. 'Here I am again, Agent Dalton. Nice to see you.' They waited as the helicopter drifted away.

Dalton said, 'It'll be back in the morning.' He eased Sara's bag from her hand and led the way to the Jeep.

'President Cazalet's really pleased to be seeing you. Mrs Boulder has left out a lovely supper in the conservatory.'

'The President? Is that how you still address him?' Sara asked.

Ferguson said, 'Technically, all former holders of the office retain the title for life, but I think it's a matter of individual choice. Cazalet says there can only be one Mr President and asks that I call him Jake. I could never bring myself to do it, so I make do with "sir".'

'Then "sir"' it will be for me also,' Sara said.

'I'm looking forward to seeing Murchison again,' Ferguson said. 'That's the dog of the house, Sara, a wonderful flat-coated retriever.'

'Who once saved the President's life, as I recall,' Dillon said. 'Although there's no official documentation of that.'

'Too bad he isn't here tonight,' said Dalton. 'Mrs Boulder has taken him home with her. She gets lonely since her husband died last year, and the President doesn't mind.'

He turned off the road at a point where high-wire fencing fronted the trees. He paused, waiting for a ten-foot gate to open slowly between stone pillars, and drove through, pine trees and lots of shrubbery crowding in from both sides. To the left, they could see a terraced conservatory and they continued, circling around to a formal garden that fronted the old Colonial-style house with steps leading up to a pillared entrance, the door standing open, light pouring out, and Jake Cazalet waiting to greet them.

'Charles, my dear old friend,' he cried. 'Marvellous to see you, marvellous to see all of you.'

Then he rushed down the steps to greet them, arms outstretched.

After embraces, Ferguson said, 'Now, this was all most mysterious. It's always a pleasure to see you, sir, but why were we summoned?'

Cazalet said, 'Oh, it's nothing dire. The President

wanted to invite you to the Oval Office, but couldn't because of the publicity such a visit would have caused. He said you were in New York to meet the British ambassador and proposed that we kidnap you for a night so that I could say a heartfelt thanks on his behalf for your handling of the Husseini affair. If Iran had been able to use his work to perfect their nuclear bomb – well, it wouldn't bear thinking of. All three of you did a remarkable job, and we are in your debt.'

'Please tell the President how grateful we are,' Ferguson said. 'But it's all in the game these days, and a damn ugly game it is.'

'You've got that right,' Cazalet said. 'It's a complete mess. Jihadists allied to Al Qaeda have infiltrated international terrorism like the plague, linking groups worldwide, each controlled by that anonymous leader always known as the Master, a shadowy figure, a voice on the phone. Backed by millions obtained from oil-rich states in the Middle East. They're extremely dangerous.'

'As Captain Gideon can attest to first-hand,' said Ferguson.

Cazalet turned to Sara, who said, 'Dillon and I were targeted by Al Qaeda in London, with orders to dispose of us.'

'I notice you're still here,' Cazalet said.

'You should see her in action, sir,' Dillon told him.

'So there's a Master responsible for London?'

'He also handled affairs in Paris,' Dillon said. 'And later in Beirut.'

'And turned out to be General Ali ben Levi, the commander of the Iranian Army's Secret Field Police.'

'He was killed in London, though we weren't responsible,' Ferguson said. 'But we had his body disposed of. We couldn't see the point of sending the details to the Iranian military, and they're still looking for him. They had no idea of his Al Qaeda connection.'

'And I'm sure he has already been replaced,' said Cazalet. 'That there's a new Master out there now. Terrorism has completely changed warfare as we know it. Enemies without uniforms, bombs everywhere.' He shivered. 'End of an era. But enough of that for this one night. Tonight, let's go out on the terrace and have some champagne. Or perhaps you'd prefer a glass of port, Charles?'

'Now you're talking, sir,' Ferguson said, and led the way out.

The dining room opened into the conservatory, where great sliding doors gave access to the terrace with tables and lounging chairs, the garden crowding in, flowering shrubs of every description, tall pines and palm trees that someone had experimented with over many years. The scent of flowers, the sound of grasshoppers chirping in the lights, all combined to create a kind of tropical splendour.

'Wonderful,' Sara said. 'I love the smell of it.'

Cazalet said, 'It's a bit of a jungle really, but at my age I can do as I please, so I let it run riot. Reminds me of my tours in Vietnam. Come, have something to eat.'

CHAPTER 2

Yanni and Khalid had reached the house without the slightest trouble, following the beach, passing the occasional barbecue, sometimes a fire. There were lots of other people in the darkness, laughter, guitar music, but there was no one by the Cazalet house.

They passed it, turning up the left side of the estate through a marshy area with reeds growing high, found a place where the fencing gaped and squeezed into the garden. They could hear conversation and laughter, light through the trees and shrubbery.

They had taken pills before leaving the cottage and were feeling the effects. 'Are you getting high, brother?' Yanni whispered.

'I'm floating, man,' Khalid told him.

'Then put on your face.'

Yanni pulled the ski mask on, and grinned as his brother did the same. 'You look like a clown.'

'So do you,' Khalid told him, and took his Glock out and dropped the shoulder bag to the ground. 'Let's do it,' he said to Yanni, and led the way cautiously.

★   ★   ★

18

On the terrace, they were at the coffee stage, Ferguson and Cazalet sitting down and Dalton pouring it out. Dillon was standing by the open window, enjoying a cigarette. There were three stone steps leading up to the terrace crowded with overgrown shrubbery, and Sara stood there waiting for her coffee. Yanni crouched, watching her admiringly. His brother stood a few feet away in heavy bushes behind the balustrade.

They could have killed everyone if they'd fired without hesitating, but the drugs had taken full control and they were shaking with excitement, and it was Yanni who made the first move.

'Let's go!' he shouted, and took three quick steps up to the terrace. Sara half turned and he hit her sideways in the face, pulled her against him, and rammed the barrel of the Glock into her side. 'A present from Osama, with regards from the Master.'

'Oh God,' she moaned, as if terrified, and closed her eyes, apparently fainting, starting to slide to the floor so that he was losing his grasp.

Dalton was already drawing his weapon and jumping in front of Cazalet. Khalid stepped out of the bushes and shot him in the chest. In the same moment, Dillon drew the Colt .25 he always carried in a rear belt holder and fired rapidly three times, the hollow-point cartridges tearing Khalid apart, hurling him back into the shrubbery.

Yanni howled in rage, allowed Sara to slide, and fired once at Dillon, denting the wall. Sara withdrew the flick knife from the sheath she always wore around her right ankle, sprang the blade, and stabbed him under the chin. He dropped his weapon, fell back down the steps, and lay in the middle of rosebushes, kicking as he choked to death.

There had been surprisingly little sound, just the dull thud of silenced weapons, and Cazalet was already on his knees with Ferguson, examining Dalton, Dillon standing over them, his gun still in his hand. Dalton groaned and Cazalet looked up in relief.

'Thank God, he was wearing his vest. I'll leave him to you, Charles, while I raise the alarm.'

He found Dalton's cell phone and called in. 'This is Cazalet. Empire down. Two intruders down. Request Nightbird Retrieval.'

He said to the others, 'Which means a cover-up job by the CIA. It should be easy enough, since all the weapons were silenced, so the neighbours shouldn't have any idea what's been going on, and as you know, the occasional helicopter landing is nothing new here.' He turned to Sara. 'I can see why they awarded you a Military Cross in Afghanistan, but your suit will never be the same again. It's badly bloodstained.'

'No problem, sir, I have another in my luggage. If you'll excuse me, I'll go to my room to shower and change.'

'Of course,' he said.

As she moved out, Dillon murmured, 'Are you okay?'

She held up a bloodstained hand. 'As usual, not even shaking.'

'Just like in the Bible. The sword of the Lord and of Gideon.'

'Which doesn't help me in the slightest,' she said, and went out.

Cazalet eased Dalton onto a chair and gave him some brandy to sip. Dillon poured champagne for himself and Ferguson, who said, 'God knows why we're drinking this, but it's a pity to waste good stuff.'

'That's what I was thinking.' Dillon toasted him.

Cazalet cut in: 'Did you two hear what the one she killed said to her?'

Dillon nodded. 'A present from Osama, with regards from the Master.'

'It appears that Al Qaeda has found us, right here in Nantucket.'

The Nightbird was of medium size, black in colour, the engine noise remarkably quiet. A dozen men in black overalls got out. The officer in charge, wearing the same black uniform, was calm and efficient.

'Colonel Sam Caxton, Mr President. We'll be treating this as a crime scene, although it's not a police investigation. If you would, I'd like you all to wait inside and two of my men will record interviews with you, both individually and together, to cover all the bases. We also have a doctor with us, just to check you all out.'

'We're at your service, Colonel,' Cazalet said.

'If you could move in, we'll get started. It goes without saying that we're delighted to find you in one piece.'

He went out, and Cazalet said to Dalton, 'How do you feel, Frank?'

'The vest I'm wearing can stop a forty-four.'

'You deserve a medal, jumping in front of me like that.'

'That's what I'm paid to do, sir.'

Cazalet clapped him on the shoulder. 'Let's all return to the kitchen and have a cup of coffee. It's going to be a long night.'

On the *Dolphin* out at sea, the lights of Nantucket had faded when Kelly entered the wheelhouse with two mugs of tea and gave one to Tod, who was listening to a jazz trio.

'Sounds good. Who is it?' Kelly asked.

'No idea. It's Nantucket local radio. I was waiting to hear if there were any news reports.'

'What are you going to tell the Master?'

'I'll think of something.' He sighed. 'Probably better get it over with.'

'I'd like to hear that,' Kelly said. 'Put it on speaker.'

In a moment, they were connected.

'This is Tod Flynn.'

'I've been waiting to hear from you. Are you still in Nantucket?'

'We're at sea. Couldn't contact the Chechens,

and there didn't seem to be any sign of action at the Cazalet house. Nothing on local news, either, so I decided the smart thing to do was leave.'

The Master cut in. 'Then I have news for you. Yanni and Khalid are dead, bagged, and waiting to be flown away.'

Shocked, Tod made an instinctive response. 'That's impossible. How could you know that?'

'Because I provided backup that even the Chechens did not know about. A woman sympathetic to our cause that I had in place. After I phoned you, I called her. She had seen you casting off to go to sea and smelled a rat, went after the Chechens herself, and was right behind when they entered Cazalet's jungle of a garden. There was no time to warn them.'

'So what happened?' Tod asked.

'The Chechens were butchered. Dillon shot Khalid, and the Gideon woman stabbed Yanni with a knife. When a CIA black unit arrived by helicopter, she slipped away.'

'A hell of a cool customer,' Tod said.

'Yes, a remarkable lady – but to business. Admit it, you were doing a runner. You never even attempted to warn those boys.'

'Okay, we were. We know Dillon from way back in the Troubles. Nobody messes with him, he's a killing machine and the Gideon woman is the same. If we had tried to find them, we'd be lying dead next to the Chechens.'

'Nevertheless, that was your charge. You owe me a quarter of a million dollars.'

Tod said, 'We didn't sign up for any of this. You lied about everything. It wasn't our fault that things turned out the way they did.'

'Don't think you can shirk your responsibility. Everybody is accountable. But you can keep the money.'

Tod was astonished. 'What do you mean?'

'You and Kelly are men of a mercenary persuasion, as the song goes. Go home to Drumgoole, to your horses and the stud and your aunt Meg – she runs things there, correct? Oh, and you'll be losing your niece Hannah; she just heard yesterday that she's been accepted by the Royal College of Music in London.'

'Damn you, how do you know all this?'

'I know everything, Tod, I thought you knew that. I just want to make sure you realize that there is nowhere that you – and yours – can go that I can't touch. Now, I have tickets waiting for you at the airport. When you get home, shave off the beards and it will be as if you never left Ireland, and I'm sure you'll have plenty of friends to swear you never did. Good luck and try to stay sober. I'll be in touch soon, and this time you are going to earn the money you have from me.'

He faded away, the *Dolphin* plowed on, rain bouncing off the screen. Kelly said, 'Is he for real?'

'Oh, yes, and a barrel of laughs, too. I admire his fine turn of phrase.'

'Well, he's going to want something for his quarter of a million bucks, God knows what. Here, you take the helm. I'm going below to try to get a little shut-eye.'

Sara Gideon lay in bed in a dressing gown, unable to sleep. Outside, the wind howled, rain rattled against the window. There was a knock at the door, which opened and Dillon peered in. 'What's happening?' she asked.

'Ferguson and Cazalet are downstairs and there's an intermittent flow of information about the two people we knocked off. They're Chechen brothers, but American, brought into the country as refugees with their grandparents, who have since died. Shouldn't be long before we know everything about them.'

'Wouldn't be too sure about that.'

'Why?'

'It was all so wild, weird even. It was as if a piece of foolish nonsense came to an unlooked-for end.'

'That's really quite literary,' Dillon told her. 'Are you by chance regretting the fact that you had to kill that maniac?'

'Not at all, he'd have finished us all off. Dammit, Sean, he got a shot off at you that just missed.'

'And you put the knife in to save my life, girl,' Dillon said. 'So bless you for that.'

'Anything else happening?'

'Well, Ferguson's spoken to Roper in London,

25

and I'm sure he's been put to work. You can feel free to contact him on your mobile if you want.'

In the Holland Park safe house in London, Major Giles Roper sat in his wheelchair in the computer room, wearing a dressing gown, a towel about his neck, his bomb-ravaged face shining with sweat. He was smoking a cigarette and drinking a glass of whiskey when Sara called.

'My goodness, love, so you've been playing executioner again?'

'No choice, Giles, not this time. Sean was his usual deadly self.' She shivered. 'Seconds, Giles, just seconds. It could have turned out so badly for all of us.'

'Well, it didn't, and that's all that counts.'

'So who do you think was behind them? You're the best that I know at squeezing answers out of cyberspace.'

'I have to agree with you, but these things take time. Besides, you have to remember that what happened tonight in Nantucket *didn't* happen. Nobody heard a thing, nobody saw a thing. And if nothing happened, then no one can claim responsibility. I'm certainly not going to go online saying there's a rumour that there was an assassination attempt on former President Jake Cazalet. Then everyone would know – and all the wrong sort of people *would* claim responsibility.'

'So what can you do?'

'Just wait and watch, see if anything unusual

pops out. You never know. Anyway, get some sleep. I'll see you when you get back.'

Dalton had reluctantly gone to sleep on a couch in the sitting room, and Cazalet and Ferguson sat in the kitchen, drinking coffee and turning things over between them.

'I'm almost flattered that someone feels I'm worth being a target,' Cazalet said.

'Nonsense, you were a great President. Your death would have made headlines around the world.'

'Maybe,' Cazalet admitted grudgingly. 'Anyway, there was one matter I was asked to raise with you before you leave.'

'What's that?'

'Colonel Declan Rashid. He was an enormous help in the Husseini business, so disgusted at the way Husseini was treated by the Iranian government that he deserted their army and supported your people in everything.'

'And took a couple of bullets in the back doing it. He's agreed to work for us when fit again,' Ferguson added.

'Well, apparently the CIA would like to talk with him. They're really quite keen on it, though I expect I know your answer. I told them I'd pass it along, but wouldn't promise anything.'

'And you were right. You know Rashid's history. He was a paratrooper at sixteen and, during Iran's war with Saddam Hussein, made his first jump

27

into action without training. Over the years, he has been wounded many times, and now his doctors, including our own Professor Bellamy, say enough is enough. He needs time to recuperate. The CIA will just have to retire gracefully from the conflict.'

Cazalet laughed out loud. 'That'll be the day. Anyway, let me just check my office messages. I've given Mrs Boulder the morning off, so when it comes to breakfast, we'll all have to pitch in.'

He went out. Ferguson boiled the kettle, made tea, and Dillon entered. 'You look fit,' the general said.

'Didn't sleep worth a damn, but I dry-shaved and had a cold shower. I could kill for a cup of tea.'

'Help yourself,' Ferguson told him. Cazalet came in. 'Your helicopter arrives at eleven. Also, photos of the Chechens have just come through. The machine's pumped out some extra copies.'

'Goodness me,' Ferguson said. 'They look like any young convicts from about a century ago.'

Dillon helped himself, took one of the sheets and slipped it in a pocket. Cazalet said, 'Right, who's for bacon and eggs?'

'Sounds good to me,' Ferguson replied, but Dillon said, 'I think I'd prefer a last walk on the beach, sir. I can get something down there.'

So he left them to it, tiptoeing past Dalton – still sleeping heavily on the couch – and letting himself out on the drive, and was soon walking along the beach. Plenty of tourists were out already, for it was a particularly fine day.

He wandered through them, uncertain about what it was he was looking for. The Chechens fascinated him. Two real wild boys, and how had they got to Nantucket? Looking at the crowded harbour, he found a very possible answer. The sea, because that's what he would have done.

He went up on the jetty and started to walk along past people working on the decks of the boats, others diving into the harbour and swimming. A young man with a money satchel around his neck and a register in his hands was working his way along the line of boats. The name tag on his shirt said 'Henry'.

Dillon said, 'Can you help me? Have you ever seen these guys?'

He unfolded the sheet with both photos. Henry stopped smiling. 'What have they done, are you a cop?'

'I work for a security firm,' Dillon said. 'They've been leaving unpaid bills all over the place.'

'Sure, I've seen them. Yesterday evening, they were around here really high on something and drinking booze, and they had an argument with people on one of the boats. Went off making a hell of a row.'

'Show me the boat involved.'

'I saw it leave last night as it was getting dark, which was strange, because the mooring fee was paid until Friday. It was a sport-fisherman, a rental from Quogue. Two guys on board named Jackson and Hawkins. I brought them passports. Maybe they're just cruising about out there.'

'I don't think so. Did you do any copying of their passport details, photos and so on?'

'No, that would be illegal. Anyway, the national agency just tells me either it's okay or not okay.'

'It's just that I'd been wondering whether you could use a fifty-dollar bill.'

Henry smiled. 'Only if you'd be happy with a picture I took of them on my phone. They were chatting on deck.' He took the phone out of his pocket.

'Why did you take it?'

'Because jazz and swing are my thing, and Mr Hawkins plays a great clarinet. He turned an old Irish folk song, "The Lark in the Clear Air", into pure Gershwin, special enough to bring tears to the eyes. That's him with the white beard.'

The disguises, which in effect the bearded faces were, had succeeded brilliantly. Not for a moment had Dillon recognized them from the photo, but Henry's musical anecdote was unique. It related to the deepest and most poignant moment in Dillon's life, which meant the man in the white beard was Tim Kelly and the other was probably Tod Flynn.

'Does it ring any bells, sir?'

'Not really, it was a hell of a long time ago. I'd like to have a copy of the photo anyway, if that's okay with you. Can you email it to me?' Dillon held out the fifty and gave Henry his number.

'You're more than welcome, sir.' Henry sent it and slipped the bill into his pocket. 'Have a nice day.'

Dillon walked away, his mind in a turmoil, never so conflicted. It was obvious that he should tell Ferguson what he had discovered, but it was impossible to discuss why at the moment, and certainly not with Sara around. She served the Crown, wore the uniform. On the other hand, they were returning to Roper, the bomb-scarred hero trapped in his wheelchair. He nodded to himself. Roper would know what to do. He hurried along the beach.

At the end of the strand across from the house, a mobile beach concession had appeared, a sandwich and burger bar on wheels with canvas chairs and fold-up tables, most of which were taken. Dillon stopped and ordered tea and an egg sandwich, sitting close to the bar.

The woman sympathetic to the Cause whom the Master had mentioned to Flynn sat not too far away, keeping an eye on the situation over the road where the helicopter had just drifted in behind the house. Her name was Lily Shah, and she worked in the dispensary at the Army of God headquarters in London.

She was quite small, wore sandals, a Panama pushed down over fair hair, her blue linen shirt loose over khaki shorts. She removed her Ray-Bans to scratch her nose, revealing a calm, sweet face. She was forty-five and looked younger. On seeing Dillon, she replaced her Ray-Bans, took a sound enhancer from her shirt pocket, slipped it into her right ear, and adjusted it as Sara Gideon crossed the road.

'Anything special happen while I've been out?' Dillon asked as he finished his tea.

Lily could hear perfectly as Sara answered. 'The President wants Cazalet safe. The black team from last night is coming in tomorrow to start doing all sorts of security things to the house. Since it's been in the family since before the Civil War, Cazalet is not pleased. Even more, the staff have been suspended. Dalton's going to hang on to hand over to the team, and Mrs Boulder keeps Murchison, bless her. And I'm here to tell you to get a move on – we're boarding the helicopter in minutes.'

They hurried across the road and entered the drive, cutting it very fine, for it seemed no more than five minutes later that the helicopter lifted above the trees and turned away, causing a certain excitement among the tourists.

Once things settled down, Lily wandered along the beach, turned across and down the side of the house, the marshy area with the reeds growing high. She stood looking at the place where the fencing gaped and, on impulse, scrambled through into the garden, and then ventured a little further cautiously to where the carnage had taken place.

The windows on the terrace slipped open and Dalton walked through, comfortable in shirt-sleeves, a can of beer in one hand, and sat down on the swing chair. He opened the newspaper, and she pointed her right index finger at him, thumb raised, then smiled, eased back through the jungle of the garden, and left.

Walking back to town, barefoot at the sea's edge, she phoned the Master and told him what happened. 'So Ferguson and company will be back to trouble you again very soon.'

'And trouble is the right word. He's been a thorn in our side for much too long. I'm sure he was responsible for the disappearance of General Ali ben Levi. We know that he flew in here, to Northolt, in pursuit of the traitor Declan Rashid. This is a fact.'

Referring to Ali ben Levi as flying 'in here, to Northolt' Airport had been an unfortunate slip, for his choice of words had indicated that the Master was speaking in London. Come to that, Lily was sure she'd once heard Big Ben chiming in the background of one of his calls. Lily was intrigued, but concentrated on the matter at hand.

'The Russians tried to eradicate Ferguson and his Prime Minister's private army some years ago. All they got was a bloody nose,' she said.

'Who told you that?'

'Dr Ali Saif, when he was head of education at the Army of God.'

'What a damn traitor he turned out to be. Another turncoat.'

'But not to Ferguson. As far as I know, MI5 claimed him. Perhaps he found it preferable to facing twenty-five years in Belmarsh under anti-terrorism laws,' Lily said.

'A traitor is a traitor. And as far as Ferguson goes, I've received an order from the Grand Council. They want revenge for ben Levi. Nothing less than assassination. Bullet or bomb, I'm open to either.' He laughed. 'I suppose I could put it to Tod Flynn.'

Lily was shocked at the implication. 'The political upheaval would be enormous.'

'And so it should be. That would be the point. That no one is safe, not even those working at the highest level for the Prime Minister himself, and *there's* a thought.'

Lily tried to sound enthused, but managed only a muted 'I hear what you say.'

'Good. With luck, you should be back in London tomorrow. Give my sincere thanks to Hamid Bey for allowing you the few days' leave to assist me as you have. He has been a revelation once he took over as imam. AQ acknowledges its debt.'

'I'll speak to him as soon as I get back. Is there anything more I can do for you?'

'Yes, I'd like you to look up Tod Flynn's niece at the Royal College of Music. She interests me. It seems that when she was fourteen, she lost her parents to a car bomb on a trip to Ulster and was crippled.'

'Dear God,' Lily said, genuinely shocked.

'Her father was Flynn's elder brother, Peter. Flynn became her legal guardian, and she's been raised by him and her great-aunt. I want to know more about her. Something tells me it'll come in handy for keeping Mr Flynn in hand.'

'The usual file?'

'Exactly, now be on your way. God go with you.'

She continued to walk at the water's edge, thinking of Pound Street Methodist Chapel, now converted to the mosque and the headquarters of the Army of God charity. She was a cockney girl who from childhood had only wanted to be a nurse, had qualified against the odds and then joined the Army Medical Corps. In the seven years that followed, one war after another had given her an unrivalled experience of the barbarism, the butchery, that people could inflict on one another.

In Bosnia, she'd seen open graves with hundreds of Muslim bodies tumbled into them, as if the Nazis had returned to haunt Europe. In Kosovo, you had to get out of the ambulances to pull the corpses of mothers and their children to one side of the road so you could continue. In northern Lebanon, she had served with the Red Cross and UN with only a handful of soldiers to try to control the rape and pillage outside the mission hospital.

It was the only time she'd fought, and that was in desperation, picking up a dead soldier's Browning pistol and emptying it into savage faces one after another, and then the trucks had roared up with the men and rifles. Al Qaeda, ruthlessly shooting wrongdoers, bringing order where there was none.

Two years later and out of the army, a nursing sister at the Cromwell Hospital in London, she'd met the love of her life, Khalid Shah, a handsome Algerian charge nurse, married him, and they'd moved to the dispensary at Pound Street, where it became clear that he was a follower of Osama bin Laden.

It was a year later that the cruelty of life took him away from her, when Al Qaeda called him in for service in Gaza, an Israeli air strike a month later ensuring his stay was permanent. She couldn't hate Jews because of what had happened, for her dark secret, even from Khalid, was that she was only a Christian through her father, because her mother was a Jew and had married out. Hamid Bey, the imam at Pound Street Mosque, seemed a reasonable man, and as the dispensary was multi-faith, Lily's Christianity caused no problem. The fact that he also looked the other way where Al Qaeda was concerned was understandable, when one considered that the greater part of his congregation supported it. She had yet to realize that she was entirely wrong in her assessment of Hamid, a savage zealot, who supported the Cause as much as the Master.

As her husband Khalid had been very open about his dedication to Al Qaeda, Lily had, to a certain extent, been drawn in. After all, it was the ruthless actions of Al Qaeda in Lebanon, saving many lives, including her own, which had made it possible for the most important relationship of her life to take place. And when that had ended, the telephone call from the Master to commiserate had opened a door into what followed. When General Ali ben Levi had been killed, she had not wondered why the Master's voice had suddenly become different, for it was her place to serve without question.

But what had taken place here in Nantucket was like a bad dream that wouldn't go away and not like anything that had happened before. Not even like Lebanon and the massacre and the intervention of Al Qaeda, which had saved so many lives.

She glanced at her watch and saw the time. If she was going to catch the ferry, she'd have to run. She slung her beach bag over her shoulder and started to do just that.

NEW YORK

LONDON
IRELAND

CHAPTER 3

The helicopter was comfortable enough, three tables with bench seats around the windows and a room in the back for privacy, into which Cazalet and Ferguson vanished on boarding. A young man and woman were in attendance, wearing identical dark blue suits and ties, and they ushered Dillon and Sara to one of the tables, belted themselves up for takeoff, and afterwards indicated that coffee or tea and a selection of sandwiches were available.

'Would there be anything stronger?' Dillon asked the woman, her colleague having gone off to serve the back room. 'Like Bushmills, or would that be too much to ask?'

'Of course not, sir, we keep a full range of spirits. And you, Captain?'

'You must forgive my friend being so particular, but he's Irish and not as other men. I'm probably being just as awkward by asking if you have any English breakfast tea.'

There was the ghost of a smile as the woman said, 'Of course, Captain, I think I can manage that.'

She returned with their drinks on a tray and served them, and Sara thanked her. There were three double miniatures on Dillon's small tray, a glass, but no water. 'That should make you happy,' Sara said as she poured her tea. 'It's almost as if she knows you.'

Dillon had opened his first miniature as she spoke, poured it, and tossed it down. 'Maybe she does,' he said as he opened another.

'I don't understand you, Sean,' Sara said. 'You were fine earlier when you came to tell me you'd had a word with Roper and so on, but now you're in another place.' She drank some of her tea. 'You seemed okay when you went off to have a walk on the beach, but since then, not even a smile. What's wrong? Are you upset about something?'

'You mean like shooting a guy three times in the head last night? Why should I let a little thing like that bother me? You, on the other hand, the sword of the Lord and of Gideon.' He picked up the third miniature, started to open it, and slammed it down.

Sara reached over and put her hand on his. 'What is it, love? This isn't you. Just tell me. It's what friends are for.'

'Damn you, Sara, for being so bloody nice. I'm truly sorry, but let's leave it. If you'll excuse me, I'm going to the toilet.'

She sat there thinking about it, thoroughly worried, then he returned fifteen minutes later, a fresh face on him, hair combed. He smiled. 'If I do that again, punch me in the mouth. I don't usually stress up that easily, but I seem to have done so this trip.'

Not that she believed him, but she couldn't take the matter any further when the young man appeared from the back room and told them that Cazalet wanted to see them.

It was comfortably furnished, some chairs clamped to the floor, a desk, a large television screen, a computer. Cazalet sat behind the desk, Ferguson to one side. Ferguson said, 'We'll be in New York pretty soon, so this is the last chance for the four of us to discuss what's happening. Sit down.'

Which they did, and Cazalet said, 'The President has decided to be guided by the CIA in this matter, and their advice is this. They agree that the attack was sponsored by Al Qaeda, but they want to keep it under wraps. They'll immediately start investigating, but want to keep Al Qaeda off balance by not saying a word about it publicly. All they'll know is that I'm obviously alive and walking around. Al Qaeda won't know what to make of it, won't know what did occur.'

'Only that their two assassins have gone missing?' Sara nodded. 'That makes for an interesting situation.'

'Well, they love their martyrs,' Ferguson said. 'We all know that, so handled this way, it denies AQ the oxygen of publicity.'

Cazalet said, 'Maybe they'll slip up, make a

mistake, try to communicate with each other. That's helped us before.' Cazalet smiled grimly. 'And we have a lot of drones.'

'Which still requires us to know where the bastards are in the first place,' Dillon said. 'To be able to score.'

There was a slight pause. Sara glanced at Dillon, then said, 'Thank you for being so clear, sir.'

'Very weird.' Dillon shook his head. 'We were in New York at the UN to discuss the Husseini affair with the British ambassador, then got yanked out for an evening with you, and it was that which screwed up Al Qaeda's plan. I'm surprised they didn't get wind of our trip to Nantucket. The UN's a sieve, all those countries crammed into that building on the East River. Don't tell me Al Qaeda doesn't have its fingers in that pie.'

'That may be,' Ferguson said. 'The point is how we handle it now. I've had word from London. It seems the President has spoken to the Prime Minister, who has agreed to all this but with some reluctance. So that settles it. As far as the public is concerned, none of this ever happened.'

He turned to Dillon. 'Have you anything to say? You usually do.'

'About the dream I had last night? It's fading rapidly.'

'Go on, back to your seats. We need a last few words together, don't we, sir?' he said to Cazalet.

Dillon and Sara turned to go. He had his hand

on the door handle when Cazalet called, 'Just a moment, you two.'

They turned, and Sara said, 'Yes, sir, was there something else?'

'Yes.' Cazalet was smiling. 'Very private and between us. Frankly, I don't give a damn about the CIA. Thank God you were there last night. It's people like you who guard the wall for all of us, and I, for one, am extremely grateful.'

There was a silent moment as his words sank in, and then Sara smiled and said, 'It's been a privilege to serve, Mr President,' and she followed Dillon out.

Later that day, in the Gulfstream heading home, Ferguson stayed towards the front of the cabin video-conferencing while Flight Lieutenant Parry moved along from the cockpit, visited the kitchen area, and came out with coffee.

'We've got some storms threatening in the mid-Atlantic, so make sure you belt up if you go to sleep. And' – he looked a little uncomfortable – 'could you advise Dillon to watch his drinking?'

He and Sara exchanged a look, then he moved back towards the cockpit. She reached up to a locker and found a couple of blankets, and Dillon, who'd been to the toilet, returned with a glass in one hand. She tossed one blanket to him and draped herself in the other.

'I'd be careful with your booze intake, Sean,' she advised. 'Rough weather forecast.'

They sat with their backs against the rear bulk-head on either side of the aisle, and he touched her. 'Just the one, and then I'll probably have a sleep.'

'So you've still got problems?'

'As a matter of fact, I've been thinking about what Cazalet said about people like us guarding the wall.'

'That was a fine thing for him to say, but then he's a fine man.'

'I agree, but it made me feel ashamed.'

She frowned. 'But why should it do that?'

'Oh, not living up to the image, in my case allowing a mental aberration to cloud my judgment, but I see sense now. I've been wrong, but at least when you see you have, you can put it right.'

'Are you going to talk to Ferguson about it?'

'Eventually, but I need to consult Roper first.'

Ferguson switched off the screen, turned, and called to them, 'That's it for me. I'm taking a pill. With any luck, I'll sleep through to Farley Field,' and he pulled out a blanket and settled down.

Sara lowered her voice. 'Come on, Sean, what's going on?'

'Well – I believe I know the identity of two people involved in the Nantucket business.'

She was astonished. 'But you haven't said a word of this to anyone. Why not?'

'There's an Irish connection, a question of mistaken loyalty to family on my part. It has to do with the death of my father in Belfast in 1979, when he blundered into a firefight with British paratroopers and was killed. I can see now I was wrong. It will be put right, that's all that counts. God knows what Ferguson will do, but I'll take that as it comes.'

'Sean, what are you talking about?'

'Well, if you'll shut up for a while, girl dear, I'll tell you,' Dillon said. 'In my early years in Collyban, my father in London trying to make a place for us, I was raised by my uncle, Mickeen Oge Flynn. His son Tod and I were like brothers. We tackled the old upright in the front parlour together, learned to play passable barroom piano, accompanied by our friend, Tim Kelly, on clarinet. A boy with a real gift, believe me. Then I went to London and got involved with the theatre, as you know.'

'Sean, what on earth has this to do with anything?'

'It has to do with *everything*,' Dillon said. 'Be patient. What with the Troubles, we just kept in touch with the family by phone from London, and I knew that Tod and Tim Kelly had made something of their music, played in bars and clubs, and it was Uncle Mickeen who phoned me with the news of my father's death. He said that nobody from Collyban would be going up to Belfast for the funeral, as it would be too dangerous.'

Sara said, 'And I imagine he thought the same for you.'

'I suppose so, but I told him I'd be there, and

he said he ought to warn me that Tod and Kelly, who were going to take care of the funeral, were Provisional IRA and on the run as far as the army and police were concerned.'

Sara shook her head. 'So, needless to say, you went?'

'A rushed flight, Belfast greeted me with pouring rain. Taxis were available, though expensive. I was dropped at St Mary the Virgin Church in Samson Street near the docks. Three vans had men standing around them under umbrellas, watching. I hurried through a decaying graveyard and entered the church.'

'And what did you find?'

'It was like most of them, half dark, burning candles, an effigy of Mary and the Christ child by the door. I remember putting my fingers in the holy water – habit, I suppose. There was the aisle between the pews towards the altar, a closed coffin on trestles, an old priest in a cassock, no vestments. Tod stood there, obviously startled by the door opening, a Browning ready, and Tim Kelly was opposite, a clarinet in his hands.'

'"God in heaven, you've come." Tod stepped forward and gave me a hug.

'"It's where I should be," I told him, "But there are vans outside, and we seem to be attracting attention."

'"UVF Protestant bastards," Kelly told me. "They'd hang the lot of us if they could."

'"Never mind that now," Tod said. "Father

Murphy's done with his prayers and will see to the burial with the sexton after we've gone. It only remains for Tim's tribute."'

'Tribute?' Sara said. 'What was that?'

'My father had a favourite old Irish folk song, "The Lark in the Clear Air", and the sound of that clarinet played in the Gershwin style, soaring up to the roof, was the most poignant thing I'd ever heard, has remained with me forever. There were voices outside, but the music stilled them. There was a moment of silence as Kelly finished – then a brick came in through a window. Tod pulled a Smith & Wesson revolver out of his pocket and pushed it into my hand. I'd done a training course on the use of weapons on stage.'

'Which was your only experience of handling a gun?' Sara said.

'Exactly. Father Murphy shouted, *You know the way out, boys. Don't worry about me. They wouldn't dare to harm a priest.* The church door swung open, men burst in, the first one already firing a pistol,' Dillon continued. 'He hit me in the left shoulder. I staggered back, firing blindly, and caught him in the throat. Tod shot the man behind them, driving the others back, then got an arm around me, hustled me into the vestry, Kelly following, down some steps to a cellar. There was a manhole in a corner, they opened it, and we scrambled into a sewage tunnel, big enough to walk along, all the way down to the docks.'

'And obviously, you got away,' Sara said.

'That part of the city is an underground network of similar tunnels. I remember us surfacing in some sort of large garage full of trucks and vans, and then I blacked out, so I can only tell you what I was told later.'

'And what was that?'

'The Provos had the trick of using ambulances they'd got their hands on, manning them with their own people wearing hospital uniforms. Tod told me they had a real nurse pump me full of morphine, then he and Kelly scrambled in the back wearing hospital scrubs and we were away, sailing through every roadblock.'

'To where?' Sara asked.

'Over the border into the Republic, to a charity hospital called St Mary's Priory run by the Little Sisters of the Poor, a nursing order.'

'Strictly speaking, that was illegal.'

'Of course, but how far do you think they'd get putting nuns in court in Ireland? Tod and Kelly left me to it, then came back three weeks later when I was fit to leave.'

'An amazing story, the whole business, changing your life like that. You were forced into killing that UVF man, I can see that, but why did you join the PIRA and set foot on such a course?'

'It was nothing to do with the death of that UVF man, everything to do with what happened to Father Murphy. He and the sexton buried my father as he had promised. A week later, somebody ran him down one night, left him dead in the road.'

Sara was distressed. 'It *could* have been an accident, Sean.'

'You don't believe that any more than I did at the time. But never mind. You've been so gripped by my story that you've lost sight of why I told it to you.'

'What are you saying?' she asked.

He showed her the photo on his phone. She examined it, frowning. 'Who on earth are these two?'

'Supposedly their names are Jackson and Hawkins, two Americans visiting Nantucket in a sport-fisherman out of Long Island. I got that photo of them from a nice kid named Henry working out of the harbourmaster's office. Remember I went for a walk on the beach down to the harbour? I found Henry checking boats and showed him the Chechen photos. He recognized them as having had a row with Jackson and Hawkins the previous evening, told me he was surprised to find that they had already left in their boat, which was booked to stay until Friday.'

'Are you trying to say you know these men?'

'I certainly don't recognize them, but beards and bushy hairdos are a very successful disguise, so I've always found. But some things can't be disguised. What if I told you that Henry's a jazz enthusiast and heard Hawkins, the one with the white hair, playing the finest clarinet he'd ever heard but didn't recognize the music. When he asked what it was, Hawkins told him it was an old

51

Irish folk song called "The Lark in the Clear Air", which he'd played in the style of George Gershwin.'

Her eyes widened as she stared at him, stunned. 'Oh, my God!'

'Yes, my love, my cousin and Tim Kelly can disguise themselves as much as you like, but no one could disguise that music from me, wouldn't you agree after hearing my story?'

'But what would they be up to?'

'Obviously I don't know, but what I do is that they were both released from the Maze Prison during the peace process. I heard some talk of them being in the security business, so called. As we know, that could mean anything. It gave me the greatest shock of my life when Henry spoke to me. It was so strange, brought everything back. My first thought was that I'd have to turn them in. I couldn't face that, but I've got my head round it now. I'll have to tell the General and face the consequences.'

There was a stirring up in front of them and Ferguson looked around. 'No need, Dillon, I heard the whole bloody saga – taped it, as a matter of fact. How lucky for me that my pill box was empty so I hadn't been knocked out as I usually am on these flights.'

'So it's the Tower of London, next stop?' Dillon said.

'You certainly deserve it. You've given me all sorts of problems now. What do I do about the CIA, what will the Prime Minister have to say?

I'm going to send it all on for Roper to digest. In the meantime, we have another four hours to Farley. May I suggest we dim the lights and try to get some sleep?'

At the Holland Park safe house, Roper, seated in his dressing gown in his wheelchair in the computer room, was ecstatic and laughing to himself as he reached the end of the recording. He reached for the Bushmills Irish whiskey bottle and poured a large one.

He tossed it back, broke into laughter, and said, 'God bless you, Sean Dillon. When my day is dull, I can always rely on you to brighten it up.'

Tony Doyle, the military police sergeant on night duty, had just pushed in a trolley with bacon sandwiches and a tea urn, his bomb-devastated boss being unable to drink coffee any longer.

'You're a happy man, Major, what's caused that? Have there been developments?'

He had been in the computer room the previous night with Roper when Ferguson had come on screen from Nantucket to mention the assassination attempt and Dillon and Sara's part in it. The Holland Park safe house operated outside the normal security services such as MI5 and 6, who hated the fact that, thanks to Roper's genius, a great deal that passed through his coded computers stayed private except to Ferguson and his people, all sworn to secrecy.

Roper said, 'You've got to hear this, Tony, fresh

from the Gulfstream. Pass me a bacon sandwich and a mug of tea. No pictures, just audio.'

When it was finished, Tony Doyle shook his head. 'That was a bad thing some bastard did to Father Murphy.'

Roper, taking a more sober attitude now, agreed. 'The Troubles were not only hell on earth, they were disgusting morally.'

'Yes, but you only realized that by being there,' Doyle said. 'Take me. A Jamaican Cockney born and bred in London. I wanted to see the world, so I joined the British Army, and what did I get?'

'Seven tours of duty in Northern Ireland.' Roper took another sandwich. 'And what did *I* get out of it? This wheelchair.' He switched on multiple screens. 'Let me see if there's anything interesting I can find about the Flynn clan.'

Doyle said, 'Yes, Major, *you* really are a casualty of war.'

'So are you,' Roper told him, not looking at him but scanning the screens. 'And so were Dillon and Tod Flynn and Tim Kelly, who marched to the beat of the wrong drum. Hmm. Apparently, the only person in this affair who showed good sense was Tod's elder brother by ten years, Peter. He avoided the Troubles by moving to the Republic to work for a distant relative on his horse farm and stud at a place called Drumgoole.'

'A sensible option, I'd say.'

'I'd agree, especially as seven years later, the relative died of a heart attack and left the farm to

54

Peter and his wife, on the condition that they gave a home to his widowed sister, Margaret Flynn, known to the family as Aunt Meg.'

'Some people have all the luck,' Doyle said.

'Especially when Tod and Kelly were released from the Maze and he was able to offer them a home.'

'To work on the farm?'

'Some of the time. It's also the address of a security firm. Obviously, it didn't take them long to get down to business.'

'So you think Nantucket was part of their agenda?'

'I don't know.' Roper was frowning, manipulating his control. 'Not good,' he said. 'That was unfortunate. There's a daughter, Hannah, who was eighteen in June. Four years ago, on a trip to Belfast, she lost her parents to a car bomb. She was badly injured and in hospital for months. Her father died intestate.'

'What does that mean?'

'No will. She inherited everything, but as she was only fourteen, the court appointed Tod and Aunt Meg as joint guardians.'

'Well, as I wouldn't trust that Provo bastard an inch, I'm happy the aunt's around to keep an eye on him,' Doyle said.

'There's some personal stuff here on her Facebook page,' Roper said. 'Good news. She must be a real hotshot on the piano. She's just been accepted as a student at the Royal College of Music.'

'Sounds like you're taking a personal interest.'

Roper switched off most of the screens, leaving only one, the emergency cover. 'Enough already. I could do with a steam, shower and shave and fresh clothes, then I'll doze until our lord and master appears.' He was very cheerful. 'Can you assist me, Sergeant?'

'That's what I'm here for, Major,' Doyle told him, and followed as Roper switched on his wheelchair and led the way out.

And in Ireland, high on a hill that loomed above Drumgoole Place, Hannah Flynn reined in a mare named Fancy as she saw the Land Rover approaching the house in the far distance. It was raining lightly, evening drawing in, and she wore an Australian drover's coat, a broad-brimmed hat pulled down over auburn hair that framed a calm and serious face. She spoke into a cell phone.

'They're here, Aunt Meg.'

Margaret Flynn took the call in the kitchen. At seventy-six, she was a handsome woman still, in jerkin and riding breeches, hair white, face tanned. There was still a hint of the actress she had been in her youth.

'Wonderful, but when your uncle Tod called from Dublin Airport, he said they wanted to change as soon as possible.'

'More cloak and dagger again,' Hannah said. 'When are they going to learn that the IRA is past its prime and nobody wants to know any more?'

'Of course, love, Tod and Kelly know that. It's just security work they do these days. Anyway, I've given the stable hands the night off, so you get here when you can. We'll have dinner a little later.'

There had long been a dark suspicion that the car bomb which had killed Hannah's parents and injured her so badly had been meant for Tod. Perhaps someone was settling an old score? Hannah frequently remembered that possibility with some bitterness.

She sat there for a moment longer, stroking and patting the mare. 'That's men for you, Fancy, still playing games in the schoolyard and then never seeming to learn that sometimes people get hurt.' She shook her head. 'Security, my arse,' and she rode away.

Tod and Kelly showered in the wet room on the ground floor of Drumgoole Place, then set about shaving their beards, which took quite some time. After that, they sat side by side and Meg cut their hair in turn.

'Will ye watch what you're doing, woman?' Tod said.

She cuffed him. 'You're in good hands. I learned everything there is to know about hairdressing in my theatre days. I'll see to the cuts first, then use the right solvents to treat the colour.'

Hannah moved in from the corridor, limping, a walking stick in her right hand. 'What a couple of beauties.'

'You show some respect, girl,' Tod told her. 'We've been away earning a crust. Takes money to run this place.'

'Where to this time?'

Kelly looked hunted, but Tod said, 'Nothing much, just inspecting the security system for the company that runs the ferries from Harwich to the Hook of Holland. No big deal.'

'A pity.' She tossed some matches into Tod's lap. 'I found those in the kitchen. They advertise a café in Nantucket. That would have been much more exciting.'

She went out, and Meg picked up the matches. 'I wonder where these came from?'

'Don't ask me,' Tod said. 'I don't know.'

She said, 'You told me you were dressing up to put one over on a rival firm for someone you were working for?'

'So we were,' he said. 'Just business, Meg. Is she pleased about the Royal College of Music?'

'I'm not really sure. It's not residential, so accommodation is going to be a problem with it being London.'

'Don't worry, these days we've got plenty of money. Just keep on cutting and bring back my auburn hair.'

Which she did, cut Kelly's very short and darkened the white to grey.

'Marvellous,' Tod said. 'I feel human again. Let's have dinner.'

★   ★   ★

Ferguson's Daimler and driver were waiting when the Gulfstream landed at Farley. Dillon had left his Mini Cooper there, but Sara had nothing.

'I've decided not to go home tonight,' Ferguson said. 'I'd like to have words with Roper sooner rather than later, so I'll stay in the guest wing at Holland Park.'

Dillon often did the same, and said, 'I'd like to join you.'

'That's fine by me, but I expect you'll be wanting a lift to Highfield Court to see your grandfather?' he said to Sara.

'He won't be there, he's touring the lecture circuit. "God and the Mind of Man," his favourite topic. Everyone wants Rabbi Nathan Gideon these days.'

'And so they should,' Dillon told her. 'He's a great man.'

'Actually, I'd welcome your input, Captain,' Ferguson said, 'So jump in and we'll be on our way. We'll see you there, Dillon.'

When Roper returned from the shower, it was to find that Ferguson and the others had arrived and had gone upstairs to unpack, but he had another visitor waiting.

Dr Ali Saif was an Egyptian with an English grandmother who'd not only sent him to Eton but supplied him with a UK passport under filial law. A brilliant scholar, a senior lecturer in archaeology at London University, he had initially found

59

Osama's message attractive enough for him to offer his services to the Army of God charity. As with others, one could be drawn into the activities of Al Qaeda without realizing it, especially with the hypnotic tones of the Master on the telephone to guide you.

He'd been caught in a bad situation, however, and his decision to act on the side of right had not only saved lives but impressed Ferguson enough to save him from prison and find a use for his talents as an interrogator of Muslims suspected of terrorism, at Tenby Street safe house run by MI5.

'Have they arrived?' Ali enquired, and before Roper could answer him, Ferguson, Sara, and Dillon walked in.

'Ali, it's you,' Ferguson said in surprise.

'We were talking earlier,' Roper told him. 'He's been fully informed about the latest development. After his past services to us, I felt he could be trusted to keep it to himself.'

'Your account of Belfast 1979 was extraordinary, Mr Dillon,' Ali said. 'It's certainly possible that these men, Flynn and Kelly, could have something to do with the affair. I've already learned in my short time at MI5 that individuals from dissident Irish groups have used their past experience in all kinds of violent situations, from Eastern Europe to the Middle East. Does anyone else know?'

'No, actually, which is rather interesting.' Ferguson said. 'I haven't mentioned them to anybody, not even the Prime Minister.'

'So what are you going to do?' Roper asked. 'Keeping the PM uninformed seems risky to me.'

'You'll have to wait and see.' He turned to Ali Saif. 'I need hardly remind you that what you've heard is privileged and not for your masters at MI5. Now, meanwhile, you've had personal experience with AQ in London. What's your take?'

Sara said, 'Considering it's not very long since the last Master died, this new one seems to have got to work pretty quickly.'

'But Al Qaeda is organized for such situations,' Ali told her. 'There is a Grand Council, nobody knows where, which issues its decisions in Paris. General ben Levi was killed in London, and nobody outside the Council knew his true identity until the day he died. His replacement, from what little we have discovered about this worldwide cult, will have been put in place instantly.'

'So what was the purpose of the attempt on Jake Cazalet's life?'

'He looked like easy meat, and they would have destroyed an American icon, shown the world they could get away with it, given two fingers to the Great Satan.'

'Only they didn't,' Ferguson said.

Ali nodded. 'Because of the coincidence of your visit, General.'

'Ironic, really,' Dillon said. 'If the President hadn't decided to have us privately thanked, Cazalet would be dead now.'

'Exactly.' Ali shrugged. 'Of course, the Grand

Council will want revenge. They will attack us here in London, a spectacular, perhaps. You notice I say *us* because I must include myself now. I'm a turncoat of the first order, as far as they're concerned. If I dared to show my face at Pound Street, I'd be stoned.'

'Come, come, Ali, we mustn't exaggerate. The Army of God is a legally organized charity. Their dispensary serves all denominations, and the imam of the mosque, Hamid Bey, is highly respected.'

'Smoke and mirrors, General. As you say, I have had personal experience with AQ. The City Corporation, the police, tread carefully for political reasons. In my time when I was on the wrong side, the Master spoke to me on a regular basis, and I'm not naive enough to think I was the only one. As for Hamid Bey, he is a dog and not to be trusted.'

'All right, I'll take your word for it,' Ferguson said. 'We'll have to take extra care from now on.'

Ali opened his jacket to show a Walther in a shoulder holster. 'I'm also wearing a nylon-and-titanium vest. I hope the rest of you are.' He smiled, leaned down, and kissed Sara's hand gallantly. 'You always astonish one, Captain Gideon. God is good to you.' He nodded to the others. 'If you'll excuse me, General, I'm on night duty at Tenby Street.' He turned and walked out.

'My goodness,' Ferguson said. 'He's really come on. It was a wise choice to take a chance on him. I'm sure you'll all take heed of his advice. His experience with this cult of the Master thing is obviously unique. Anyway, I think we could also do with some supper. Let's see what the kitchen's got for us. As for Hamid Bey, I always thought the bastard was too good to be true.'

There was a loud bang, the front door crashed open, and Doyle shouted, 'Help, man down!'

Dillon and Sara ran out into the hall, to find Doyle dragging a hospital trolley out of the hallway and outside.

The Judas gate had swung open and Ali Saif was lying half outside it. As they raced toward him, Doyle said, 'He told me he was going to walk back to Tenby Street, so I accompanied him, opened the Judas gate, and somebody shot him. He bounced off the gate, half turning. There was a second shot, he staggered into me and went down. Silenced weapon, just a couple of coughs. God knows I've heard enough of those in my time.'

Sara appeared with two wound packs and ripped one open as she examined Ali, who was obviously in shock, eyes staring.

'The vest seems to have stopped one round, but the other has ploughed into his right thigh, no protection there.' She staunched the blood flow as best she could. 'Help me, Sean, there are morphine ampoules in the pack, get one into him.'

Ferguson was talking briskly into his phone, and Ali reached and clutched Sara. 'You must take care, Sara. I told you the Grand Council wants revenge and I'm the first to be punished. The traitor . . .'

He fainted, and Ferguson said, 'Rosedene's alerting Professor Bellamy. Let's get Saif into the Land Rover and get him up there.'

A couple of hours later, the matron at Rosedene, Margaret Duncan, approached the group, still in theatre scrubs and looking tired. 'My goodness, General, another one. When will somebody say enough is enough?'

'Not in the world as it is today, I'm afraid. How is he?'

Professor Charles Bellamy walked in and answered for her. 'Alive, and that is one good thing. The vest did exactly what it was supposed to and stopped a heart shot.'

'Which, if successful, would have killed instantly, but Ali started thrashing around, so the shooter put a random round into him and cleared off,' Dillon said. 'What's the verdict?'

'A serious wound in the left thigh, damage to bone and sinew,' Bellamy told him.

'Just how bad?' Ferguson asked.

'He'll be here for several weeks, and recovery and therapy will take some time.' He smiled at Sara. 'As you know only too well, Captain, better than anyone else here, including myself.'

'God help him,' Sara said. 'While I'm here, can I ask how Declan is?'

'He's asleep. You can see him tomorrow.'

'We'll leave them both in your good hands.' Ferguson turned to the others. 'Back to Holland Park, I think, and may I point out that we still haven't had any supper.'

It was much later that they rejoined Roper in the computer room and discussed the attack.

'Takes me back to Afghanistan,' Sara said. 'All the trappings of high security mean nothing once you step outside base where some fifteen-year-old with an AK can take a pop at you at any moment.'

'And get away with it,' Dillon said. 'Though I'd say in this case whoever was responsible tonight was aware of Ali's habit of walking to Tenby Street after visiting us. It's not much more than a mile. Lots of trees on the other side of the road.'

'I agree,' Roper said. 'Looks like the work of a silenced AK with a folding stock, probably carried in an ordinary supermarket shopping bag.'

'A reinforcement of Ali's warning earlier about Al Qaeda's Grand Council seeking revenge, and that means full alert, people,' Ferguson said.

There were a few moments of silence as they all thought about it, and it was Sara who spoke first. 'There is the business of Flynn and Kelly, sir. What are we going to do about that?'

'Yes, you left it hanging,' Roper pointed out.

'Perhaps somebody should go and see them,' Sara said.

'Maybe we all should.' Ferguson laughed out loud. 'That could be fun.'

'You mean just turn up at Drumgoole out of the blue?' she asked.

'It's a thought.' Ferguson was considering it, a slightly wicked smile on his face. He looked at his watch. 'Just after eleven. A man like Flynn's bound to be up. Find the number, Major. I'll leave it to you what to say, Dillon.'

In the parlour at Drumgoole Place, they were sitting by a log fire, Tod Flynn and Kelly, Aunt Meg and Hannah, a film just finishing on television. Hannah was nearest to the house phone when it rang, and she answered.

'Drumgoole Place.'

'Put me on to Tod,' Dillon said.

She bridled. 'And who the hell are you, mister?'

Dillon laughed. 'From the sound of you, you'd be Hannah.'

'Aren't you the cheeky one.' Meg had turned off the television and they were staring at Hannah. 'I'll only ask you once more, then I'm putting the phone down. Who are you?' She put it on speaker so they could all hear.

'Your second cousin, girl dear, Sean Dillon. Now, put him on.'

The look of incredulity on her face was quite something as she held out the phone to her uncle. 'He says he's Sean Dillon.'

There was silence for a moment, Kelly in immediate shock, but Tod took a deep breath and the phone. 'Is this a joke?'

'No, it is me, you old sod. How did you enjoy Nantucket?'

'I don't know what you're talking about.'

'Stop being stupid, it doesn't suit you. Tell Kelly if he'd not been noticed playing "The Lark in the Clear Air" on his clarinet, I'd never have known you were there. I work for Charles Ferguson these days, but I'm sure you know that.'

'Sold out to the Brits, Sean, didn't you?' Tod said.

'Oh, we all sold out to somebody, in your case the Master and Al Qaeda. We'll be over to see you in a few days, and don't try to run away. There's nowhere to go.'

He cut off the call, leaving Tod sitting by the fire, numb with shock, the others staring at him. It was Meg who shook her head and spoke first. 'The Lord help us, Tod, what have you done now?'

But Hannah was already on her feet, leaning on her walking stick. 'The glory days are back, is that it, Uncle Tod? Well, you and the damn IRA and Al Qaeda can go to hell,' and she limped out of the room, banging the door shut behind her.

In the computer room, it was all smiles. 'Good work, Sean, you've stirred the pot there,' Roper said.

'Excellent, Dillon, you really put the boot in,' Ferguson told him. 'I would judge he's in a state of total shock, but we must strike while he's still off balance, give him time to get really worried,

67

then we'll take the Gulfstream to Ireland and descend on him.'

'On them, sir,' Sara said. 'I thought the young girl was pretty feisty. I liked the sound of her.'

'Well, just remember she might be the enemy, Captain, but I'm for bed. It's been a rough old week.'

'Tomorrow is always another day,' Sara said. 'Hang on to that thought.' They filed out, leaving Roper to doze in his wheelchair, his screens still on.

CHAPTER 4

Half past midnight, Hannah sat on a stool in Fancy's stall in the stud stable at Drumgoole, a horse blanket over her shoulders, the mare content with an occasional glance at her. It had been a refuge during four years of pain from the car bomb – the dim lights, the stable smell of fourteen horses, always had a deeply calming effect. She leaned back and closed her eyes, allowing her rage to ebb away, heard the door open at the other end of the stables, then voices.

Kelly said, 'What happens now?'

'You're forgetting he presented us with one of his coded mobile phones.' Tod's smile was mirthless. 'I'm going to call him right now.'

'At this time in the morning?'

'He boasts that he can operate from anywhere, doesn't he? Let's see if he does.'

Kelly laughed harshly. 'Put it on speaker, I don't want to lose a word.'

A couple of minutes, no more, and then the voice echoed, calm and full of authority. 'Say who you are.'

Tod told him. 'So we can cut the crap.'

'Why, Mr Flynn, you're angry,' the Master replied. 'An emotion that leads to stupidity, and that's not to be recommended in our line of work. Is there a problem? If so, tell me.'

'With pleasure,' Tod said. 'What would you say if I'd had a phone call from Sean Dillon a couple of hours ago, asking me if we'd enjoyed Nantucket? They know about you, Master-whoever-you-are, and the Al Qaeda connection – everything.' There was a perceptible pause. 'Are you there?'

'Oh, I'm here, Mr Flynn, and considering what act of human stupidity has brought us to this situation.'

Kelly broke in, shouting, 'Trying to find somebody to blame, are you?'

'Because there usually is,' the Master said calmly. 'Do get your friend to shut up, Mr Flynn, then you provide me with a sane explanation and don't leave anything out.'

Which Tod did, and when he was finished, said, 'And that's the truth of it, so what do you think?'

'That it was just bad luck. It was pure chance that sent them to Cazalet's house, and pure chance that Dillon made the connection to the two of you.'

'One hell of a coincidence,' Tod said.

'Chance, Mr Flynn – life is, in many ways, ruled by it. Of course, sometimes it's fate. It wasn't by chance that your father was Sean Dillon's uncle. There's something almost karmic about it.'

Kelly intervened again. 'We've no time for all this shite. What do we do when Ferguson and his crew turn up here?'

'Wrong question,' the Master told him. 'It should be, What can *they* do? There's no evidence the attack even took place, and Cazalet's walking around as if nothing had happened. So what can they do to you? It's rather amusing when you think of it, Ferguson couldn't even get you arrested.' Somewhere in his background was an unmistakable sound.

At that, Hannah erupted from Fancy's stall and took a few steps toward them, leaning heavily on her walking stick.

'There's nothing amusing about it, because I've heard everything.'

Kelly tried to grab her, and she slashed the walking stick across his shoulders. Tod dropped the phone on the table and caught her as she tried to get past him to the door.

'It's all right, Hannah love, I'll handle it.'

'It's not and you won't.' She shook her head. 'I don't know who this Master of yours is, Uncle Tod, but I've heard enough to recognize an evil bastard when I hear one.' She raised her voice. 'A bastard who lives in London! You should keep your window closed. Everybody knows the sound of Big Ben.'

She pulled away from him and returned to the other end of the stable, leaning heavily on her stick, and disappeared into Fancy's stall. Kelly watched her go, then picked up the mobile and handed it over.

'Are you still there?' Tod asked.

The Master replied calmly, 'Do we have a problem with your niece?'

'No, I promise you. Since the car bomb that took her parents four years ago, pain has been her constant companion. She's stressed about it, and now this. I'll take care of it.'

'Such sentimentality comes rather late in the day from a man who has been responsible for as many deaths as you have. But it's understandable, considering there are those who think the bomb which killed her parents and crippled her was meant for you.'

Tod said gravely, 'There was always that possibility.'

'Not in this case, Mr Flynn. In fact, I know the names of the two men who set that bomb.'

Tod was very still. 'And what must I do for those names?'

'Dillon told you he'd be coming within the next few days. I wouldn't be surprised if the Gideon woman and possibly even Ferguson himself came with him. Those people have been a running sore in Al Qaeda's side for long enough. I'm sure a man of your expertise, and Kelly's, can find a way to dispose of them one way or another.'

Kelly shook his head. 'The man's crazed, Tod.'

'Not at all,' the Master said. 'I happen to know that at the back of Drumgoole Place, at the foot of the mountain, is a bog – the Bog of Salam, isn't that what they call it? According to legend, it could swallow a regiment.'

'And it could swallow you,' Kelly told him.

'Or Hannah Flynn. I trust we're clear on that. Now, Ferguson and company, can I tempt you?'

Tod's face was bone white, eyes dark. 'Not in a million years. But I'll tell you what I will do. Never leave Hannah's side for a moment, as long as you walk this earth. And I'm keeping your money. So to hell with you, Master-whoever-you-are, and bring it on as soon as you like.'

He switched off, slipped the phone into his pocket, turned and found Hannah, standing outside Fancy's stall, face tearstained. He walked toward her, passing Kelly, who simply smiled grimly and nodded.

She managed a smile. 'That was telling him.'

He put an arm round her. 'You know what I've been, girl, the terrible things I did. My excuse was that I was fighting for a cause. True or not, it made a bad man out of me, but as far as this bastard is concerned, I'll be his worst nightmare.'

She nodded, then hugged him suddenly so that she dropped her stick. 'Dammit to hell,' she moaned, and tried to bend.

He picked it up and gave it to her. 'A nice Catholic girl and such language. Come on, child, we'll find Aunt Meg and see you both to bed. Things will look better in the morning.'

Not that he believed it, not for a single moment.

*　　*　　*

On the Belfast waterfront the following day, it had rained early and the fog came later, rolling across the docks into Cagney Street, the Orange Drum at one end. The pub was long past its prime, a leftover from the great days of the Victorian era. It would be a haven for hard drinkers and drug users later that day, but it was empty at that moment except for Fergus Tully, drinking scalding-hot tea laced with Irish whiskey at the end of the bar. He was reading the *Belfast Telegraph*, while Frank Bell, the publican, worked his way through the sports pages.

They had served time together in the Maze Prison for multiple murders, men of a Protestant persuasion, the PIRA's bitterest enemies, Tully of such fearsome reputation that newspapers nicknamed him the Shankhill Butcher. The peace process had unleashed them into the world again.

Tully emptied his glass and pushed it across the bar. 'I'll have another, Frank,' and his mobile phone sounded.

'Is that Mr Frank Tully?'

'Who the hell wants to know?' Tully said, immediately offended by the English accent.

'I've just credited your bank account with one hundred thousand dollars. Check for yourself. I'll call you back in fifteen minutes.'

Tully banged his fist down on the bar. 'Stupid bastard.'

'What was all that about?' Bell asked, and when

Tully told him, said, 'Well, all you have to do is call the bank. They opened at nine.'

Which Tully did, and was staggered to be told that such a sum had only just been deposited from a bank in Geneva. He barely had time to inform Bell, when his phone rang again.

'Who are you?' Tully demanded.

'The people I serve had dealings with you some years ago. If I say AQ, do you understand me?'

'I certainly do,' Tully said. 'Al Qaeda. I dealt with the Master then, four years ago, but he wasn't you from the sound of it.'

'He has passed on, I have replaced him. You were given the task of disposing of a man named Tod Flynn. Instead, you car-bombed his elder brother Peter, killing him and his wife and injuring the daughter.'

Tully was immediately indignant. 'I don't know who told you that, because it's completely wrong. I'd have loved to have stiffed Tod Flynn. He gave us hell during the Troubles, but my orders from the other Master were quite clear. Peter Flynn was trying to take over the drug scene in Belfast and was seriously displeasing a lot of people. Al Qaeda wanted it sorted, and me and my friend Frank Bell took care of it as ordered.'

'I get the impression that the family and those around them have always believed Tod Flynn to have been the intended target, especially as his brother had borrowed his car for the trip to Belfast.'

'Are you saying it left Tod feeling guilty? If that's true, you've made my day.'

'Did your orders include the girl?'

'No, and they didn't include her mother either,' Tully said. 'Fortunes of war. They're always going on about collateral damage these days, aren't they? Anyway, what's this all about?'

'You've already got one hundred thousand dollars in your account, and it's yours if you and your friend get yourselves down to Drumgoole Place and take out Tod Flynn and Tim Kelly.'

The look on Tully's face was pure delight. 'You've no idea how much of a pleasure that would be.'

'And another hundred thousand if you dispose of the girl.'

Tully stopped smiling. 'Is that necessary?'

'She could be a serious threat to us. If there is a difficulty here, I must go elsewhere.'

Bell was looking grim, ran a finger across his throat and nodded slightly. Tully said, 'No problem, we can see to the girl, too.'

'I'll place the second hundred thousand in your account and on hold for three days. After that, all bets are off. In the glove compartment of your Jeep at the pub, you will find a package containing a mobile linked only to me. It also contains photos of everyone who could be linked in any way to Tod Flynn.'

'What a bastard,' Tully said when the call ended. 'He sounded just like one of those Brit judges who used to sentence us.' He laughed harshly and reached to take the very large whiskey that was pushed across the bar.

'Two hundred thousand dollars.' Bell was smiling. 'He can look like the Queen of Sheba, as far as I'm concerned. Happy days, my old son.' He raised his glass and then emptied it in one quick swallow.

Hannah Flynn was a remarkable young woman harmed by life, but she had threatened to expose Al Qaeda and had to be eliminated. Which still allowed the Master to feel nothing but distaste where Tully and Bell were concerned. It was time to move on, so he tapped in a highly secret number in Tehran.

With his blue suit and striped tie, the Iranian Minister of War, seated behind the mahogany desk in the comfortably furnished room, would not have been out of place in the White House or Downing Street. But this was Tehran, his phone number so secret that when it rang, it was usually a matter concerning the highest levels of government.

He picked up the phone and said in Farsi, 'Yes, what is it?'

The Master replied in English, 'You've been trying to trace the whereabouts of General Ali ben Levi since his disappearance.'

The minister said, 'To whom am I speaking?'

'I am the man who replaced him. He was killed on a private mission to London in pursuit of his deputy, Colonel Declan Rashid, a traitor to his country and its army.'

The minister was aghast. 'Rashid! His father was a fine general, but that Irish wife of his. . . . Where is the colonel now?'

'He was badly wounded in London. General Charles Ferguson is holding him in a private hospital at the moment.'

'Was Ferguson responsible for what happened to ben Levi?'

'I wish I could say that he was, but the general was shot by one of our own people, a malcontent who has since paid the penalty.'

'So why are you calling?'

'Because I believe Declan Rashid should be punished. And Charles Ferguson and his people finished off for good.'

'I suppose that would be because of their success against Al Qaeda,' the minister said. 'Sorry that I can't help you there, but my government would really prefer to rule Iran ourselves.'

'There may come a time when you regret it,' the Master told him.

'I wouldn't be surprised. I already have so many regrets. What's one more?' But he was deep in thought.

'Did you know that there are scores of language schools in London? It's true. The system is wide open if you want to pose as a student, which illegals do who simply want to live in England. We've sent young officers to such places for some time, to perfect their language skills and learn to adapt to Western society. They've all had special forces training, of course.'

'So what's your point?'

'I like to think of them as foot soldiers, men who can handle any dirty work which comes along. Now, I am not a religious man. I am indifferent to the message of Osama bin Laden. However, we live in a world of change, and who knows what may happen politically?'

'So what are you saying?'

'I'll make a deal with you. I'll take care of Ferguson and his people. You take care of Declan Rashid. It's a matter of honour, for he did betray all of us. I have two Secret Field Police for you, quite exceptional individuals. Captains Ali Herim and Khalid Abed.' He followed with a phone number. 'I shall speak to them and make plain what I expect. They can pass as Westerners without the slightest trouble, and frequently do. However, don't call me again. Let your results speak for themselves.'

Ali Herim and Khalid Abed were cousins, the sons of upper-class families in Iran, educated at an English public school, Winchester. They'd entered the army in Tehran together, the icing on the cake provided by a special year for foreign students at Sandhurst Military Academy in the UK.

There was always action somewhere in the Middle East, particularly on the borders of their own country, and they had seen plenty, but a transfer to the army's Secret Field Police, the SFP, had appealed to both of them and they had never regretted it. Recently, their orders had taken them to London, supported by excellent fake passports that turned Ali into Lance Harvey and Khalid, his younger brother by eighteen months, into Anthony. Dark-haired and handsome, in their late twenties, they looked exactly like what they were supposed to be, two young English gentlemen of means, out for a good time and determined to have one, a role that Ali and Khalid fitted perfectly, as they had a background of family wealth, easily tapped into in the City of London. Seated on either side of the fireplace in the parlour of their mews cottage, they were stunned at the information they'd had to absorb from two phone calls.

The first, from the Minister of War, had been concerned with the new direction they were to take. The shock of that had barely sunk in when the Master had phoned. Religion had never been important for either of them, but orders were orders.

'Colonel Declan Rashid, the Irishman, as they called him when we joined the SFP.' Ali shook his head. 'His record in the Iraq war was amazing.'

'It doesn't make sense to me,' Khalid said. 'The man is a true hero.'

'That's not what they are saying when words like *traitor* are flying around,' Ali told him.

The door to the study stood open, a computer beeped, there was the sound of the printer working. Ali stood up, went in, and returned with a sheaf of papers. Khalid sat beside him.

'Holland Park,' Khalid said. 'We'll have to have a drive past. Photos of everyone connected to the affair. It would seem we are to consider them all as possible targets. For the time being, totally familiarize ourselves with everyone connected, visit where they live and so on, and be ready when needed.'

'An interesting bunch of people Ferguson has,' Ali told him. 'This Major Roper, the bomb expert, is a legend in his own right, and the IRA veteran, Sean Dillon, would appear to be ready to kill anybody.'

'And usually does,' Khalid pointed out. 'Gangsters play an active role, too – this is Harry Salter and his nephew Billy.'

'Obviously much in demand,' Ali said. 'But let's not forget the lady. Captain Sara Gideon, the Military Cross in Afghanistan. But don't get any ideas about her, Khalid. She's entirely the wrong persuasion for you, my son. Sephardic Jewish. Her people have been in England since Oliver Cromwell.'

'Well, I could say we're all people of the book,' Khalid told him.

'Well, we don't need to argue about it.' Ali shrugged. 'If she finds out who we are, she'd probably reach for her Glock and shoot us both. To shoot back is something I refuse to contemplate, but enough for now. Let's go along to the Ivy, have a bite to eat and discuss a plan of campaign. Bring the information file and the photos with you, so we can study them again.'

'You're on.'

It was raining hard, their Mini Cooper parked around the corner. 'Umbrella time,' Khalid said, picked one out of the stand, stepped outside, and opened it. Ali joined him. They moved into the street where the Mini Cooper was parked, found a hole in the road, three workmen sheltering in a doorway smoking cigarettes and talking. Two of them were older, rough and brutal-looking, badly shaved, wearing pea jackets. A youth in a yellow oilskin had been telling a joke and stopped as the Iranians approached.

'Look what we've got here, a couple of bleeding nancy boys.' His companions roared with laughter.

Ali said, 'Isn't nature wonderful? That thing can actually talk.'

The youth ran up behind, grabbing him by the shoulder. 'Come here, you.'

Khalid dodged out of the way with the umbrella, leaving Ali to turn, grab the youth's wrist, twist it into a rigid bar, and run him into the yellow van. The nose crunched, the youth cried out, falling to his knees, rain washing the blood down over his face.

There was a roar of anger from the two men. The first out of the doorstep reached for Ali, who spun around and stamped on his kneecap. As the man started to go down, Khalid raised a knee into the descending face, lifting him back to fall across the youth. The other man retreated.

Ali said, 'Chalk it up to experience, boys. Now, if I were you,' he said to the standing man, 'I'd shove them in the back of your van and get round to accident and emergency at St Wilfred's. They do a lovely job, and it's for free.'

Khalid was already behind the Mini Cooper's wheel, and he started the engine. Ali climbed in beside him.

'Now, where were we? Oh, yes, the Ivy for a bite to eat and a discussion on a plan of campaign.'

At the same time, the Master was phoning Hamid Bey. 'I bring you some interesting news, An attempt was made on the life of Dr Ali Saif last night as he was leaving the Holland Park safe house.'

'Allah be praised,' the imam said. 'Who was responsible?'

'Better not to know,' the Master said. 'There's such wildness around these days, and so many of our young people become angry and disturbed when they hear what is happening to our people in Syria, Somalia or Egypt.'

'I agree wholeheartedly, but Allah will forgive me for branding Ali Saif as a black-hearted traitor to his religion and people.'

'To put it mildly, he has faltered on his spiritual

journey, but he may yet be saved, and I believe you could assist in this regard.'

'I am at your command.'

'He was badly wounded and is at present in a private hospital named Rosedene, where General Charles Ferguson provides treatment for those injured in his service.'

'Ferguson, as I hardly need to remind you, is one of Al Qaeda's most implacable enemies, he's done great harm to us on occasion,' Hamid Bey said. 'What do you suggest I do?'

'Ask to see Ali Saif. A not-unreasonable request. As imam, you were his spiritual guide.'

'Until he betrayed the Cause,' Hamid Bey said.

'Yes, but you will put Ferguson on the spot with your request. He looks upon the Army of God and the Brotherhood that goes with it as the enemy.'

'Which we are,' Hamid Bey said.

'You are missing the point. We must at all times appear to be what we claim, which is a spiritual and educational organization, offering the services of a multi-faith dispensary to the local population. I also suggest you take Lily Shah with you.'

'Why would I do that?' Hamid asked.

'Because the fact that she is a Christian may smooth the way, indeed make things rather awkward for them. She is already something of a saint in Muslim eyes. All this helps to wrong-foot the police and the city authorities. A whole range of municipal workers are members of the Army of God Brotherhood – a Muslim trade union, if you like – but to us, a private army. And there is little they can do about it.'

'I am proud to serve,' Hamid Bey said.

'Prove it by having one of your vans call on Captain Sara Gideon at Highfield Court tonight,' the Master told him, and switched off.

Next, he phoned Lily Shah. 'There's something I want you to do,' and he told her what he had just arranged with the imam.

'What will be the purpose of this?' she asked. 'If Ali Saif has gunshot wounds, he will be laid low for some time, but when he left the Army of God to join Ferguson, he must have been an invaluable source of information. About me, for instance.'

'Every embassy in London has an intelligence unit. People like us know who they are and they know who we are. The real work is trying to find out what the other people are up to and what their next move will be.'

'I see, so it doesn't matter that Ali Saif has told Ferguson what kind of people we are at Pound Street?'

'Exactly, because that's quite different from knowing what we intend to do next. So you'll help?'

'What do you want me to do?'

'Just keep your eyes open, if indeed you are allowed in to Rosedene. Any information about the place could be important. Another patient

85

there and suffering gunshot wounds is Colonel Declan Rashid, once deputy commander of the Secret Field Police, now a traitor to Iran and an associate of Ferguson's. I especially want to know about him.'

He sauntered off, leaving her anxious and troubled, mainly because she was no longer sure that she wanted to do this and was beginning to query what was happening. It was a new experience, but it was real enough. She shook her head, pulled herself together, and moved downstairs to reception, where help was always needed.

Major Max Shelby, superintendent of MI5's Tenby Street safe house, was sitting alone in the lounge at Rosedene when Sara arrived. An old Intelligence Corps hand, he was, like Sara, a Pashto and Arabic speaker. Although in his sixties, he'd returned to the army because of the pressures of terrorism, and been glad to do it. His only son, a Household Cavalry captain, had been killed by a roadside bomb on his third tour in Afghanistan.

He stood up and kissed her on the cheek. 'You're looking wonderful, as usual. Ferguson is in Bellamy's office, discussing Ali's condition.' He and Sara had first met in Afghanistan.

'Have you seen him?' she asked.

'Only through the window of his room. He's all wired up, but Bellamy's confident he'll pull through.'

'But what as?' she asked.

'God knows, but at least he's alive.' There was pain in his voice.

She reached to squeeze his hand. 'How's Mary?'

'When she discovered that the Taliban had displayed the body parts of my son in a thorn tree, she became a walking corpse and overdosed on sleeping pills. I got a closed court order and had her cremated eight days ago. I didn't see the need to advertise.' He shrugged. 'Price of war, as they say.'

She gave him a sudden fierce hug. 'Come on, Max, remember what we used to say in Helmand Province about the Taliban? Don't let the bastards grind you down.'

He said gravely, 'The trouble is, love, that some days I think they've succeeded.' There was real pain there for a moment, and then he hugged her. 'What a marvellous woman you are.'

'Allow me to second that.' Declan Rashid emerged from the corridor in a tracksuit, a towel around his neck, a walking stick in his right hand. 'How are things at Tenby Street, Max?' he asked, for they had become good friends.

'We'll miss Ali for sure. He's got a real gift for interrogation,' the major told him, as Ferguson and Bellamy appeared.

'What's the situation?' Sara asked.

'He'll occasionally surface, say a few words, then sink back again. I do believe he'll recover eventually, but we're not talking a week or two like the colonel here, more like a couple of months.' That was Bellamy.

'That's all I wanted to know,' Shelby said. 'I've lost my best interrogator, so I'll leave you to it and get back to Tenby Street.'

'Give me a moment, Major, if you don't mind,' Ferguson said. 'I'd like your opinion on a rather important matter.'

'And what would that be, General?'

'What would you say if I told you I've had Imam Hamid Bey on the phone asking permission to visit Ali Saif?'

'You mean here?' The look on Shelby's face was one of amazement.

'Yes, and he'd also like to bring someone from the dispensary with him, a Mrs Lily Shah, who is apparently a Christian.'

'I don't see what that's got to do with anything,' Shelby said. 'I know her. She married an Algerian charge nurse who worshipped Osama bin Laden, went to Gaza a year ago when AQ ordered him, and was killed in an Israeli air strike. But she stayed a Christian. Mind you, she's popular at the mosque in spite of that.'

'So, taking that into account,' Ferguson said, 'what would you do?'

'Shoot Hamid Bey, but that not being viable, I suppose it might be useful to allow them in. Know thy enemy, my old colonel used to say.'

'Very sensible,' Ferguson said. 'I think we'll give it a whirl.'

Shelby shrugged. 'You're in charge, General, but if you'll excuse me, I've got to get back to Tenby Street. A bit of a situation there at the moment with what's happened to Ali Saif. We're short-handed, yet I'm expected to turn up at the Ministry of Defence umpteen times a day to talk to idiots. Sometimes I despair.'

'Off you go, then, watch your back. Difficult days ahead, I think, Major.'

'I suppose that's what we joined for, General.' Max Shelby smiled and was gone.

Ferguson sighed and murmured, 'Yes, but we were younger then.'

Finding Declan and Sara missing, he pursued the sound of voices along the corridor and found them standing at the reception window to Ali's room, peering in. He was unconscious, festooned with electronic equipment, his body connected to tubes injecting him with fluids of one kind or another.

'He looks more dead than alive,' Declan murmured.

'You mustn't say that,' Sara told him. 'It's bad luck. Never forget, he saved our lives at the Park Lane shoot-out when that creep Rasoul tried to ambush us.'

Ferguson moved forward. 'He certainly did, and it won't be forgotten, but I've told Roper to call in the troops. We're due to get together in the computer room in an hour, so I need to get moving.' He turned to Sara. 'My Daimler is waiting, can I offer you a lift?'

'No need, sir, I came in Dillon's Mini.'

'I'll see you there.' He turned to Declan. 'As for you, Colonel, an early night is indicated. You must take it slowly. After all, you've had a good innings.'

He hurried away, and she turned and smiled. 'I'd better get going.'

'My dear Sara, I know you're Wonder Woman and will be armed to the teeth as usual, but I suspect things are really stirring again, and two of us in the Mini would look better than one if someone is taking the wrong kind of interest in you.'

'And what's Ferguson going to say to that?' she enquired.

'Who cares? Just let me get suitably dressed.'

He hurried along the corridor to his room, found a bomber jacket, pulled it on, took a Colt .25 from its inside pocket, checked that the weapon was loaded, and returned to her.

'You really are a lovely man.' She smiled and patted his chest, feeling the gun. 'I thought so. What am I going to do with you, Colonel?'

'Oh, we'll have to leave that until later. Let's get moving.'

She laughed, allowing him to take her arm, and they moved out of the front entrance into the car park, pausing beside the Mini while she found the keys. All this, Khalid Abed, sitting in the Mini Cooper beside Ali Herim at the wheel, saw clearly through Nightstalker binoculars.

He shoved them into Ali's hands. 'The couple getting in the old Mini. Declan Rashid and Gideon.'

'I do believe you're right,' Ali said.

'So what do we do, shoot them?' Khalid produced a silenced Walther PPK.

Ali pushed his cousin's hand down. 'Let's see where they're going, but if it's Holland Park I won't stop. After what happened the other night, their surveillance cameras will be working overtime.'

But Holland Park it was, for they had driven past it earlier in the day, so Ali carried on, turning into the main road traffic.

'So what do we do now?' Khalid asked again, exasperated.

'Well, there's nowhere we can wait to follow them when they come out. A close read of a lot of that stuff the Master sent us makes clear how much AQ rely on the Army of God people to handle surveillance.'

'What do you suggest? That we knock off some yellow van, posing as street cleaners in yellow oilskins, and take to the streets?'

'No, we can always get people like that to do our bidding,' Ali told him.

'So what *do* we do?' Khalid asked.

'Not waste our time sitting in the car. I suggest we adjourn to the Dorchester Bar, split a bottle of champagne, indulge in a delicious light supper, and give the matter some thought.'

'Sounds good to me, especially if you find time to answer the most intriguing question of the evening, which is why wouldn't you let me shoot them when they were such easy targets?'

'Because they were,' Ali said. 'Will that do?'

'Ah, now I understand. You've been suborned by being educated at an English public school and finished off with a year at dear old Sandhurst, the finest military academy in the world. An indifferent education for a spy.'

'I would point out that the same applies to you, Cousin,' Ali told him as he swung out of Park Lane and roared up to the entrance of the Dorchester. 'So just shut up for a while and give me time to think.'

CHAPTER 5

The Salters were talking to Roper when Declan and Sara went in. The Salters' minders, Joe Baxter and Sam Hall, were there, too, and Tony Doyle was leaning against the back of Roper's wheelchair. Dillon and Ferguson came in together, and the general frowned on seeing Declan.

'Do you think this is wise, Colonel?'

'Well, it seems to me that since I've got to join the human race sometime, I might as well do it with something really important. On top of that, I need the exercise. What I call alternative therapy.'

Harry Salter laughed harshly. 'Just listen to him. I know all about you, old son, shot so many times over the years that you've lost count. You're just as bad as Billy here. Bellamy's put him back together again a few times, I can tell you.'

'Leave it out, Harry,' Billy told his uncle. 'I'm still here, aren't I, serving Queen and country?'

'Only because the general paid a discreet visit to Scotland Yard and got your police records wiped clean,' Harry told him. 'Otherwise, the security services wouldn't have touched you.'

'Enough already,' Dillon said. 'Let's get on with it.'

'Here we go,' Billy Salter said. 'It's nylon-and-titanium waistcoat time unless I'm very much mistaken. I know I should have bought more shares in the Wilkinson Sword Company.'

'Shut up, Billy,' Ferguson said. 'Just so everybody here knows exactly what happened on Nantucket, I'll go through it.'

When he was finished, Harry said, 'Dillon, you were a right bastard as usual, and you, Sara, are getting better all the time, but you've seriously annoyed Al Qaeda, I can see that. Not only did you dispose of their two hit men, but Al Qaeda doesn't even get brownie points for trying. They won't forgive us for that.'

'Which is why we are meeting, Harry,' Dillon put in. 'They're going to need some sort of revenge to keep their credibility in the world.'

'What could we expect, do you think – some kind of spectacular?' Billy demanded. 'Another bombing in London, an attempt on the Prime Minister?'

Roper said, 'No, this is personal. Once they get their act together, they'll come after us. I've never been more certain.'

'So Billy was right,' Ferguson said. 'I want you wearing bulletproof vests at all times, and armed. No exceptions. What you haven't got, pick up in the supply department before you leave.'

He turned to Harry Salter. 'You're completely

legit these days, but for years, you were one of the most successful crooks in the London underworld. There's not much that happens in this town that your associates don't know about. Squeeze them dry.'

'Done. I don't have many Muslim sources, though.'

'We have to be careful there,' Roper put in. 'The Brotherhood and the Army of God handle themselves cleverly. They're a legitimate charity.'

'But that's just a front,' Harry said.

'We all know that,' Roper said. 'But they've played it well. We've just got to learn to box a little more cleverly than they do.'

'What about Imam Hamid Bey's request to visit Ali Saif?' Sara said. 'Have you made a decision?'

Ferguson nodded. 'I think Max Shelby was right to point out the value in keeping your enemies close, so I'm going to allow it. Lily Shah, too.' He raised a hand. 'And yes, I know her husband was Al Qaeda.'

'And Drumgoole?' Dillon asked. 'You seemed interested in going yourself.'

'I'd have enjoyed doing that, believe me, but the Prime Minister insists I stay available.'

'So Sara and I will have to manage on our own,' Dillon said.

'That won't do at all, you need a third gun.' Ferguson nodded to Billy Salter. 'Do you feel up to it? I know you've been through the grinder this last two or three years, and Bellamy has his concerns about you.'

'Time I got out in the fresh air,' Billy said. 'And don't listen to Old Father Time here.'

Harry Salter scowled. 'Silly young bastard. They'll be sending you home in a box one of these days.'

'Well, keep me out of Highgate Cemetery if they do,' Billy told him. 'I don't want to be anywhere near Karl Marx.'

Ferguson nodded. 'That's settled, then. You'll leave tomorrow morning. When you get to Dublin, drive straight to Drumgoole without warning. That should put the fear of God in them.'

'The Tod Flynn I was raised with didn't do fear,' Dillon said. 'He was too busy getting a gun out fast.'

'And after Dillon's phone call, we *are* expected,' Sara pointed out. 'So what are we supposed to do, try to recruit them?'

'They certainly can't be arrested,' Dillon said. 'We've established that.'

'Just trust your instincts,' Ferguson said. 'I think your move will become clear once you're there. Now, time to rest up.'

Roper moved off in his wheelchair, the others got up to follow, and Declan lurched badly, almost dropping his stick, and Dillon caught him.

'There you are,' Ferguson said. 'You've got to take it easy, Colonel, and since you were shot on my behalf in a manner of speaking, I'm going to make that an order. You will retire to bed in the guest wing at once, and Professor Bellamy can

96

have you recovered by the Rosedene ambulance in the morning.'

'He's right,' Sara said. 'You should be in bed.'

He was obviously in pain, and nodded. 'Okay, so I've been stupid.'

Tony Doyle appeared with a wheelchair and eased him into it. The others had moved on, their voices drifting back calling good night.

'I'll be in touch. Off you go.' Sara turned to Dillon. 'What about you?'

'I'm staying overnight, and so is Ferguson. I'll check on the colonel later.'

'I'll need clothes for our trip,' she said, 'Can I borrow that wonderful supercharged old Mini of yours again? I think I've fallen in love with it.'

He smiled. 'Of course you can, but in view of what Ferguson said, take care.'

'Always do.' She produced a Colt .25 from her rear belt holster. 'See what a good girl I am. From here to Highfield Court is seventeen minutes in that Mini of yours, Dillon, I've timed it.'

'Then I suggest you take double care.'

She holstered the Colt. 'You know what they say? To the hero of Abusan, anything is possible. How many Taliban did I slaughter with that machine gun?'

'Your citation said twenty.'

'And what has it achieved where Afghanistan is concerned?'

'Not a thing, and if you expected something different, you were seriously misinformed. As the army leaves Helmand Province, the news is that the Taliban are moving back in, so you're entitled to ask what the war was supposed to be about.'

'Damn you, Sean Dillon.'

'Already taken care of,' he told her, 'So go home and get a good night's sleep. I need you sharp on this one. Tod Flynn and Kelly have been playing the great game for more than thirty years and they're still in one piece. I'd remember that if I were you. Night bless, Sara.'

He turned and walked away.

At the Dorchester, Ali and Khalid had enjoyed their meal, shared a bottle of Krug champagne, and were debating whether to order another one.

'It's been rather an abortive evening,' Khalid said. 'First, you prevent me from making the easiest hit in my career, then the targets drop in at what must be one of the best-guarded safe houses in London.'

Ali glanced at his watch. 'It's been about an hour and a half since they went in.'

'And could have left at any time. I think we may as well go home.'

'Just give me a moment.' Ali had brought the folder containing the information file and photos of Ferguson's people, from the car. He made a quick check. 'I thought so. Sara Gideon lives at her grandfather's house not far from here. Let's go and have a look. You never know.'

'Then let's get on with it.' Khalid turned and beckoned to a waiter.

Outside, they turned into South Audley Street, lined with parked cars all the way to Grosvenor Square. Just before the square on the right was a side street, Highfield Place, an enclave of several mid-Victorian properties, the largest being Highfield Court, standing back from the road, an imposing gated property.

Ali managed to find a space in South Audley Street and they looked across, Khalid using his Nightstalkers. 'That's the address, the large one with the garden.' He stiffened suddenly. 'Well, I never, cousin. There's a van parked at the end of the street.'

'Is it yellow?' Ali demanded.

'Difficult to say in this light. What I can see is "Public Works" painted on the side in large letters. Ah, that's it. A guy just got out and he's definitely in yellow. He's crossing the road to the gates. Interesting that they're open.'

'Even more interesting,' Ali said, 'is the fact that he has just stepped inside without any security lights coming on, which can only mean one thing.'

'And what's that?'

'I'd say an ambush has been set up for Captain Sara Gideon.'

'The bastards,' Khalid said as the man stepped back out into the road, leaving a brief glimpse of two others behind him in the garden who merged into the dark as he crossed to the van.

'Why, Khalid,' Ali said. 'This time it is I who am asking *you* whose side you are on.'

'My own,' Khalid said. 'I don't like anybody butting into our business. And I don't like complications.'

'Then let's uncomplicate it.' Ali rummaged in the glove compartment, pulled out two ski masks, and tossed one to him. 'Get that on fast. It's late, so I suspect she could turn up at any minute. We only move in if she's alone. If Dillon or Ferguson is with her, we stay out of it. If we do have to interfere, you're – let's say, a rough Cockney putting the boot in. Okay?'

At that moment, Sara passed them, swung into Highfield Place, turned into the open gates, and braked to a halt.

'She smells a rat.' Khalid pulled on his ski mask.

The security lights in the garden came on and she took the Mini forward. 'They've done that to draw her in,' Ali said, also pulling on his ski mask.

The man from the van hurried down the street and entered the gate, and it was Khalid who said, 'What are we waiting for, Cousin?'

He kicked open the door and ran across the road, pulling a Walther PPK from his pocket, and reached the gate, Ali right behind him, both of them looking quite terrifying.

The plan had been cunning enough, its main purpose confusion. The open gate, the darkness to arouse suspicion, and then the lights suddenly coming on, a false indication that everything was all right. She'd braked at the bottom of the terrace steps, opened the driver's door, and had immediately had two large men in yellow uniforms burst from the shrubbery to grab her from behind the wheel, one of them with handcuffs. She was fighting like a tiger when the third man arrived.

'Get the cuffs on her and let's get out of here,' he said as they struggled.

He turned at the sound of footsteps running behind them and faced the terrifying sight of a masked man arriving, arm swinging to slash him across the face with the Walther. The man with the handcuffs looked up from Sara in alarm, and a second masked man booted him under the chin. The third man tried to scramble to his feet, and the first one gave him the same blow across the face he'd given the handcuff man, vicious and brutal, no pity.

Sara, roughed up and confused, got to her feet, scrabbled for her Colt and drew it, slightly bewildered. 'Who are you?'

'Just a couple of Good Samaritans,' Ali said, 'helping a lady in distress. I don't think you'll need your pistol. We'll just get these nasty men out of your hair. Why don't you go into the house and just forget it ever happened, darling. It's a good job we were passing.'

'A nice hot bath, love, that's what I'd recommend,' Khalid said as he hauled the third man to his feet to join the other two. 'What are we going to do with them?' he asked his cousin in as close to a Cockney accent as he could manage.

'Kneecapping's as good as anything, but just get the bleeders to their van and we'll see.'

At that moment, the front door opened on the terrace and Sadie Cohen, the housekeeper, called, 'Is that you, Sara, is everything okay?'

'I'd say yes if I were you,' Ali said. 'We'll be going now.' He turned and followed Khalid as he pushed the men towards the van, Walther in hand.

When they got there, Khalid said, 'Now what?'

'One at the wheel, the other two behind, windows down so you can lean in and shoot the one on the left in the kneecap. I'll do the one on the right. With luck, it should cripple them.'

It was over very quickly, the dull thuds of the silenced pistols, the groans of the two victims. The gibbering fear of the one behind the wheel. 'Lucky for you they need a driver. I suggest you try the dispensary at the Pound Street mosque. They offer care, even to scum like you,' Khalid told him.

They drove off quickly. The cousins walked briskly away, removing their masks as they turned the corner and crossed the road. Ali said, 'You certainly passed that test with flying colours. You've got a bit of a flair for acting, if you ask me.'

'Yes, but you won the Oscar, Cousin.' Khalid smiled as they got into the Mini Cooper. 'I suppose it comes of having been a prefect at Winchester.'

'In my opinion, we've earned a treat. That second bottle of champagne we were considering?'

'You mean return to the Dorchester?'

'Why not?' Ali said. 'The night is young.'

So he swung the Mini Cooper around and drove back down Great Audley Street.

Sara's call brought Ferguson and Dillon instantly, followed by Roper in the van driven by Tony Doyle, who unloaded him in his wheelchair. A grim-faced Sadie Cohen admitted them.

'Has it always got to be like this, Major?' she enquired.

'So it would appear, Sadie.'

Angry, she strode along the corridor, opened the large mahogany door, and led the way into Rabbi Nathan Gideon's Victorian library, where Sara was sitting on one side of the period fireplace, faced by Ferguson and Dillon.

For once, Roper was missing his usual lazy smile. 'Have they hurt you?'

She got up, went to take his outstretched hand, and kissed him on the cheek. 'No, I'm fine. They were disguised as Public Works men in one of those yellow vans. I saw it flash by afterwards. My mysterious saviours followed on foot and went the same way. Perhaps they had a car waiting.'

'And the saviours, you said, kneecapping was mentioned?' Dillon said. 'That's an old IRA custom.'

'There was nothing Irish about them,' Sara said. 'A couple of Cockney hard boys. They certainly didn't take prisoners. They dished out some very rough stuff and laughed about it. I got the impression they'd seen it happening and just got stuck in for the hell of it. Mind you, they were armed.'

'Well, a lot of people are these days,' Ferguson said.

Roper, who had been examining a computer built into his wheelchair, said, 'There's some interesting news here on the Scotland Yard night report. A Public Works yellow van collided with a cleansing cart in Wigmore Street. The driver's skull was fractured in the incident and two passengers were found to have gunshot wounds in the knee.'

Sadie, who had just pushed in a trolley and was pouring coffee, said, 'So at last we're getting somewhere.'

'I'm afraid not,' Roper told her as she handed him a cup. 'The wounded men will undoubtedly be members of the Brotherhood, who will claim that those who attacked them had a racial motive. They'll disclaim all knowledge of the van, which was probably stolen anyway.'

'One thing's for certain,' Dillon said. 'Obviously, the Irish flight will be postponed.'

'Certainly not,' Sara said, before anyone could speak. 'I think I'd probably be safer there than I am here.' She turned to Ferguson. 'I want that clearly understood.'

'And so it is, Captain,' he said gravely. 'You have a clear sense of duty, and I admire that.'

'Which is all very well, but I really would like to get to bed now.'

'So you shall,' Ferguson told her. 'But there is one proviso. Staff Sergeant Doyle moves in now and stays on until you return. I don't want Sadie left on her own.'

Sadie said, 'Why, General Ferguson, I didn't know you cared, and yes, I'd appreciate the sergeant being on hand. In fact, there are a number of things around here that could do with a man's touch.'

'I'm yours to command, Miss Sadie,' Doyle said.

'Never mind that. I'll sort you later, but for the moment, I'd like the rest of you to move out and allow Sara to go to bed.'

So they went, leaving Tony Doyle to guard the wall, as he would have said, Dillon taking over the duty of getting Roper into the van and back to Holland Park.

They departed, and Sadie turned to Doyle. 'You, into the kitchen and we'll discuss the regime.' Then she turned to Sara: 'I think you're crazy to go on this Irish trip tomorrow, but you certainly won't unless you get some sleep tonight, so off to bed with you.'

And Sara, yawning, climbed the stairs obediently.

There was not much difference between night and day for Giles Roper, sitting in his wheelchair, his shoulder-length hair pulled back in a pigtail from his bomb-ravaged face. A man who should have died many times, the great survivor, kept going by the right drugs and a diet of whiskey, cigarettes, and bacon sandwiches.

But he was king of cyberspace, also kept alive by those dozens of screens in his computer room, constantly presenting new information to his fertile brain. At five-thirty in the morning, he was filling a mug from the tea urn and considering the day's venture to Drumgoole and Tod Flynn, whose career was on his main screen, when Dillon appeared in a tracksuit, a towel around his neck.

'You're up early, considering what happened last night,' Roper told him.

'Couldn't sleep, too much on my mind,' Dillon said. 'Thought I'd have a swim and some steam, shake myself up a bit. You, of course, never leave the chair.'

'Need assistance for that, but when I want to, I can summon the whole world to my screens. As you see, I've been looking at our target for today, your cousin Tod Flynn.'

'So I notice,' Dillon said. 'And that's Aunt Meg with him, young Hannah when she was fourteen, his brother Peter and his wife.'

He turned away, poured tea into a mug, laced it with whiskey, then helped himself to one of Roper's cigarettes.

'Poor old Sean,' Roper said. 'Family is everything when you come down to it. You don't like to think about what happened shortly after that photo was taken. The car bomb that killed your cousin Peter and his wife and crippled their daughter.'

Dillon showed no emotion. 'It was Tod's car they were in, the bomb obviously meant for him. He was a big name in his day and very important to the Provos. There would have been plenty of people with a score to settle.'

'And what do you know about this?'

The screen showed Tod's brother standing before a pillared entrance, a neon sign above it that said *Flynn's.*

'Do you recognize that?'

'Only by the photo. Although he'd inherited Drumgoole Place, it was never enough for him. He left his wife and Aunt Meg in charge and made for Belfast, which was a wide-open town during the Troubles. He hadn't the slightest interest in politics. Everything was business and making a buck.'

'Which was why he leased an old cinema and converted it into a ballroom?'

Dillon nodded. 'It was also during the final two years of the peace process, which finally released men like Tod and Kelly from the Maze. I'd moved abroad by then to assist other people with their problems.'

'Yes, well, we won't go into that,' Roper said. 'Were you aware that the ballroom business was only a front for Peter Flynn, who controlled a mini drug empire from the premises, made a great deal of money, and got away with it?'

'No, I didn't. I was too busy being chased by the Royal Ulster Constabulary and the British Army while I was still in Ulster.'

'Do you think Tod Flynn knew?'

'I've no idea. Life was confusion in those days. I heard that Peter closed down the ballroom and returned to Drumgoole, where he eventually offered a home to Tod and Kelly when they got out of prison. They worked on the stud farm and used the address to offer their services as security specialists.'

'So what do you think about what happened to Peter and his family?'

'I've told you. It was Tod's car which Peter had borrowed. Whoever it was got the wrong target.'

'Which must have left Tod riddled with guilt and feeling somehow responsible, especially since he had to know others in the family saw it that way, too, including the niece.'

Dillon poured another cup of tea. 'I'm sure that's true, but what's your point, Giles?'

'That my screens tell another story. Try this one.'

The film that appeared showed the Orange Drum, and was obviously a few years old and in black and white. An old Rover saloon appeared, braked to a halt, and Fergus Tully got out, followed by a teenage girl. Frank Bell came around from the other side to join them and they walked toward the camera, smiling and chatting.

'You'll know these people, I presume?'

'Oh yes,' Dillon said. 'The ugly bastard is Fergus

Tully, known to the press as the Shankhill Butcher, one of the most feared hit men in the UVF. The teenage girl is his daughter Myra, so that footage must have been taken many years ago. She'd be about forty now.'

'She is indeed. Has lived in London for some years, but we'll leave her for the moment. What about the other?'

'Frank Barry, the brains of the duo, also UVF. But what's the point of all this?'

'Peter Flynn had decided to return to the drug scene, but times had changed, there were others in the gang now, and he wasn't wanted. At that time, most of the good stuff was coming in from Holland, where Al Qaeda had organized the delivery system very successfully. Now Peter was going to ruin everything by trying to muscle in, so AQ decided he had to go.'

'So that's where Tully and Bell came in?' Dillon asked.

'I'm afraid so, Sean,' Roper said. 'Who owned the car had nothing to do with it. Peter was the target, Al Qaeda behind it.'

'And the fact that his wife and fourteen-year-old daughter were with him didn't bother those bastards in the slightest.' Dillon's face was dark.

Roper said, 'What goes around, comes around, but we've got other fish to fry today. We'll think of something special for Tully and Bell another time.'

'You can count on that, I promise you. What were you going to say about Myra?'

'She went to London years ago and married a cousin, Brendan, so she's still a Tully. He was more Cockney than Irish, a gangster from childhood. He's working his way through a fifteen-year sentence for a failed gold robbery at Stansted Airport two years ago. They've got him in Belmarsh.'

'So what's she up to?'

'Running the crew while he's away, from a dock-side development about half a mile down-river from the Salters. Irish Wharf. What used to be an old pub called the Sash. She's turned it into a nightclub.'

'God save us, with a name like that, it can only be a Protestant pub.' Dillon laughed. 'Just like Belfast. Are you sending a digest of all that up to Ferguson's office?'

'He isn't there. He got a text at one o'clock to say the Prime Minister wanted a breakfast meeting at Downing Street, so he decided to clear off to Cavendish Place. I'll send it to him there.'

'And do the same for Sara and Billy. Some of the facts you've uncovered do make the situation at Drumgoole rather difficult. I'd like them to know exactly what they are getting into.'

'That makes sense,' Roper said.

'I'll see you later.'

In the kitchen of the Orange Drum, Fergus Tully made toast and tea with a shot of whiskey in it and stood at the kitchen window in pyjamas and a dressing gown, looking out at a grey morning which threatened rain, not that such a prospect bothered him. He liked rain, always had, and his daughter had been the same, and the thought made him decide to phone her, and he took out his mobile and did just that.

During her husband's first year in prison, Myra Tully had taken the opportunity to completely refurbish the Sash, and that had included a bedroom for herself, very luxurious although a touch gaudy.

She reached for her mobile and said, 'It's only six o'-bloody-clock. Who is this?'

'Sorry, my love, have I disturbed you?'

The Belfast accent alerted her at once. 'What is it, Da? Is there a problem?'

'Not at all. I've got a busy day ahead and I just wanted a word.'

The man next to Myra was around forty, with a military moustache and a boxer's face and a lot of muscle, an East End hard man of the finest vintage. 'Stir yourself, Terry, and get me some coffee. It's me da.'

Terry Harker made no complaint, simply rolled out of bed and made for the door. She pulled a pillow behind her, reached for a cigarette, lit it and sat up. She was handsome rather than beautiful, with jet-black hair framing a fierce face.

'Are you in trouble, Da?'

'Not at all, my love, just bringing you up to speed.'

At eight, she had lost her mother to pancreatic

cancer, which had taken only three months to kill her. Fergus Tully, a monster to everyone else, was to her the perfect father and she was fiercely protective of him. There were no secrets between them, and they'd discussed his doings from an early age.

'Something's happening. What is it?'

'Remember the job Frank and I did for Al Qaeda four years ago, where that Master fella rang up out of the blue?'

'Course I do. The car bombing. Peter Flynn.'

'Well, I've heard from them again, a different Master, that they want us to get rid of Tod Flynn, the brother. A damn Provo who was in the Maze same time as me and Frank.'

The door opened and Terry appeared in his underpants, with a coffee and tray that he put down beside her. She waved him away and he went out. 'So what's the score, Da?'

'One hundred thousand dollars down and another hundred to come if we fix Tod Flynn and the girl, his niece.'

'Is that necessary?'

'He said she was a serious threat and if we didn't want to do it, he'd go elsewhere. He only gave us three days to make up our minds, so we're going today. It's a horse farm in Drumgoole well over the border in the Republic. Three or four hours' drive if we're lucky. Do I have your blessing?'

'You always have that, Da, and this is a big one, so take care.'

'One thing – believe it or not, but Tod Flynn's cousin is Sean Dillon.'

'God in heaven, does that Provo bastard have anything to do with this?'

'Not that I know of, but I imagine he wouldn't be pleased with what we're about to do. I'll stay in touch.'

He was gone, and she sat there thinking about it. A big payday, no doubt about that, and the girl's involvement didn't bother her in the slightest. The door opened and Terry entered.

'Everything okay?'

'Couldn't be better, so get back in bed and find something useful to do.'

When Dillon reported to the computer room just before nine, he was wearing a dark blue Bugatti anorak, weatherproof country slacks in the same colour, paratroop boots, and a tweed cap, Irish-style.

Roper said, 'You should offer yourself out to do whiskey adverts in the better magazines.'

'Very funny,' Dillon told him. 'But the kind of country we're visiting, and in this kind of weather, can be very unforgiving. I'll need transport, so you'll have to find me a driver.'

'Sara called in. She's on her way now in your Mini. You're carrying?'

'Of course.'

'Canvas holdall by the door. I spoke to the armourer. You'll find two AK-47s, the silenced versions with the folding stock.'

'Do you think we're going to war, then?' Dillon asked.

'I'd say Flynn's too sensible to start one. All he's got to do is stand his ground. After all, there's nothing he and Kelly can be charged with.'

Dillon shrugged. 'But we know differently, and no harm in making that clear.'

Sara walked in, wearing a French beret and a Gucci coat in black leather. She looked fresh and alive, as if last night hadn't happened.

'I overslept, and Sadie left me to it. We'd better get a move on. Where's Ferguson?'

'Breakfast at Number Ten,' Roper told her. 'Did you get my message?'

'It was the sound of my laptop receiving it that woke me up. I must say it makes things even more interesting.'

'So let's get moving.' Dillon was impatient. 'Billy will be wondering where the hell we are.'

'Actually, Billy *and* Harry will be wondering,' Roper told him. 'Apparently, the old sod read the stuff I sent Billy and decided he should join the party himself.'

'And what does Ferguson think about that?' Sara asked.

'Why bother the man, and him breakfasting with the Prime Minister?' Dillon demanded.

Roper smiled wickedly. 'Exactly, so off you go and enjoy yourselves. I'll give him the good news at a more appropriate time.'

★　　★　　★

114

They found Harry and Billy waiting in the small departure lounge at Farley having a coffee. Billy, like Dillon, wore a tweed cap but a black bomber jacket and jeans. His uncle had preferred a brown country suit of Harris tweed, a Burberry mac, and a rain hat.

'Why, Harry, the complete country gentleman,' Dillon said. 'I'd never have believed it.'

'Don't mock,' Sara told him, and kissed Harry on the cheek. 'I think you look terrific.'

'And so do you, darling, but Dillon here. How would he know any better? I mean, he's bleeding Irish, isn't he?' He tucked her hand in his arm. 'So let's get this show on the road,' and they led the way out and walked towards the Gulfstream.

CHAPTER 6

At the Orange Drum, after his conversation with Myra, Tully went in search of Bell and found him in the garage in the back courtyard loading up the old and battered Jeep with the baskets and rods.

'So that's our cover?' Tully asked. 'Fly fishermen bent on a day out in the country?'

'Can you think of anything better when we're venturing into a part of the Republic where strangers stand out like a sore thumb?' Bell asked. 'So look the part of the tourist fisherman, wear your waterproofs, anorak, leggings, rain hat, the works. The way the weather's shaping up, it will probably pour down at some stage anyway.'

'And what about weaponry? What have you decided?'

'Well, a car bomb is out. We'd never get close enough, and with the family history, I shouldn't think any of them would get into any vehicle without giving it a thorough check.'

'So what do you intend?'

'Maybe I'll go back to good old-fashioned sniping, and you know how good I am at that. I could use the weapon that got my dad through the Korean War with the Ulster Rifles.'

'Here we go again. The Lee Enfield bolt-action, standard-round, 303 rifle. Isn't it time you moved on?'

'He killed a lot of Chinese with that weapon, and it saved his life on more than one occasion. You being such a lousy shot, I've got you a Mac 10 machine pistol. All you have to do is spray the target, but you'd never get close enough, so my way is better. If you look under the rear seat, there's also a couple of British Army issue Browning pistols and plenty of ammo.'

'I'll take your word for it. I'd better go and sort myself out.'

Frank Bell finished what he was doing, pulled out a pack of cigarettes, and lit one. 'How are you feeling, Fergus? Are you up for this?'

'Of course I am, why wouldn't I be? Have you spoken to the Master yet?'

'I thought I'd do that when we're halfway there. I suppose you've talked to Myra, you always do. What did she think?'

'All for it, no doubt of that, and why wouldn't she be? It's a big payday.'

'What about the Flynn girl, did you mention that?'

'She asked if it was necessary. I told her what the Master said about going elsewhere if it was a problem, and she never mentioned it again.'

'I bet she didn't,' Bell said.

'The only time she got upset was when I told her that Sean Dillon was Tod Flynn's cousin. She exploded, only quietened down when I said he'd nothing to do with our enterprise.'

'And thank God for that. Those photos of him and those others in Ferguson's crew were warning enough. Thank God we're not mixing it with them. Off you go and get ready, I'll finish off here.'

Which he did, then lit another cigarette, moved to the door in time to see the rain. He shivered suddenly and didn't know why. How many days like this had he known during the last thirty years? But that would never do, not at all, and he put his head down and ran across the yard to the kitchen door.

Ferguson came on the screen in Roper's computer room, and he wasn't pleased. 'What's going on, Major?' he demanded. 'Who gave permission to include Harry Salter in the party to Drumgoole?'

'I did, General,' Roper said. 'Knowing how important your breakfast meeting was with the PM. You've obviously seen the additional information I've discovered about Flynn. I not only sent it to you, but Captain Gideon and Billy Salter. When Harry suggested he might be of use after all, I decided to use my discretion and agree. I can't see what harm it would do. They're not visiting a war zone.'

'Yes, well, in future I suggest you be a little more circumspect,' Ferguson said. 'But to other things. I'm at Rosedene right now, awaiting the arrival of Hamid Bey. I've had words with Maggie Duncan, told her I'm leaving it to her own good sense to warn her staff to conduct themselves with caution when these people are here. Bellamy has insisted he will be present himself, and I'm expecting him at any moment, hopefully before the Pound Street couple arrive. I thought Max Shelby might be able to join us, but he's tied up at the Ministry of Defence. As usual, when the going gets rough, it's the old hands like Max who the politicians need to pull their irons out of the fire.'

'I'll certainly be interested to know what happens,' Roper said.

At that moment, there were voices off-screen and Ferguson said, 'Damn it, they've just arrived. I'll have to go,' and the screen went dark.

Maggie Duncan had been matron at Rosedene for more years than she cared to remember, but the situation in which she found herself now was unique. Following Ferguson's orders, she had hurriedly paid a visit to each section of the small hospital, ending up in Ali Saif's room, where he lay in a stupor, festooned with tubes and wires, his breathing rough. She gave him a quick examination, and Declan Rashid entered the room behind her, leaning on a walking stick and wearing the black tracksuit.

She turned, and he raised his free hand. 'Just checking, Sister, Captain Gideon and I are particularly concerned. After all, he saved our lives last time out. What do you think this morning?'

'He's very poorly.' She shook her head, deeply concerned, and her mobile sounded. 'Ah, Professor Bellamy. The imam and Sister Shah have just arrived, I believe. I thought you were coming?'

Bellamy said, 'I was, but we've just had the result of a two-car pile-up rushed into Emergency at Guy's. Four seriously damaged people. Sorry, but I must go.'

'Problems?' Declan asked.

'No Bellamy, I'm afraid. He's needed elsewhere urgently.'

'I see. So what about this visit? Is Saif fit to see visitors?'

'If it's just a look-in, yes, but nothing more. I really must make that clear to General Ferguson.'

A young nurse glanced in. 'You're needed in reception, Matron.'

'Excuse me, Colonel,' Maggie Duncan said, and hurried out.

It was quiet then, only the electronic beeping from the machines monitoring Ali Saif's vital signs. He was breathing very deeply, and Declan moved close, leaned on his walking stick, reached down and held the wasted hand. Saif's eyes, sunken into his face, flickered open, stared, and he managed the weakest of smiles. His lips moved, but speech eluded him. Declan was aware of

Ferguson's voice approaching down the corridor and another, deeper voice that could only be Hamid Bey. There was bewilderment and then alarm in Saif's eyes.

Declan squeezed his hand again. 'Don't worry. I won't leave you, I'll be close by.'

He moved quickly into the bathroom, went inside, closed the door, and stood behind it. He left it open an inch or two, enough to observe and hear clearly.

The outer door to the corridor was open and there was the observation window. Imam Hamid Bey, dramatic in his robes, stood waiting with Lily Shah, wearing a navy blue raincoat over her uniform. Maggie was obviously explaining to Ferguson that Bellamy wasn't coming, and he eased her away from the others while he listened. Hamid Bey watched them go, took Lily by the arm, urged her into the sickroom, and approached Saif, staring down at him, his rage and anger clear. Saif's eyes flickered open and his instant terror was plain.

Lily said, 'This is not good. Leave him. He is obviously very ill.'

But rage had consumed Hamid Bey to an extent that left him without caution. His face contorted, he leaned over Saif and said in Arabic, 'Foul apostate, turning against your race and religion. May Allah send you to hell, where you most truly belong, you pariah dog.'

For a moment, his hand poised as if to snatch

away the life-saving lines attached to Saif's body, and at that instant, the bathroom door crashed open and Declan Rashid stepped out, right arm extended and holding a Colt .25.

'There is only one dog here,' he said in Arabic. 'Step back very gently or I'll leave your brains on the floor.'

Hamid Bey glared. Lily grabbed him with both hands and pulled him away.

Ferguson rushed in. 'What's happened?'

Declan told him, returning the Colt to his rear waistband. 'I never liked the idea of bringing these people into Rosedene in the first place, but at least you know now exactly where you are with the Army of God. Pity you can't put him on the next plane out.'

Hamid Bey had recovered now. 'Just try, Ferguson, and see where it gets you.'

'I know, you'll deny everything, your lawyer will mention your human rights, and you'll be left free to blow up Parliament if you want to.' Ferguson turned to Lily. 'You seem a decent kind of lady. Can't you do better than this?' He shook his head. 'Just go away, both of you.'

'You haven't heard the last of me,' Hamid Bey shouted, but Lily reacted forcefully for once, grabbing his arm and hurrying him along the corridor and out the front door to the car park. She urged him into the rear of their car, got behind the wheel, and drove away.

'Such rage is bad for your heart. Calm yourself,' she said. 'That's sound medical advice.'

'Surely you see now that there is only one way of dealing with these people,' he told her. 'The sword.'

But the truth was she saw no such thing and drove back to Pound Street, more troubled than ever about the situation into which she had got herself, while he glowered beside her at this latest reversal on top of the failure of the attack on Sara Gideon. He was convinced Dillon had been responsible. Who else would have kneecapped them?

Tully and Bell were over the border and well on their way when Bell pulled into a parking area at the side of the road. 'Time I had a word with the Master,' he said, took out the mobile, and pressed the button.

'Who is this?'

'As if you didn't know, but if you want to play games, this is Frank Bell. We've taken you up on your offer and we're on our way.'

'I'm glad to hear it,' the Master said. 'Where are you?'

'A mile outside Castletown. We'll stop there for a drink and a sandwich, then we should be in the Drumgoole area within half an hour after that.'

'My regards to Mr Tully. I wish you every success with the enterprise. We'll talk again later.'

Tully had been leaning close to him to catch the conversation. 'I hate that English accent,' he said. 'A posh bastard, that fella. Anyway, Castletown, a drink or two at the pub, and then Drumgoole and Tod Flynn and his niece.' His smile was evil. 'You know, it's been a long time, Frank, and I'm really looking forward to it.' He shook his head. 'I've never been happy with peace.'

At Drumgoole, Hannah had ridden Fancy partway up the hill behind the buildings, then paused as a few drops of rain indicated the chance of a shower. She half turned and saw a Land Rover approaching on the country road that led to the Place.

The fact that it was an unfamiliar vehicle alerted her, and there was also the fact that since Dillon's phone call, the stable hands had been sent off on holiday while Tod and Kelly, Aunt Meg, and Hannah waited to see what would happen.

She produced her mobile, called Aunt Meg, and found her in the kitchen. 'There's a Land Rover I've never seen before heading straight for the Place. It may be Dillon.'

'Well, if it is, he'll be just in time for lunch,' Meg said. 'But I'll warn Tod and Kelly, and you better get back here quick, girl.'

Hannah muttered, swung Fancy around, and urged her into a gallop.

* * *

Dillon was driving, Sara beside him, Billy and Harry in the rear. He turned into the front court-yard of the fine old building and found Meg in her apron, Hannah in riding breeches, leaning on her walking stick, Tod and Kelly in work shirts and jeans, standing one on each side of the ladies.

Dillon got out, followed by Sara, who had brought her own stick in anticipation of rough country.

Billy and Harry got out, the two groups confronting each other.

It was Sara who broke the ice, by limping up to Hannah and holding out her hand. 'Sara Gideon, and you must be Hannah. We seem to have something in common.'

Hannah's smile was instant. 'This is my aunt Meg.'

'Who hopes you've all brought an appetite with you, as we were just going to sit down to lunch,' Meg said, and turned to Dillon and kissed him on the cheek. 'A long, long time, Sean. So good to see you.'

He turned and pulled in his companions. 'This is Harry Salter, a friend.'

Harry was gravely polite. 'A real pleasure,' he told Meg. 'And this is my nephew, Billy, who works for the government.'

'But doing what?' Tod asked, coming forward, flinging his arms wide and hugging Dillon. 'You ould bastard. You're looking well.'

Dillon reached and shook hands with Kelly. 'And so are you, and without leaving it another minute, we're on a peace mission, so there are things that must be said.'

'Of course there are, but that can wait until you've all eaten your fill,' Meg said. 'So inside this minute, the lot of you.'

Billy trailed behind to admire the Montesa on its stand beside the front door, the Spanish dirt bike developed for high country and beloved by shepherds all over the world, because it could go at half a mile an hour on rough ground and roar away like the wind when needed.

Tod had paused. 'Are you a bike man?'

'I think you could say that,' Billy said. 'I've heard of these.'

'Give it a try after lunch if you like, but let's go in.'

It was a farmhouse meal at the kitchen table, and afterwards tea and cake in the parlour, Irish-style, which Sara insisted on helping Meg and Hannah get ready.

Hannah said, 'What happened to your leg?'

'I was shot in a Taliban ambush in Afghanistan.'

Hannah was astonished. 'Do you mean you're a soldier?'

'For ten years now. I'm a captain in the Intelligence Corps. They let me still serve because I speak some useful languages, so as the army says, I'm fit for purpose.'

'I was blown up by a bomb in Uncle Tod's car.

My parents were killed, but I think it must have been meant for Uncle Tod,' Hannah said. 'He was big stuff when he was in the IRA.'

'Actually, Hannah, we've just investigated that. You've heard of Al Qaeda, of course,' Sara said.

'Oh, yes.'

'It was they who targeted your father. They thought he was going to be a threat to their business, so they had a couple of contract killers from the UVF, named Fergus Tully and Frank Bell, do away with him. They're the kind who didn't care that his wife and daughter were with him. I can show you photos of them.' She opened her shoulder bag, found the print of the information Roper had sent her. 'There you are.'

Hannah looked, then wiped slow tears from her eyes and said, 'Just excuse me for a moment,' and she limped out.

Meg said, 'Are you certain that's the way of it?'

'Yes, there can be no doubt of it.'

'God help us, but that will relieve Tod of a terrible burden. Give me a hand with the tea and cake and we'll see what's going on in the parlour.'

Tod was bitterly angry as Meg entered with the large tray, which she put down on the table. Sara paused by the door and listened as he spoke.

'Fergus Tully and Frank Bell were responsible for the car bomb, Aunt Meg. Sean's just been telling me. An Al Qaeda hit, and they weren't out for me at all. It was Peter they were after.'

127

'I know, love, Sara was discussing it with us.'

'So where is Hannah?' Tod asked.

She entered the room at that moment, reached for Sara's hand, squeezed it, then crossed to Tod and kissed him on the cheek.

'Are you okay?' he asked.

'Definitely.' She smiled and turned to Sara. 'Do you ride?'

'Indeed I do.'

'What do you say to taking a turn up the hill?'

'I'd love to.'

'Then let's go and find you a nice mare and the right kit and leave them to it.'

It was companionable enough in the parlour. Tod drank his tea, his mind obviously still on what he'd just heard. 'So here we are. You've not come to lift us, Sean?'

'According to the official story, you've done nothing, and Jake Cazalet is alive and well to prove it.'

Kelly said, 'For God's sake, will you tell him how it all happened, Tod?'

'Why not?' Tod shrugged. 'Like we all do, I knew of the existence of Al Qaeda, but I'd never had any kind of dealing with the Master until he came on the phone and waved a big payday at me.'

What he went through was a reasonably honest account of what had gone on on Nantucket. When he was finished, Harry said, 'So the moment you heard who was arriving for dinner with Cazalet, you dumped the Chechens and headed for home?'

'That's it. Doesn't bother me in the slightest. They were lunatics.'

'Never mind that,' Dillon said. 'It's the woman who interests me, the one that even the Chechens didn't know about, who followed them into Cazalet's garden and witnessed the attack. Can you tell me any more about her?'

'The Master described her as a woman sympathetic to our cause, that's all I can say.'

There was silence for a moment, and Billy said, 'What a story. You'd have difficulty improving on that.'

'Actually, I can,' Tod said. 'After Dillon's call referring to Nantucket, I called the Master with the happy news.'

'And how did he take it?'

'Wanted me to dispose of Ferguson and any of you who turned up here, pointed out that the Bog of Salam is close by. He also tried to bribe me by saying I could keep the quarter million dollars I owe him and offering to give me the names of the two men who were responsible for the car bomb that killed my brother.'

'Did he?' Dillon asked.

'No, and as I'd taken his call in the stable, Hannah overheard it and told him what she thought of Al Qaeda, which wasn't much.'

'And what was his response to that?' Harry Salter put in.

'He threatened her life, which was a stupid thing to do, because it now means that I'll have to kill him the first chance I get.'

'Which isn't very likely,' Dillon said. 'Meeting him, I mean, but I know how you feel.'

Meg had sat there without a word, but she spoke now. 'Hannah's got a week to sign in at the Royal. How can she be left there on her own?'

'We'll sort it,' Tod said. 'I'll be her shadow.'

'Well, I can tell you now, she won't fancy that.'

'We'll get a decent place for her, that quarter of a million dollars will see to that.' He turned to the others. 'Come and see the stables. We've got some fine horses this year.' They all got up to go.

'You'll excuse me, the kitchen calls,' Meg said, and left.

But as the men were walking around to the stud stables, Hannah emerged on Fancy and Sara on a white mare. They both wore Australian drover's coats and broad-brimmed hats.

'It's going to rain,' Tod told them.

'I know, that's why we're dressed for it,' Hannah told him, and they cantered away.

The Jeep had arrived much earlier than expected at roughly the same time as the Land Rover. High on the hill were a few ancient stone walls and a copse offering shelter. Tully had been reading a tourist handbook of the area, purchased in Castletown.

He peered down into the valley below. 'The Great Bog of Salam. The things these turnip-heads believe. It says here: *To be avoided at all times.*'

'Well, that seems sensible to me.' Bell turned in the other direction to Drumgoole Place below. 'Very nice, I must say, you have to admire that. Tod Flynn has done well for himself.'

Tully said, 'Well, this is payback day, but what's that big silver vehicle driving towards the house?'

'A Land Rover,' Bell told him, and at that moment saw Hannah, mounted on Fancy, much lower down the hill. She looked towards the Land Rover, took out her mobile, spoke into it, then she turned the horse and galloped back down to the house.

Bell took great care reversing into the trees of the copse and checked to confirm that the Jeep was hidden from view. Then he produced a pair of high-powered Nikon binoculars and put them to use.

'That's Tod, his aunt Meg, Kelly, and the niece Hannah, still in riding breeches,' he said, focusing on the front door as they emerged.

'By God, I'd like to have those off her,' Tully said.

Bell ignored him and turned to the Land Rover. 'Let's see what we've got here.' He watched for a long moment as Dillon and the others got out, was stunned at the sight of them. 'I don't believe it!'

'Believe what?' Tully asked.

131

'Those photos we got have just come to life stepping out of that Land Rover. There's Sean Dillon, the Gideon woman, Harry Salter, and his nephew, Billy. All Ferguson's people.'

Tully shook his head. 'That isn't possible.'

Bell handed over the binoculars. 'See for yourself.'

Tully watched as the greetings took place below and everyone moved into the house. He turned to Bell. 'What's going on, Frank, it doesn't make sense.'

'That's just what I'm going to find out,' Bell told him, and led the way back to the Jeep, where he climbed inside, retrieved the mobile, and punched the button as Tully followed him.

The Master answered at once. 'Who is this?'

'Well, I'm not sure anymore,' Bell said. 'We're established here on the hill overlooking Drumgoole Place, where we've been privileged to watch a Land Rover drive up and disgorge Sean Dillon, and Captain Sara Gideon, plus Harry Salter and nephew. They've now gone inside after a warm welcome from Tod Flynn and family.'

There was a slight pause, unlike his usual behaviour, then the Master said, 'A warm welcome, you say?'

'Absolutely. The men hugged each other, the women kissed. Happy families time, as far as we could see. What's going on? Is there something you haven't told us? What are Charles Ferguson's four best operatives doing here?'

'I haven't the slightest idea,' the Master lied,

cursing the fact that Ferguson had moved a lot faster than he had anticipated. 'It appears that my information was incorrect this time. I assume Dillon and his friends will be armed to the teeth. In the circumstances, the sensible choice would be to leave them to it. We'll discuss the possibility of further action at a later date.'

'And here's me thinking you were infallible,' Bell told him. 'What a disappointment. The thing I hate is wasting my time, so we'll hang on for a couple of hours. There's a chance we can get by here, parked in the trees. The Flynns and their guests are probably enjoying lunch. Remember, I've got my rifle. If I wait until they step out of the front door again, I could probably knock off three or even four of them, before they knew what was happening.'

'You'd be taking a chance. The odds are stacked against you.'

'Just the way I like it,' and Bell switched off.

'So what do we do?' Tully asked.

'We wait as long as we can get away with it. Get the fishing tackle out and lean the rods against the Jeep, that sort of thing. Lucky we got all those sandwiches at the pub in Castletown.'

'That's true,' Tully said, 'And plenty of booze in the storage locker.'

'Well, go easy on that, I know you,' Bell told him. 'If it ain't going to work, then that's the end of it. Two hours tops, and if there's no kind of movement, we're out of it.'

★   ★   ★

Dillon snatched a chance to bring Holland Park up to date. 'Is Ferguson around?' he asked Roper, whom he had called.

'He was for a while, handling the business of Hamid Bey's visit to Rosedene.'

'How did that go?'

Roper told him in some detail. 'I've got a strong feeling that the imam is Al Qaeda to the core.'

'Should I be surprised? Sister Lily's husband was, that's common knowledge.'

'True, but all my reports indicate that people speak nothing but good about her. Having said that, it's fascinating what Tod Flynn had to say about the Master's lady, sympathetic to the Cause, who witnessed the entire assassination attempt. Could it be Lily Shah?'

Dillon said, 'It would need a tough lady to carry that through, but it's worth keeping an eye on her.'

'I agree,' Roper said. 'Can I notify Ferguson that Flynn and company are on our side?'

'Yes. For many reasons, but the threat to Hannah Flynn was enough on its own. You'll like her.'

'I'm sure I will. Term starts in three and a half weeks. They'll expect her on day one like everyone else. Is that a problem?'

'There's a question of her security, where should she stay, that kind of thing. It all needs serious consideration. She and Sara have bonded already.'

'I can imagine they would,' Roper said. 'They've

got a lot in common. You get surprisingly used to disability, even when the pain is constant. Sara discovered that a long time ago. I hope Hannah has. If not, the relationship could be good for her.'

'You frequently astonish me, Giles,' Dillon told him.

'Stop it now, Sean, I'm beginning to sound maudlin,' Roper said. 'Off you go.'

Up on the hill, Bell had moved into a position where a couple of boulders offered some conceal- ment that gave him a clear view of the house and the front entrance and the courtyard. He lay there, the rifle on the ground beside him, the Browning pistol tucked into the front pouch of his anorak. He had been watching for an hour with no movement below.

Suddenly, Tully called out loudly. 'How much longer? What the bloody hell is going on?'

Bell got up, went back into the trees, and discov- ered Tully standing beside the Jeep, the Mac 10 in the crook of his left arm. He was drinking from a bottle and the distinctive smell of whiskey said it all.

'What are you playing at? You're drunk, you damn fool. God save us, but you never change, Fergus.' He slapped him across the face. 'Just like the old days. It's always you who has to go and cock up a good thing.'

Tully staggered, almost falling, clutching the

Mac 10 in both hands now. 'Keep your damn hands to yourself or I'll blow you away.'

'So who would you get to drive you back to Belfast, you shite? You're too drunk to do it yourself, that's for sure. Get back to the Jeep, we're leaving. I'll get my rifle and we're out of here.'

He turned back to the boulders, and Tully cried drunkenly, 'No, don't be like that, Frank,' and went after him.

Bell leaned down to pick up the Lee Enfield and saw Hannah and Sara Gideon cross the yard, passing Dillon standing in the front door, watching Billy astride the Montesa, talking to Tod. It seemed a golden opportunity to strike, then Hannah and Sara emerged from the stables, cantered across the yard, and urged their mounts up the track.

Tully lurched forward, mesmerized. 'Would you look at that?'

Bell pulled him out of sight. 'Get back to the Jeep. Just do as you're told and we might get somewhere with this.' He punched him hard. 'Go on, do it!' he ordered.

As Tully stumbled away, Bell turned back with his rifle, but at that very moment, Hannah charged from around the boulders and brushed him to one side, so that he dropped the gun. Sara followed, knocking Bell down again, and was so close that she recognized him as he tried to stand up. She swerved her mount, raised a booted foot, and stamped him in the face.

Hannah called, 'Follow me!'

Tully shouted in anger, ran a few yards, aiming the Mac 10, stumbled and fired into the ground. Sara, gripping her reins tightly in one hand, pulled out her Colt .25 and fired as she moved past, catching him on the side of the face, the hollow-point bullet tearing his cheek open.

Hannah swerved close to her. 'Follow the track; we'll circle and try to keep out of the way until help comes. I see they've got a Jeep parked in the copse. If they want to chase us, you'll know how good they are over rough country.'

At that moment, Sara's mobile buzzed and she fished it out of her breast pocket. It was Dillon. 'Sara, what's going on?'

'Frank Bell and Tully are parked up here in a Jeep. They tried to grab us, I shot Tully, who loosed off a Mac 10 into the ground as he fell. He's up again now.'

'Billy and Tod are coming up fast on the Montesa as we speak. The rest of us will try to get as close as we can in the Land Rover.'

Grabbing Tully by the collar, Bell pulled him up, ran him to the Jeep, yanked him into the rear, grabbed a towel from a locker, and shoved it into his hand. 'Hold that against your face and shut up. I'm going to get those two bitches.'

He scrambled behind the wheel, switched on the engine, and burst out of the trees, aware of Hannah and Sara galloping away. He went after them at high speed, driving one-handed while he called the Master.

'Where are you, what's happening?' the Master demanded.

'Tully got pissed out of his mind,' Bell said. 'A bad habit of his. Tried to have a go at the women, tripped and fired the machine pistol into the ground, which must have alerted them at the house. The Gideon woman shot him in the face. He's bleeding all over the back seat now. I'm chasing after them, but I can see a bike in my rear-view mirror coming up fast, and Ferguson's people aren't in the habit of taking prisoners.'

'Is there anything I can do for you?'

'Yes, tell Myra Tully that they were responsible for the death of her father. She won't like that, so she could be exactly what you're looking for. As far as you're concerned, I hope you get your reward in hell, you bastard.'

He rammed his foot down hard. The distance between him and the girls diminished rapidly. Driving one-handed, he reached out of the side window and fired his Browning to little effect as they turned off the track. As he bumped across rough country, the Montesa closed on him, and in his large rear-view mirror he saw that Tod Flynn, seated on the pillion, was using Billy's right shoulder to steady his aim.

It worked. Fergus Tully took a bullet in the head that drove him forward across the passenger seat, two more through the windshield. The final round was like a hammer blow high in the back, next to the spine, and had Frank Bell rearing in his seat in agony.

The Jeep rolled to a halt at the very edge of the scree of loose stones on the rim of the slope that slid down into the bog. Tod got off the pillion of the Montesa and walked forward as Billy raised it on its stand. Hannah and Sara sat their horses, not speaking, just watching, like figures in some medieval morality play. There was the sound of distant thunder across the valley and it started to rain.

Tod leaned down and saw only carnage, Fergus Tully's devastated face, Frank Bell calm and somehow detached from the blood soaking into his clothes at the back of his neck.

'You should have got rid of Tully years ago. I told you that when we were in the Maze,' Tod said to him.

'So you did. Too late now. Myra won't be pleased.' Bell coughed, and a trickle of blood oozed from the corner of his mouth.

'I can live with that.'

'One question. Were you expecting Dillon and company to turn up?' Bell croaked.

'Dillon phoned me and said they'd be coming, but didn't say when. I told the Master, and we quarrelled, but he knew they intended to come sometime.'

'You were a total surprise to us. He just told me he wanted us to take out you and Hannah,' Bell said. 'Didn't mention Dillon at all.'

But Tod was coldly angry. 'Last time you had a go at the Flynns, you killed my brother and his wife and crippled my niece. Now you tell me she was to be targeted again – I was going to put a bullet in your head to ease your going, but not now.'

The engine of the Jeep was still on. Tod opened the door, reached over Bell to release the hand brake, and Bell slipped a bloody hand around his neck, holding on fast as the vehicle started to move. Tod tried to kick free in vain, and the front wheels scattered an avalanche of stones over the edge of granite at the bottom of the slope, taking the Jeep with it into the bog. The amazing thing was how quickly it disappeared.

Billy ran forward, too late, Hannah screamed 'No!' and fought to control her horse, and the Land Rover turned off the track toward them. Dillon and Kelly, Harry and Meg, got out and hurried to meet them. Sara and Hannah stayed mounted, calm now, but grave and subdued by the horror of it.

Meg reached up to Hannah to touch hands. 'What's happened?'

'Ask Billy. We'll see you back at the Place.' Hannah put her heels into Fancy and galloped away, and Sara went after her.

Meg appeared dazed, frowning in bewilderment. 'What is it, I don't understand. Where's Tod?'

So Billy told her.

★   ★   ★

If there was one thing Dillon and his cousin had in common from youth, it was a County Down accent. It was this that he intended to use, as everybody gathered in the parlour a couple of hours later and he announced that he meant to contact the Master using the special mobile given to Tod for that purpose.

'He may have cut the line, as it were,' Dillon said. 'But chances are he hasn't quite yet, out of curiosity. I'll do the talking, but I'll put it on speaker so you can hear everything.'

He made the call, and within seconds the Master's voice boomed out. 'I was beginning to think you'd gone the way of all flesh, Mr Flynn.'

'No, but I *am* the bearer of bad news,' Dillon told him, the actor in him taking over, his Down accent very pronounced. 'Frank Bell and Tully came to a particularly unfortunate finish, swallowed up by the Bog of Salam. As it's never been known to reject anything, that's an end to them.'

'The end of nothing, Mr Flynn,' the Master replied. 'To ally yourself with Charles Ferguson and his people is a grave error on your part. They are declared enemies of Al Qaeda, have done great harm to our organization.'

'I'm sure General Ferguson will be delighted to hear that,' Dillon said.

'But not so pleased when the news of Tully's murder reaches the ears of his daughter. Myra is a formidable lady, as you'll find out.'

Harry could not contain himself 'What a load of bollocks. The only big thing about Myra is her mouth. A right little tin-pot dictator. I could go back on the streets tomorrow and walk all over her.'

'Let him rant and rave,' the Master said. 'London can be a dangerous place for female students even at the best of times, but particularly for one so handicapped.'

It was Sara who spoke now. 'If you had seen the way she handled herself with the two thugs you sent to murder her, you would not waste your time making stupid threats. When I return to London, she goes with me.'

Hannah's angry smile said it all. 'You can go to hell, Master-whoever-you-are.'

The Master's voice stayed calm. 'Not me, Hannah, but you and all your friends.'

The phone died as he departed, and there was only silence as if no one knew what to make of what had happened. It was Dillon who said, 'So there we are. Tod is a threat for him, played by me, of course. But what are you suggesting, Sara?'

'Hannah needs to go to London as soon as possible, to make ready for her new life, and she'll need a safe and secure place, with people who will make her welfare a priority. I think I have just the one.'

Dillon was already smiling. 'Highfield Court, is that what you're suggesting?'

'Absolutely,' Sara said, 'If a nice Catholic Irish girl can adjust to a Sephardic Jewish establishment. It's where I live when I'm in London, Hannah, with my grandfather, Rabbi Nathan Gideon, and our housekeeper, Mrs Sadie Cohen. An early-Victorian house with a music room.'

'You mean with a piano?' She was almost pleading. 'Oh, say that there is, Sara.'

'All right, but not just any old piano. You'll have to wait and see. Your induction week at college starts on September the fifteenth. That gives you four clear weeks at Highfield to settle in and prepare.'

Meg seemed uncertain and worried about the whole thing, but Hannah immediately made it clear that it was what she wanted. 'It takes care of all the problems, Aunt Meg. I owe it to Uncle Tod, you must see that. It would be a waste not to, after what happened to him.'

'The Gulfstream could fly us back to Farley in the early evening,' Dillon said. 'You can stuff as many of your personal belongings in it as you like.'

Kelly cut in. 'It solves too many problems to say no, Aunt Meg. We've four mares in foal. We'll have our hands full with the stud, and you can go and visit once she's settled in. No one will query Tod's absence. God rest him, he was away more than he was here for years.'

Meg nodded sadly. 'Well, let's get you packed,' she said to Hannah, and they went out together at once, and Kelly followed to take care of chores in the stables.

The Salters, Dillon, and Sara were left together, and Harry smiled. 'It's certainly been a lively day out. That Master's a right bastard, I must say. He really needs sorting.'

'Easier said than done,' Billy told him. 'She's quite a girl, Hannah. Is Ferguson going to be okay about you having her on board, Sara?'

'He'll have to be,' she said. 'I'll just take a walk outside and have a word with my grandfather and Sadie and warn them to expect us, then I'll speak to Roper. I'll leave you to call Lacey at Kilmartin to arrange our departure, Sean.'

Rabbi Nathan Gideon was the kindest of men by nature, and accepted the prospect of his world being turned upside down with his usual equanimity. Sadie, while admitting that Tony Doyle had been a real asset about the house, warmed to the idea of taking Hannah in after Sara gave her a brief account of what to expect, and then called Roper.

After an account of the day's events, he was astonished. 'Honestly, Sara, when you lot get stuck-in these days, you don't take prisoners.'

'I can't see the point, Giles,' she said. 'The new rules are that there are no rules any longer. Bullet in your target's back on a dark and rainy night, then call Mr Teague with his van and body bags and the crematorium waiting. Play dirty seems to be the name of the game.'

'And are we winning?'

'Don't ask me. I've had a hard day, which included shooting Fergus Tully in the face, then watching him and his associate get swallowed by an Irish bog and taking a good man with them. The prospect of facing Ferguson with an account of the day's events is beyond me. I'll leave it to you, but when you've explained Hannah's presence to him, tell him one thing is a given. Staff Sergeant Tony Doyle stays on in the house as an armed guard and chauffeur.'

She was stressed and weary, Roper could sense it. 'Well, why didn't I think of that! Lie back and enjoy the flight. I'll see you soon,' and he switched off.

In her bedroom at the Sash, Myra Tully was dressing for her usual evening appearance, splendid in exotic underwear, easing a dress of scarlet oyster satin over her head, when Terry entered, wearing a well-tailored black suit, a white shirt, and a Guards tie. There was a glass of champagne on the tray he carried, and he put it down.

'You didn't knock, did you? Honestly, Terry, you're hopeless. Go and make sure there's no rubbish in the saloon bar, good dressers only.'

He withdrew without a word and she reached

for the champagne, drank half of it inelegantly, and was starting to touch up her make-up when her mobile sounded.

She turned it on and said, 'Myra Tully. Who the hell is this?'

'This is the Master speaking. You're aware, I'm sure, that I've been dealing with your father, Myra?'

His use of her Christian name offended her, and she bridled. 'Well, you're bleeding familiar for a start. Anyway, how's my da getting on?'

'Not too well.' He was deliberately goading her. 'Like the Scarlet Pimpernel in the French Revolution. Is he in Heaven or is he in Hell?'

'What are you trying to say?' she demanded hoarsely.

'That your father and his good friend Frank Bell are dead. It was the work of the Flynn family and Charles Ferguson's people – Sean Dillon, Harry and Billy Salter, Captain Sara Gideon.'

She had to struggle to speak. 'It can't be true. How could you know?'

'Don't be silly, Myra, it's all out there.'

'Dillon,' she croaked. 'And Ferguson.' Her voice rose. 'I'll have them all, if it's the last thing I do on this earth.'

'Excellent,' the Master said. 'I'll go now, but we'll speak again. And get one thing clear – if you want revenge, don't make a move unless I tell you to.'

She threw her phone at the wall, the door

burst open, and Terry entered. 'Myra, what is it?' he demanded.

She pushed him away from her. 'He's dead, my da's dead, and it's all Charles Ferguson's fault. I'll have his eyes before I'm through,' and she fell on the bed, sobbing bitterly.

WASHINGTON

PARIS
LONDON

CHAPTER 7

The helicopter from Nantucket that had dropped off Ferguson and his people in New York continued its flight to Washington, landing in a reserved area of the airport, where Jake Cazalet found Blake Johnson waiting with a driver and limousine. During Cazalet's two terms at the White House, Blake had served him well and had become a loyal friend.

'Great to see you in one piece,' Blake said as they shook hands.

'Thanks to the Prime Minister's private army,' Cazalet told him. 'Where are we going?'

'We've booked you into a suite at the Hay-Adams. You like it there, don't you?'

'Who wouldn't?' Cazalet said. 'Frankly, I was worried he might have decided to have me stay at the White House, so I'm glad he hasn't. After all, we were never bosom buddies.'

'Well, I can't think of the right answer to that,' Blake said.

'Forget it, I don't want to embarrass you. Your job is to serve the President, which you did brilliantly for me, and now you do it for him. So the situation makes you feel uncomfortable. What's so surprising? After all, we don't even vote for the same party.'

Blake laughed. 'Well, I suppose that might explain it.'

They pulled up at the hotel entrance, the driver got out to pass the luggage to the doorman, and Cazalet turned, smiling.

'So I take it I'm not due to see him for dinner tonight?'

'He said he wanted to give you time to settle in.'

'That's considerate of him, so that's exactly what I'm going to do.' He scrambled out of the Mercedes and turned, leaning down. 'Is he still taking the CIA line over the Nantucket affair?'

Blake looked strangely helpless. 'What do you want me to say?'

'Not a thing, old friend, I'll handle it. See you later.'

He went up the steps and the doorman saluted him. 'Great to see you again, Captain.'

Cazalet patted his shoulder. 'You're still here, George. You must be seventy if you're a day.'

'Just don't tell anyone, Mr President. I need the job.'

'I won't let you down,' Cazalet said. 'We old Vietnam vets have got to stick together,' and he walked inside to where the hotel manager waited.

'A great pleasure to have you here once again, Mr President,' the manager said formally. 'Let me show you to your suite.'

He led the way, people staring in recognition

as they passed. When they reached the lift, a white-haired old man in a tan suit was leaning on a cane, waiting.

'Good afternoon, Professor Khan,' the manager said. 'Going up?'

Khan seemed mesmerized by Cazalet's presence. 'Mr President, I wouldn't dream of intruding.'

'Nonsense,' Cazalet told him as the door opened. 'Join us by all means. Are you on vacation?'

'No, I've lived in Washington for many years. I'm staying here while my house is being renovated. This is a great honour, sir.'

'Not at all. Nice to meet you.' Cazalet shook his hand, Khan got out on his own floor, and the lift continued.

'The Penthouse, sir,' the manager said. 'The White House insisted.'

'Top of the world, eh?' Cazalet said cheerfully. 'Well, isn't that kind of them?' And as the door opened, he followed the manager out.

The suite was perfection, and the views of Washington from the balcony were extraordinary. Standing there, taking it all in, tiredness washed over him in a great wave. In a few short hours, his life had totally changed. The assassination attempt, the gunplay and deaths, the uncertainty of what lay before him. There was only one sensible answer to that, so he went to bed and slept soundly until ten o'clock the following morning, when he awoke to a day of heavy rain.

There were no messages when he tried reception, so he spent some time in the pool and sauna and worked his way through a selection of newspapers. Just after lunch he was surprised to see himself on local television arriving at the hotel the day before. No reason was given for his presence in Washington. Cazalet didn't like that and thought about reaching for a phone, but there was pride to consider, so he hung in there as if nothing was wrong, dined openly in the restaurant that night, and went to bed early again.

Three days of this was definitely enough, four if you included his day of arrival. A rerun on television of him arriving at the hotel was the final straw, and he phoned Blake Johnson.

'I presume they can't decide what to do with me, but I object to find myself playing the invisible man. If he won't grant me an audience, I'm out of here tonight.'

'Calm down, Jake, it's the President we're talking about.'

'I've been there and done that, Blake. I'm sixty-five years of age, lost the two most important women in my life to cancer and my beloved daughter to a car accident in Spain. So what have I got? The fortune my mother brought into the family when she married my father. When I last checked, that stood at four billion, and the board is clamouring to have me as chairman. I'll leave you to decide.'

He was smiling when he went up to his suite, smiled again half an hour later when his phone sounded. He picked it up and said, 'That's what I call service, Blake.'

A familiar voice replied, 'Can't help you there. This is Charles Ferguson.'

'Where are you calling from?'

'London. You've got the number.'

'Of course I have. How did you know I was here?'

'Well, we do have an embassy in Washington, and I was just curious to know what the President is doing with you.'

'Absolutely nothing. Haven't even seen him, only Blake when I arrived. I've been killing time for four days. What about your end?'

'The four days since we parted have been filled with death and destruction. Among other things, we discovered who was behind Nantucket.'

It took Ferguson some time to cover everything. When he was finished, there was a long pause before Jake Cazalet said, 'So Dillon's pretending this man Tod Flynn's still alive whenever the Master phones, Sara Gideon has taken his niece Hannah to live at her place, and the Salters are alive and well?'

'And on the other side, this woman, Myra Tully, and her gang are likely to be trouble,' Ferguson said. 'And, of course, there's still Hamid Bey and his Army of God.'

'And the two men in ski masks who saved Sara when she was attacked. That was certainly lucky. It'd be nice to know who they were,' Cazalet put in. 'But enough, Charles, I've got to hear from Blake and the President. I'll get back to you when I can. And Charles? Thank you, old friend.'

Three hours later, angry that he still hadn't heard from the White House, he changed into a black tracksuit, went down to the hotel entrance, and passed the night doorman. It was dusk, still raining, street lights on in Lafayette Square. Running head down as he pulled up his hood, he emerged through trees and bumped into another man in a tracksuit who stumbled to one knee, came up fast, and punched him on the side of the face.

Larger than Cazalet, he snarled, 'Stupid bastard!' and struck out again. Cazalet could smell the alcohol, parried the blow to one side, and delivered two savage knuckle strikes under the ribs that had the man yell, stumble over a bench, and fall to the ground. He pulled himself up, groaning.

'Get the hell out of here or I'll break your arm,' Cazalet told him.

'Sorry, bud,' the man croaked. 'My mistake.'

He limped away, and Cazalet stood there shaking his head, the rain pouring down. 'What comes next, Jake?' he asked softly. 'Are you going to kill somebody? Vietnam was a long time ago.'

He turned away through the trees, started back towards the hotel, and saw a Mercedes parked outside the entrance, Blake Johnson in a trench coat and rain hat standing under an umbrella being held by the night doorman.

'So there you are!' Blake called. 'What are you trying to do? Drown yourself? You're expected in the Oval Office.' He shook his head as Cazalet got close. 'You're soaking. I'm driving you myself in case you want to talk.'

Cazalet said, 'Wait for me in the hall.'

He jumped out of the car and made for the lift on the run, to the astonishment of those seated in the reception area, among them Professor Ali Khan, at a table enjoying a coffee and reading the *Washington Post*. Blake moved in out of the rain and stood waiting for him.

Within ten minutes he reappeared, wearing a tweed jacket over khaki pants.

'Will I do?' he demanded.

'Of course you will,' Blake told him.

'Then let's get going. One shouldn't keep Potus waiting.' He hurried outside, Blake following.

Two white-haired ladies were enjoying coffee at the table close to Ali Khan, and one said to the other, 'Potus? That's a strange word. What on earth does it mean?'

Khan beamed at them over his newspaper. 'It's an acronym, ladies. President of the United States.'

They were surprised and a bit shocked. 'Well, I must say that's very clever, isn't it, Mary?' She nodded to Khan. 'Thank you so much.'

'My pleasure,' he said, and returned to his newspaper.

★   ★   ★

When Blake ushered Cazalet into the Oval Office, it was in shadows, a table light on the desk, the President sitting behind, papers scattered in front of him, which he had obviously been reading. He looked up, didn't bother to smile, just nodded.

'Ah, there you are.'

There was the hint of reproof, and Blake said, 'Shall I wait outside, Mr President?'

'No, I'd like you to stay.'

The door to the Chief of Staff's office stood slightly ajar, although the room itself was in darkness. In spite of that, it probably meant that someone was in there, not that the possibility bothered Cazalet in the slightest, although he could see there was no light on.

'Now then, Jake,' the President said stiffly. 'Bad business, this Nantucket thing. What's to be done, that's what I'd like to know.'

There was somehow a suggestion that it was all Cazalet's fault, which he quickly countered. 'It was lucky for me that you wanted me to thank Ferguson on your behalf. I'm pretty certain I'd have been dead meat if Dillon and Captain Sara Gideon hadn't upset Al Qaeda's apple cart.'

'Yes, it goes without saying that was fortunate. Anyway, the thing is, what are we going to do with you now?'

'I understood the idea was that I hang around Washington on display to prove I'm alive if any false rumours of my death started to circulate, while our experts do all the work needed to make my house in Nantucket totally secure.'

'Which can't be done, I'm afraid,' the President said. 'Apparently, the house is far too old, and I can't possibly allow you to go back to living in it. I was going to discuss that with you when you arrived, but all the current fuss with Ukraine got in the way.'

'It usually does,' Cazalet said.

'On top of that, there's a UN committee, chaired by the French President, meeting in Paris at the Elysée Palace to discuss the plight of Syrian refugees. When their business is done there, they intend to carry on to London and repeat the process with the British Prime Minister.'

'Were they hoping you might put in an appearance?' Cazalet asked.

'There's no way I can do that. I've made my decision to run for re-election. Life's going to be busy from now on.'

'Congratulations,' Cazalet said. 'But maybe I could sit in for you in Paris and in London if you want – simply as an observer, of course. The kind of international coverage it'd get would certainly make it clear that I was in the land of the living.'

'Trying to get your face on screen again, Jake? Thanks for the offer, but the CIA, with the FBI, have now concluded that a repeat of the Nantucket affair is unlikely.'

Cazalet laughed out loud. 'You mean that Al

Qaeda won't have another try at shooting me? Well, thanks very much. There's a comforting thought.'

The President didn't like it. 'You know what your problem is? You're *you*, which is sometimes a handicap. The gallant war hero bit doesn't cut it any more, or your attempt at a man-of-the-people image. The CIA is here to protect the citizens of this country, including you, and I can't accept your constant criticism of their actions.'

'Of course, Mr President. It wasn't their fault that they weren't there when the assassins struck in Nantucket, and forgive me if I appeared to be suggesting otherwise.'

It seemed to mollify the President.

'That's understandable, Jake, you've been through a pretty dreadful experience. I think you should take some time off. As I recall, you've got a wonderful place down there in the Virgin Islands. Why don't you pay it a visit, get some diving in, try a little fishing?'

'Do a Hemingway?' Cazalet said. 'You know, that's a very good idea. Thanks for the thought.'

'What are friends for? You'll come back a new man. We can decide what to do with you then.'

'I look forward to it.' Cazalet reached across and shook his hand. 'You've been very understanding.'

'Think nothing of it,' the President said. 'Blake will drop you back at the hotel.'

★   ★   ★

As they eased into the traffic outside the White House, Blake smiled. 'I don't know why, but I get a feeling the Virgin Islands is not likely to figure in your future plans, whatever they are.'

'Careful, Blake, you could be faced with a conflict of interest here,' Cazalet told him.

'Oh, I'll do my duty for my president, just like I did for you. I seem to recall that meant taking a bullet for you on more than one occasion.'

'True enough,' Cazalet said. 'And let me assure you, Blake, nothing I do now will be detrimental to my country or its leaders.'

They turned into the hotel at that moment and parked by the entrance. 'Well, that being so, I'm your man. Maybe I can provide a little helpful advice,' Blake said.

'I'm sure you can.' Cazalet nodded. 'I have to make a couple of important phone calls, but I'll be as quick as I can.' He beckoned to the duty manager, who was standing nearby. 'Alonzo, if you could see to Mr Johnson. Nice table in the supper bar. Open a bottle of Dom Pérignon.'

'Of course, sir.'

'I'll be right back,' Cazalet said, and hurried to the elevator.

His private secretary, Carol Shaw, had been a soldier's wife, widowed by Desert Storm when she started working in Senator Jake Cazalet's office. She had moved with him to the White House, and these days was based in the chairman's suite at

Cazalet Plaza in Manhattan. Because of the time, he called her at home.

'I've finally seen the President.'

'How did it go?'

'Not too well, but never mind that. I'm going to stay here tomorrow, do some shopping, but I'll want a plane around noon. The President says I need a holiday after all the stress lately, so I've decided to take him at his word.'

'Are you going to fly down to the Virgins?'

'That was what he suggested, but I have other ideas. I need to be in Paris by Wednesday. Book me a suite at the Ritz. I should be there two days, then London. The Dorchester. See if you can get me the Oliver Messel Suite. I love the vista of London from up there.'

She was surprised. 'Is this something you're doing for the President?'

'You couldn't be more wrong, Carol. There is nothing for me in his camp, nor will there be.'

'So what's in Paris?'

'A UN meeting chaired by the French President to discuss Syria. I intend to be there.'

'In what capacity?'

'That of a concerned human being who happens to be in Paris, and like everyone else in the audience, wants to know what they're going to do about it.'

'I'm amazed the White House would allow it.'

'They won't know until it happens, will they? I'll have flown off into the wild blue yonder. I offered to observe for the President in Paris, but he turned me down flat. He's entitled to do that. I suppose he'd see me as competition.'

'So all this is about you getting back at the President?'

'It's got nothing to do with him. In Paris, I'll be an American citizen on holiday, and what I do there is my business.'

'But you're not an ordinary American citizen.' Her voice rose. 'You were once President of these United States.'

'Yes, many years ago. Since then, my red hair has turned to grey and I'm just a civilian. Last year, I spent three days in London on business, shopped in Harrods and the West End, and went to the theatre twice, and nobody recognized me.'

'Maybe, but that was before Nantucket. AQ tried to kill you, and from what I've read about them, they'll try it again because they don't do failure,' she said. 'This is all very risky.'

'You're probably right,' he said. 'I'll have to take that as it comes. The truth of the matter is that it would not make the slightest difference if I booked into the Dorchester as Mr Smith. Al Qaeda would still know it was me.'

She was suddenly angry. 'So what are you going to do? Start carrying a pistol in your pocket, waiting for them to turn up – or should I say hoping they'll turn up? This isn't 1974, and it's not Saigon, where action and passion were second nature to you.'

'Would that be so bad? At least it would show I was still alive. I'm meeting Blake now. Just go to bed, Carol,' and he switched off his mobile.

The supper bar was quiet enough when Cazalet went in, no more than twelve or fifteen tables taken, Professor Ali Khan at one of them. The two ladies who had been sitting nearby in the foyer had obviously followed him in and were within talking distance. Blake was near the palms by the window, slightly isolated and reading *Vanity Fair*. His champagne glass was half full.

Cazalet said to the waiter, 'I'll have some of that champagne, smoked salmon, and scrambled eggs. Is that all right for you, Blake?'

'Suits me fine.'

'Give us half an hour,' Cazalet told the waiter, and turned to Blake. 'I think we should talk.'

Khan was wearing a KGB sound enhancer. The clarity was remarkable and he could hear everything. More important, however, was his cane with the carved ivory handle. It contained a directional microphone, which could record at quite a distance.

'So what have you decided?' Blake said. 'Where's the holiday to be? What are you going to get up to?'

'Maybe I shouldn't tell you. If I do and you keep the whole business to yourself, perhaps it could ruin your career.'

'Screw my career, and I promise not to tell the President.'

'Okay, I'm going to Paris tomorrow.'

'What the hell for?'

'I figure I'll look in on the UN committee meeting with the French President. When it moves to London, I'll move with it. That's my excuse.'

Blake frowned. 'So why are you really going?'

'Ferguson's found out quite a lot about what – and who – was behind Nantucket. And somehow I've just neglected to pass it on to either the White House or the CIA.'

'You're frightening me now,' Blake told him. 'Tell me the worst.'

Blake had started listening with a certain foreboding on his face, which was replaced by a kind of awe by the time Cazalet had finished.

'God help us, it's better than the midnight movie.'

Two waiters arrived together with their meal, and conversation subsided while they served. They moved away, and Blake said, 'So why is it so important to go to Paris?'

Cazalet talked while he ate: 'When those Chechens attacked on Nantucket, one of them grabbed Sara Gideon, shouting his head off, and was about to shoot her when she stabbed him.'

'A soldier to the hilt, that young woman,' Blake said.

'Which I plan to take advantage of, her and the rest of Ferguson's people. They know a lot about the Master now. They know he's in London. They know he was appointed by a Grand Council in Paris. And I bet we can find out a lot more. I might not be able to do much good in the general scheme of things, but I plan to meet the Master face-to-face and shoot the bastard.'

Blake didn't know what to say. Finally, he gave a small laugh and said, 'I'd try to argue you out of it, but I know from experience that'd be useless. When your mind's made up . . . Have you still got one of those nylon-and-titanium bulletproof vests Ferguson gave us some years ago?'

'I never travel without it.'

'Then just promise me this: promise me you'll wear it at all times.'

'My word on it,' Cazalet said.

Cazalet said good night to Blake under the hotel's canopy, and as he walked back inside he met Ali Khan, emerging from the supper bar. 'Did you have an enjoyable meal, Professor?' Cazalet asked.

'Excellent,' Khan said as they walked down to the lift. 'I love the hotel and always have, but then I love Washington. I came here at seventeen with my father from Pakistan. He was a widower and a very great eye surgeon, and I followed him as a student at the medical school.'

The lift doors opened and they stepped inside. Cazalet said, 'Do you return to Pakistan often?'

166

'I have, of course, to see relatives, but Washington has been home to me for fifty years now. I'm a widower, no children. What would I do anywhere else?'

The lift stopped, and he stepped out and turned. 'Such an honour for me, sir. Good night to you.' And he walked away as the doors closed.

In his suite, Cazalet poured himself a brandy and ginger ale, dimmed the lights, opened the glass door to the terrace, and enjoyed the fresh smell of the room. Paris beckoned. He was already excited.

Fifteen years earlier, on vacation in Pakistan, relatives had taken Ali Khan to hear a remarkable new vision for Islam being preached by a man named Osama bin Laden. It was soon to be embraced by Muslims all over the world, but on that day, the crowd roared and Ali Khan roared with them, his life changed utterly.

He had found the conversation between Cazalet and Blake Johnson to be one of the most remarkable he had ever listened to. Once in his suite, he removed the recording device and the directional microphone, both incredibly small and delicate, and inserted them into what looked like a perfectly normal tape recorder. It was, in fact, a device that coded the contents for transmission, via satellite, to anywhere in the world. In this case, it was heading for Al Qaeda's Grand Council in Europe.

He waited, and after a while a green light blinked three times and the machine turned itself off. Mission accomplished and nothing to do with him anymore. What happened now was not his business. A pity really, because he'd rather liked Cazalet, but such thinking was pointless, so he went to bed.

In his apartment, Blake was sitting at his desk, going through a security report, when his phone rang. It was Carol Shaw and she was upset.

'Blake, have you got a moment? I'm desperately worried about Jake.'

'And why should you be?' he asked.

'Look, I'm aware of the attempt on his life on Nantucket. I know I'm not supposed to, and it's top secret and so on, but Jake tells me about most things.'

'Correction, Carol,' Blake said. 'Jake has been telling you everything for at least fifteen years. Do you think I don't know that? So let's start again. What is it you want to discuss, Paris?'

'So you know about that?' she said. 'Parading himself like a target, daring them to have a second go at him when the fool has no security whatever.'

If Cazalet hadn't told her what else he had in mind, Blake wasn't going to tell her. 'If he is on a hit list, he's in danger wherever he goes. Paris would be no worse than anywhere else,' Blake told her.

'I can see I'm going to have to go to the President about this,' she said.

'Well, you can, of course, but I can guarantee one thing. Jake will never speak to you again if you do. Do you want that to happen?'

She gave a long shuddering sigh. 'Of course I don't. You're absolutely right. I've been silly. I lost my husband to the stupidity of war. I've never really got over that. I couldn't bear to go through it again.'

And he was immensely sorry for her. 'Carol, he only told me what he intended to do because I promised not to tell the President. On the other hand, I didn't promise not to tell General Charles Ferguson in London.'

'Oh my God,' she said. 'Do you think he might have a solution?'

'He often does. Leave it with me. I'll ring you back.'

'But when?' she said. 'London's five hours ahead of Washington, it must be almost three o'clock in the morning over there.'

'Just go away, Carol, I'll be in touch,' and he cut her off.

There was a perfect solution to the time problem, of course, which was Major Giles Roper. The man barely slept, and Blake knew just where to find him.

Roper came on almost at once. 'Why, Blake my man, what a pleasure, especially at this time in the morning. It obviously means you have a problem. How can I help?'

Blake explained in detail, and Roper seemed amused more than anything else. 'So now he's a vigilante? Rather different from presidential days. No Secret Service covering his back, no security at all. Is he contemplating suicide?'

'What would Charles Ferguson think of it?'

'Not very much, but I'll put you on hold and see. He happens to be here at the moment, staying in the guest wing.'

'It's three a.m., Giles,' Blake said. 'He isn't going to be very pleased.'

'Well, that's just too bad,' Roper said, and rang through to Ferguson's room.

The general took it surprisingly well when he joined them in the computer room wearing a dressing gown and sat beside Roper, drinking tea plus a shot of whiskey.

'What in hell is Jake Cazalet up to?' he asked.

Blake shrugged. 'He's turned into a bit of a wild card.'

'That's an understatement,' Ferguson said.

'What will you do?'

'Bring in the DGSE, the French Secret Service, and our old friend Colonel Claude Duval. We'll keep a close eye on him, beginning when his plane touches down at Charles de Gaulle.'

'He might not be too pleased.'

'He'll get over it,' Ferguson said. 'Especially when he discovers that Sean Dillon and Sara Gideon have also moved into the Ritz.' He smiled and raised his cup of tea in salute to the screen. 'I feel quite cheered by all this, Blake. Who knows where it might take us? But if you don't mind, I think I'll get back to bed.'

Twenty minutes later, Blake was speaking to Carol on the phone, filling her in with what was going to happen.

'I'll take the blame at some future date. I'll point out to Jake that I only promised not to tell all to the President. On reflection, I got worried and as he was also due to go to London, decided it was wise to seek Ferguson's advice.'

She was overjoyed. 'I don't know how to thank you.'

'You can easily do that by letting him get on with what he wants to, otherwise you'll lose his friendship.'

She sighed. 'You're right, of course. I'd better get back to reality, see everything's properly organized for the trip. Will you be seeing him off?'

'That's the last thing I'm going to do. I just want him out of Washington before the President discovers what he's up to. I'll see you, Carol.'

In London at the same time, the Master came awake to rain rattling the windows of the penthouse apartment that had been the top floor of an Edwardian mansion in Mayfair. The living room extended into a studio, which was now furnished as a library office. There were four rooms below, serviced by a narrow lift, rooms lovingly preserved, furniture covered in drapes.

He had been sleeping on a couch, which he did frequently, and could see across to his desk, where a green light pinged softly, which meant only one thing. A communication from the Grand Council.

He got up and went straight to the desk, acknowledged receipt, then switched on the transmitter. A neutral voice detailed the provenance of the material and the identity of the players. A few moments later, he joined Jake Cazalet and Blake Johnson for supper at the Hay-Adams Hotel.

He listened to them, considering what it meant. It was certainly the coup of a lifetime. Because of it, he now knew everything that had happened to Ferguson and his people since Nantucket, including the truth about the Drumgoole affair.

So Tod Flynn was dead after all? What a clever bastard Sean Dillon was, but he'd overreached by attempting to play a dead man. That could be dealt with later. The important thing was the mine of information he now possessed. Including the fact that sometime during the afternoon Jake Cazalet was arriving in Paris to stay at the Ritz without presidential approval. This would allow the White House to pull the plug on his security, knowing that the French would be forced to assume it, which meant that when the plane landed, it would probably be greeted by Colonel Claude Duval of the DGSE.

What a coup it would be to finish the job started in Nantucket and knock off Jake Cazalet in Paris. These days, with the terrible civil war in Syria, there were plenty of men available and capable of such an assassination, either in Paris or London. Jihadists home from the war, taking a rest and available, at a price, to handle such a task.

He consulted the Grant Council and found what he wanted with no problem: Aleg Lupu, a Chechen hard man of the finest water, back from Syria for two months to receive specialist treatment for a bullet in the left thigh.

He'd been living with his woman, a French Algerian named Zahra le Ruez. The word was that he was about to return to the fray in Syria by way of Turkey, but since the only thing Zahra loved in this world more than herself was Lupu, anything that would keep him in Paris would appeal to her greatly. An actress since fourteen, she still performed when a good show was available. And when resting, as actors referred to it, she augmented her earnings by performing as a high-class lady of the night who worked only the best hotels. She lived in a luxurious barge on a lonely little quay near Notre Dame.

Asleep on the couch in the salon, Zahra came awake with a start and lay there, aware of Lupu's steady snoring from her cabin. She pushed herself up on her elbow, saw the light glowing on her mobile, and reached to the table.

'Who in the hell is it at this time in the morning?'

She had spoken French, and the Master replied in English. 'There is only one God, and Osama is his Prophet.'

She recognized him instantly and sat up. 'Master, it's you,' and she could not help the touch of fear in her voice.

'Who else would it be, Zahra? Is Lupu still with you?'

She answered in excellent English. 'Yes, he's here, but came in drunk, so he's sleeping it off. He got a false passport in Beirut for medical treatment, just in case he might run into trouble, and he'd grown a black beard when he was out there. Looks quite distinguished. He's calling himself Michael Lebrun.'

'I thought he might have returned to Turkey to cross the border and rejoin the struggle in Syria.'

A lie, of course, but he wished to make her angry. 'He's done enough for the Cause, Master. It could be the death of him if he returns.'

'Well, I bring you good news. He can serve Al Qaeda better by staying in Paris, and receive a very rich reward. I have a task for him here that would suit you two very well.'

'Oh, my God,' she exclaimed. 'Can this be true?'

'If he may be persuaded.'

She laughed harshly. 'Oh, I'll see to that, you may depend on it. What are you expecting him to do?'

'What he does best, kill someone,' the Master told her.

'I see no problem there,' she said. 'God knows, it has never given him one before. Someone special?'

'To AQ he is. Some years ago, he was President of the United States. Jake Cazalet,' the Master said. 'Perhaps you remember him?'

'Not particularly.' She reached for a cigarette from a silver box and lit it with a Zippo. 'They come and go, these people, I can't remember.'

'He's arriving by business jet at Charles de Gaulle this evening as a private citizen, staying at the Ritz.'

'Will there be cops fussing all over him?' she asked.

'I should imagine they'll keep an eye on him. Colonel Claude Duval will probably meet the plane.'

She frowned. 'That bastard. So the DGSE is involved?'

'Don't get worked up,' the Master said. 'Cazalet is dropping in on a UN committee meeting at the Elysée Palace tomorrow. He may move on to London the following day.'

'How do you want it done?'

'I'll leave that to Lupu. He can be as creative as he likes.'

'Or as dirty?' she asked.

'Well, he's always been at his best in crowds with a silenced Walther. A bullet in the back and keep on walking when the body goes down to be trampled by the mob,' the Master said calmly. 'I'll send photos of the target to your fax machine, plus

175

other information. I'll leave you to it. You've got all day to decide how to handle it. You'll find that the mobile I gave you on the last job is switched on again.'

She sat there, thinking about it, fiercely delighted that the prospect of Syria was fading fast. She got up, went into her cabin, and peered down at Lupu. He had stopped snoring, but was breathing deeply. She moved to the other side of the bed, raised the duvet, and slipped in beside him.

'What was that?' he moaned drunkenly.

She kissed his cheek. 'Nothing important at the moment, chéri. I'll tell you later. You can go back to sleep. Mama's here.'

CHAPTER 8

From her bedroom on the third floor of Highfield Court, Hannah could see the American Embassy in Grosvenor Square as she pulled on her tracksuit and old-fashioned athletic shoes that, with her lameness, helped her control the pedals when playing piano.

This was her home now, this wonderful old Victorian house, and it was just a couple of days since the affair at Drumgoole. She opened the door, checked her watch. Just before eight and quiet, as she went downstairs, her right hand sliding along the banister, leaning on the walking stick in her left.

There were faint sounds of life from the kitchen area. She started towards it, then noticed the study door ajar. She peered in, but there was no one there, so she slipped in, thrilled as she had been on the first night Sara had taken her.

It was just such a pleasure to be in there. The Turkish carpets, the library shelves, the books, and the mahogany doors that rolled to each side to reveal the music room.

She opened them now, and there was the

Schiedmayer concert grand waiting for her in the centre of the room, glass doors on the other side, the conservatory beyond, a touch of the jungle there, small palm trees, vines, exotic plants and flowers.

It was so hard to take in that this was to be her home for the next four years, with the Royal College of Music only a brisk walk away across Hyde Park. For a moment, she trembled with excitement, then took a deep breath to steady herself and sat down at the piano she had left open last night.

She flexed her fingers and launched into a Bach prelude, played very fast indeed, cold and precise and urgent. Her control was remarkable, yet when she stopped, she was shaking. Applause broke out behind her, and she turned to find Sara and her grandfather clapping, Tony Doyle joining in behind.

'Such talent,' Nathan Gideon said.

Hannah shook her head. 'Sometimes I think I show off a little bit.'

'So you've something to show off about,' Sadie Cohen said as she came up behind them, drying her hands on a kitchen towel. 'A gift from God, child, so don't knock it. Just get down to the kitchen where breakfast's waiting, everyone, including you, Rabbi. You've got seminars at the London School of Economics all day. A car's picking you up at nine.'

'You see, Hannah, no peace for the wicked,' he said.

'Since when were you wicked?' Sadie demanded. 'Just get in there, eat a good breakfast, and shut up.'

Ferguson, in the computer room at Holland Park with Roper and Dillon, was talking to Claude Duval in Paris, and the colonel was not best pleased as they discussed the Cazalet situation.

'Let me make one thing clear,' he said. 'I have nothing but admiration for Jake Cazalet, but his insistence on behaving in this fashion is absurd. The DGSE has enough on its plate without having to worry about him.'

'That's why I'm doing you a favour, Claude,' Ferguson told him. 'He's staying at the Ritz, and Dillon and Sara Gideon will stay there, too, and keep an eye on him. Didn't they do the same thing in the Husseini affair last year, and with considerable success?'

'Yes, I must admit you have a point,' Duval said.

'Well, there you are, then. They know that hotel backwards. Plus, Henri Laval's on staff, and I'm sure he'll help out.'

'You're out of date,' Duval said. 'They retired him nine months ago. I've no idea who replaced him. Anyway, make sure you have Dillon and Sara already here when Cazalet arrives so we can meet him together, although he may not find that amusing. I must go now. Lots to do.'

The picture went dark, and Ferguson said, 'Any comments?'

Dillon said, 'Do we really think Jake Cazalet could be at risk while he's there?'

'There's no answer to that, not in the world we inhabit these days.' Ferguson shrugged. 'Same applies when he moves on to London.'

'So that's a given, is it?' Roper asked.

'Afraid so. The PM's made it clear that Jake Cazalet's welcome at any time.'

'A snub for the White House, I'd have thought,' Dillon said.

'They'll get over it.' Ferguson shrugged again, and left.

When he was gone, Roper said, 'So what about you and this business of pretending to be Tod Flynn with the Master? How many times has the sod called you?'

'Three, and usually around four in the morning. Creepy stuff. "Are you still with us, Mr Flynn," and I tell him to go away, in appropriate language.'

'And with a County Down accent.'

'Of course. Anyway, you'd better tell Sara she's going to stay at the Ritz in gay Paree again. It was quite an adventure the last time we were there. I'll go and pack,' and Dillon went out.

On the barge *Rosamund*, Zahra had restored Lupu to some sort of sanity by alternating hot and freezing showers followed by large quantities of excellent coffee. His black hair was tousled, most of his face hidden by the black beard he had grown in Syria.

'You look good,' she said. 'That weight you put on in hospital, the beard. Even I, who love you, don't recognize you. Add to that your false passport and Aleg Lupu has ceased to exist.'

'Never mind that.' He reached to the coffee table for the faxes and photos the Master had sent. 'So he wants this Cazalet shot or whatever.' He reached for a walking stick from the floor, pushed himself up, and limped to the bar at the other end of the salon. 'I'm crippled.'

'No, you're not, you just can't run at the moment, but you won't have to. We book in at the Ritz because Cazalet is going to stay there. We'll take a two-bedroom suite. You'll be in a wheelchair and I'll be your uniformed nurse. With my uniform, your beard and tinted glasses, people will be very nice to us, I assure you.'

'Okay, what about your mother's half-brother, Henri Laval, the guy who used to sneak you in for the rich punters when you were on the game? We'd be finished the moment he set eyes on you.'

'Uncle Henri retired nine months ago. We don't have to worry about him.'

'And what do we do with Cazalet?'

'Depends on whatever opportunity turns up. If nothing does, we let it go. And we still get handsomely paid for it.'

'I don't know, it still sounds crazy.'

'Crazy enough that you want to get sent back to the Syrian war tomorrow? Because, the Master's promised, that's exactly what you're going to do.'

'No,' Lupu croaked. 'That won't be necessary.'
'Excellent. I knew that's what you'd say!'

Zahra smiled at Lupu, who looked strangely humble. 'I've told you before,' she said. 'Mama's here and everything is going to be fine.'

In her office at the Sash, Myra Tully was checking through the month's receipts, which were down, and her ringing mobile disturbed a lengthy calculation. She snatched it up.

'Go to hell, whoever you are, I'm busy,' she cried.

'Yes, I get that impression, Myra. It's the Master.'

'Is that so? What do you want?' she demanded. 'Or have you called to tell me you've come up with something useful, like some way of sorting out Ferguson, Dillon, and that Sara Gideon bitch.'

'I was wondering about her,' the Master said. 'It seems some Brotherhood members tried to jump Gideon as she was entering her house a few nights ago.'

'That's the best news I've had all year,' Myra told him.

'No, it isn't. A couple of Cockney thugs apparently joined in and saved her day. Kneecapped two of her assailants.'

'That sounds like Sean Dillon,' Myra said.

'Well, it wasn't. Dillon had nothing to do with that affair. I prefer to deal with reality, and here's some more of it: your precious da and Bell were shot by Tod Flynn from the pillion of a motorbike being ridden by Billy Salter. As they lay wounded in the cab of their Jeep, which had halted on the edge of a slope above a bog, Flynn leaned in to finish them off. Bell grabbed him, the Jeep moved, and they all went down to hell together. What do you think of that, Myra?'

Her face had contorted, eyes burning, the rage in her voice speaking for itself as she said, 'Billy Salter was riding that motorbike and helped murder my da? I'll have him for that if it's the last thing I do on earth!'

'Don't do anything stupid,' he said. 'If you want revenge, you'll have it, but don't make a move until I tell you.'

'Why don't you go to hell?' she demanded.

'I've been there, Myra, didn't like it, and neither would you. I'll be in touch.'

'Bastard!' she shouted as he switched off.

A door was flung open and Terry Harker rushed in from the outer office. 'Are you okay, Myra?'

She tried to pull herself together, reached for the brandy decanter on her desk, poured a large one and gulped it down, hand shaking.

'I just had the Master on telling me what really happened at Drumgoole.'

'You've got to try and put all that out of your mind, Myra.'

'Not when I hear Billy Salter was roaring round on a motorbike with Flynn on the pillion, shooting up my da and Bell. Those Salters have swaggered round too much and too long. It's time they got sorted.'

'So what do you mean by that?' Terry asked.

'We could start with that boozer of theirs, the Dark Man. Means everything to Harry Salter, that place. Get a few real wild boys in to give the car park a working-over one night and seriously damage a few cars. That'll frighten his punters away. Same deal with that restaurant of his, Harry's Place.'

'You'll be wasting your time,' Terry said. 'Harry Salter may be wealthy these days, but scratch that surface and you'll still find the gangster. He'll crush you.'

'Is that so?' She leaned back, glaring at him. 'Scared, are you? Then I'll just have to do something about it myself.'

And as always, he raised his hands. 'No need for that, love, you're the boss. If that's what you want, just tell me where and when and I'll get it sorted.'

'That's better.' Her hand shook as she poured another drink. 'I'm glad you see sense. Now, take last night's receipts up to the bank for me while I pull myself together.'

Spoiled by her infamous da all her life, vicious and cruel by nature – the Master was aware of all that about Myra, but he'd only recently realized that her greatest sin was her stupidity. He'd hoped that Harker might have more influence, but he hadn't shown any sign of that. Disappointing in a man who had served five years in the Grenadier Guards, had seen action in Bosnia, Kosovo, and Northern Ireland, and had twice been rated middleweight champion of the British Army. But that would have to wait.

He moved on to Hamid Bey and found him in his office. 'It is good to hear your voice, Master,' he said. 'What can I do for you?'

'That attack on the Gideon woman that was interrupted. Have you heard anything more about the men who interfered?'

'No, just what I've told you. They were racist in their language, unbelievably brutal, Cockney to the core, and they had no qualms about crippling two of our men,' the imam told him.

'But they weren't Ferguson's people. I'm at a loss as to who they might be,' the Master said. 'Have you any thoughts?'

'Maybe just two hard men who came upon the scene by chance, saw a woman in trouble, and decided to do something about it?'

'In the best of all possible worlds, I could believe that,' the Master said. 'But I'm not sure ours is.'

It was quiet high up in the penthouse, where the Master sat at his desk, making notes, patiently pulling things together for what he hoped would be a success in Paris. He was due to speak to Zahra and Lupu again, but it was unlikely they would have completed their preparations yet, so he called the Iranians. Best to have backup in place in case Paris didn't work.

Ali answered. 'Lance Harvey here.'

'Hello, "Lance". I assume you know who this is,' the Master said.

'Ah, it's you, we were beginning to think that you'd forgotten us,' Ali told him cheerfully.

'Don't be absurd, it's only a couple of weeks or so since we first talked. Is Khalid with you?'

'Of course, we're inseparable, but I expect you know that. He's having a shower after running round the park. It's what he does when he gets bored.'

'So what have you been doing besides living it up?'

'No need to be harsh, Master. We've been through all the files you gave us, and compiled a list of the main players and where we can find them if we want to lay hands on them. The young Irish girl, Hannah Flynn, is now living with Captain Sara.'

'At Highfield Court,' the Master said. 'I know. Gideon was just attacked by three men there.'

Ali said smoothly, 'Really? How is she?'

'I'll tell you.'

When he was finished, Ali smiled. 'I enjoyed the imam's suggestion that Sara Gideon's saviours might have been hard men just passing by who jumped in because they saw a woman in trouble.'

'So you don't think that's possible?'

'Seems more like Hollywood than real life, Master. But to other things. How much longer do we carry on playing games? Khalid is not the only one who gets bored, and my problem is I don't enjoy running round the park.'

'You must wait a little longer,' the Master said. 'But it may not be very long. Jake Cazalet is flying into Paris today and I have plans for him. But if those don't work out, he's due to come to London next, and that's where you gentlemen will be very important indeed. Enjoy yourselves while you can, I may be in touch soon.'

He switched off, leaving Ali Herim in a state of shock and still clutching the phone. That was where Khalid found him when he rattled down-stairs two minutes later, whistling cheerfully, until he saw the look on Ali's face.

'I say, old lad, you look as if the roof's fallen in,' he said. 'I think you'd better tell me.'

Which Ali did.

Sara was changing in her bedroom at Highfield when there was a knock at the door. 'It's me,' Hannah called. 'Can I come in?'

'Of course.' Sara was in her underwear, and then continued to dress, easing herself into a black Armani trouser suit with a silk blouse covering a nylon-and-titanium bulletproof vest.

'Everything okay?' she asked. 'Is there a problem?'

'No, it's just that I was practising and Sadie brought me a cup of tea and said you were having

187

to go away in a hurry. She said that you and Sean were going to Paris on a holiday.'

'No, Hannah, we're going on business.'

'Yes, I can see that.' Hannah nodded to the flick knife in its ankle sheath on the dressing table with the Colt .25 beside it. She picked up the gun before Sara could stop her and weighed it in her hand. 'A nice weapon these, especially with hollow points.'

In the act of reaching to take it from her, Sara stopped, frowning slightly. 'How on earth do you know about that?'

'Uncle Tod always worried about me and Aunt Meg being alone. Meg preferred a shotgun, but I was pretty good with one of these. He called it my dark side.'

Sara smiled and shook her head. 'What a remarkable girl you are.' She put her booted foot up on the dressing table stool, fastened the ankle sheath, then clamped the Colt in a belt clip in the small of her back. 'I'll make a deal with you. Sadie is in complete denial about what I do.'

Hannah nodded. 'I can see that.'

'I'm glad you can, but as a soldier, I always anticipate the worst that could happen. You'd be surprised how often it does. Being prepared for it has saved my life.'

'Where's this leading?' Hannah asked.

'You and Sadie will be on your own when I'm away. You'll have Tony Doyle, a decorated military policeman with twenty-one years of service behind him, but the unexpected can happen.'

Hannah was strangely calm. 'I suspect you've got an answer for that?'

Sara reached up to the back of her wardrobe and produced a box, which she offered to Hannah. 'A present for you.'

Hannah held it in both hands, frowning. 'Selected works of Charles Dickens. Published 1850.'

'I think you'll find it's interesting reading.'

Hannah put it down, opened it to reveal a Colt .25, obviously new, with a silencer and spring holster with a pocket containing fifty hollow-point cartridges.

She examined them for a moment, then looked up, smiling. 'Where should I keep it?'

'Wherever you want that's both handy and where Sadie won't find it. Now, I've got to get moving. Got the Gulfstream waiting at Farley Field.'

'Is Tony going to drive you there?'

'No, he's not to leave you alone in the house for any reason, and you or Sadie only go out if he goes with you. I'll drive myself and pick up Dillon.'

'Can I see you off?'

Sara who had pulled on a military trench coat and picked up a light suitcase, put a free arm around her. 'Just as far as the front door. We'll be back in London in a couple of days.' She kissed her cheek. 'Promise.'

'That's all right, then.' Hannah put the box under her arm and reached for the suitcase. 'Let me take that,' which she did and followed Sara downstairs, where they found Sadie waiting in the hall.

'Sergeant Doyle's outside. He's brought the Alfa round. Stay out of trouble. Don't you let Sean Dillon lead you astray.'

Sara chuckled, and kissed her. 'Take care, Sadie,' she said, and was gone. Sadie turned, slightly weepy, and blew her nose. 'Now then, young lady, what are you going to do?'

'Get back to the piano,' Hannah told her. 'I need as much practice as I can get.'

'Well, don't overdo it.' She nodded to the book under Hannah's arm. 'What have you got there?'

'Just a collection of stories by Charles Dickens. I don't think you'd be interested.'

'Too heavy for me,' Sadie said. 'I'll let you get on, then. We'll have a nice dinner tonight.'

She walked away towards the kitchen and Hannah moved into the library, went into the music room, and closed the great sliding doors. She stood there, looking for the right place, half smiling because she was enchanted at the sight of the Schiedmayer with the beautiful velvet-topped piano stool – and immediately realized she was looking at the perfect hiding place, for the stool had a storage compartment.

She raised the lid, looked inside, and found a collection of sheet music, with ample room for the Dickens box, which she placed on the piano while she removed the Colt and loaded it expertly. Then she fitted the silencer, all with great care, as Tod had always insisted, which made her sad thinking about him. She cried a little and placed the box with the Colt in it inside the piano stool and played *Pavane for a Dead Infanta* in his memory, because it was heartbreakingly beautiful and he had loved it so very much.

Dillon, in the guest room he always used at Holland Park, had showered and changed, and in deference to the Ritz, was wearing Brioni. A single-breasted black raincoat completed the outfit.

The briefness of the visit required only toilet articles, pyjamas, and a spare shirt, which fitted into a jump bag with no trouble. He opened a drawer so that he could clear unwanted items on the dressing table into it, among them Tod Flynn's mobile. He casually flicked the button and the phone came to life. He was so astonished that he dropped it.

'What in the hell's going on,' he said involuntarily, and scrambled for it, getting a reply as he raised it to his ear.

'I heard that as I was just asking myself the same question, Mr Dillon,' the Master said. 'I've known for some time about your play-acting. It was just a question of how long to allow the farce to run. Poor Hannah. She must have taken what happened to her uncle very badly.'

Dillon said, 'You're not fit to mention her name, and if you're interested, I'm just about to stamp on your mobile.'

Which, on reflection, he didn't, simply gathering his luggage together, furiously angry with himself.

He went downstairs to tell Roper what had happened and discovered Sara had arrived.

'Just a bloody stupid accident,' he said. 'Turning the damn phone on in the first place, but to give myself away like that was inexcusable.'

'No, it wasn't,' Sara said. 'Don't beat yourself up about it.'

'Anyway,' Roper said. 'What difference does it make that he knows Tod Flynn is dead? His problem is that *you* are alive.'

Dillon raised a hand defensively. 'Okay, but what do we do now?'

'Get the hell out of here. We've got a plane to catch,' Sara said. She picked up her suitcase and led the way out.

The Master had known all along that Tod Flynn was dead and Sean Dillon was impersonating him – Ali Khan's recording had made that clear. Strangely enough, he'd thought it rather amusing, all the more so now that he'd caught Dillon off guard. He had one more call to make, and he phoned Zahra.

'How are things progressing?'

'Amazingly well,' she said. 'I've been able to hire a nice blue van with "Medical Aid" on the side in gold, so we look very correct. My uniform, wheelchair, the right costume for Lupu – we're all set. It's a performance really, just like when I was a young actress, when everything and anything seemed possible.'

'Can you handle Lupu?' he asked.

'Oh, yes, he's a thoroughly dangerous man, but stupid. He needs me and always has. Can I speak frankly?'

'Of course.'

'We both know that this affair depends on sheer chance. Though I doubt it, this Cazalet might be stupid enough to answer the door with no one else there. In which case, it's two in the head with the silenced Walther, slam the door shut, and away we go. But it takes a young and dedicated believer to walk right up to his target and simply pull out a gun and do the job.'

'I know this, Zahra, what you are trying to say?'

'Guys like Lupu don't believe in sacrifice. They expect to survive, and with a wad of money in their pocket.'

'I know this, Zahra, he was fighting for money even in the Syrian war. Don't worry – as you say, everything in life depends on chance. The question is whether we control the game or it controls us. Stay with it for a couple of days, and if no opportunity presents itself, walk away. We'll have another chance in London.'

'I'll give it everything I have,' she assured him.

'I know you will.'

She went out on the stern of the *Rosamund* and found Lupu sitting under the striped awning because it was raining. He was reading *Le Monde*, a bottle of vermouth and a glass on the table at his side.

'Are you okay?' she called.

'Sure, why wouldn't I be?'

'Watch how much vermouth you're drinking,' she said. 'Don't forget we've got a big night ahead.'

'I can handle it, you worry too much,' he told her, and she shrugged and went back inside.

The rain pursued the Gulfstream to Paris and was still falling relentlessly when Sara and Dillon landed at Charles de Gaulle. Claude Duval was waiting just inside the entrance of the VIP concourse, wearing a long yellow mackintosh he'd obviously borrowed from someone in Customs, and as the plane approached and dropped its steps, he put up a large umbrella and accompanied the porters who went to meet them.

'*Bonne chance,* my dear friends.' He kissed Sara on the cheeks. 'This is getting to be a habit.'

'Especially the rain.'

'I agree, and it suits you, but let's get you in.' He turned to Dillon, who was walking with a porter holding an umbrella. 'Sean, you look fit, and it's good to see. Let's go inside. Cazalet will be here in an hour, and we need to talk.'

'Has something come up?' Dillon asked.

'I think you could say that.'

They sat in the private luncheon bar. Coffee was poured for Duval and Sara, tea as usual for Dillon.

'I think a cognac would be appropriate,' Claude said, and waved to the waitress closest, one of the two serving the bar, and ordered. 'We can speak freely. Sonia and her friend are officers of the DGSE.'

'Okay, Claude,' Dillon said. 'I suggest you tell us the worst.'

'The White House is not happy about Cazalet being here. Or maybe that really means the CIA.'

'We know that,' Sara said.

'They were already putting pressure on the Foreign Office about this, and there is little doubt the President was approached, but the feeling here has always been very pro-Cazalet, especially since his only daughter had a French mother. When she was killed in that car accident the other year, the press all ran the story with unusual delicacy.'

'So I assume you're not going to chuck him out?' Sara asked.

'We never were. But the fact is, his reason for being here has ceased to exist in the last few hours.'

'What do you mean?' Sara said.

'The committee's been cancelled. Our president doesn't have the time for it – too deeply involved in Russia, the Ukraine, Nigeria – you name it. So I don't know what Cazalet's going to do – stay here in Paris anyway, go on to London, go home. Who knows?'

'Well, that'll make our job either easier or harder, I can't decide which,' said Sara. 'What do you think, Sean?'

'That we should get a drink.' He signalled and ordered some champagne.

'Oh, and if he decides to stay,' said Duval, 'I have one message for you. You know that room-service waiter that you and Ferguson ran together for years, who retired nine months ago? Henri Laval?'

'That's right. What about him?'

'Ferguson had a word with the general manager. So Laval's back for you all, just for this stay.'

'Well, that will please the slippery old sod,' Dillon said, and raised a glass.

Just then, the far door opened and Jake Cazalet entered. He stopped dead, then laughed. 'I should have guessed I'd find the three of you here.'

They glanced at each other, then Dillon said, 'Heard the news?'

It took only a moment to explain, then Jake Cazalet sighed and dropped onto a chair. 'Is there any champagne left in that bottle, because if there is, I could do with it.'

Sonia rushed to pour it, handed him the glass, and he toasted them. 'It's good to see you, but I've got to admit I'm sorely disappointed.'

'There's always London, sir,' Sara told him.

'Is the meeting a definite there?' he asked.

'No, it's a maybe,' Dillon said. 'But the intention is genuine. Many people wish to see it take place.'

'On the other hand, no one is suggesting you rush over there,' Duval put in. 'Why not enjoy Paris?'

Cazalet brightened considerably. 'Why not indeed? Since I've come all this way, I might as well enjoy the Ritz. And I hope you'll all be my guests at dinner tonight!'

At the Ritz, Zahra and Lupu had been handled with the impeccable service that great hotels always provide. Two porters had helped them with the luggage, and they'd been whisked directly to the fifth floor instead of reception to facilitate Lupu in his wheelchair. There, a young woman from housekeeping explained about all the amenities, promising that a senior member of staff would be along shortly, then left.

Zahra was giggling like a child, moving about the room and touching things. 'This is the life, isn't it?'

'Don't be daft,' Lupu told her. 'Just get me a vermouth, a large one.'

'Don't be so miserable,' she said. 'You should be telling me to open a bottle of champagne, but if sir wants his vermouth, that's what he gets.'

As she passed him, he slapped her bottom hard. 'And keep your mouth shut for a change. Any more fancy remarks and I'll give you a good hiding, you bitch.'

So she was in trouble and knew it from past experience. He'd obviously been drinking heavily, and she was aware of a sad despair as everything crumbled around her. She took the vermouth to him, then turned away, remembering what the Master had said to her about life depending on chance. Did we control the game or did it control us?

The doorbell sounded. She stood there, frozen for a moment, uncertain what to do, and Lupu snarled at her. 'Finally, room service, I suppose, so move yourself and answer it.'

She did as she was ordered, opened the door, and got a shock when she found Henri Laval facing her. His white hair gleamed, his uniform was superb, and his smile was as false as his teeth. She stepped to one side involuntarily and he moved in.

'Madame Cornue?' he began. 'I'm Henri Laval, senior room-service waiter. So sorry you've been kept waiting,' and then he stopped smiling, the reality of who he was talking to showing in his astonishment. 'Zahra? What are you doing here?'

She found it difficult to speak. 'I thought you'd retired.'

'I have, but I've been called back in for a special client. But what in the hell are you playing at?'

Before she could reply, Lupu said drunkenly, 'Hello, you stupid bastard, still sniffing around the guests' pockets, are you?'

Henri stepped a little closer, frowning. 'Lupu, is that you? What are you doing dressed up like that?'

'And what's it got to do with you?' Lupu suddenly produced his Walther. 'Silenced version, this. I could blow your head off and nobody would be any the wiser.' He glanced at Zahra. 'What do you think the Master would say if I terminated your half-uncle?'

He laughed so hard that he dropped the Walther, and Zahra dodged past him to pick it up. She turned to Henri: 'You'd better go while you can.'

'But what about you, you're not safe in his company.'

'I'll make out. Sorry, Uncle Henri, for giving you grief.'

'But what's happening, girl, what have you got yourself into, and who's this Master he's mentioned?'

Lupu's head was down as if he were sleeping. 'We'll go,' she said. 'Go back down the service elevator to the parking lot. Just give me fifteen minutes and we'll be out of here. I didn't even unpack our case.'

'I can't afford any trouble,' he said. 'It's important at my age. I'd never get a job again, you know what the hotel trade is like.'

'Then just give me fifteen minutes and I'm out of your life.'

'Damn you, Zahra, where's your case, the bedroom? I'll get it while you push him out to the service elevator, and I'll follow on with the luggage. If we see anybody, just behave normally.'

But they didn't see a soul, having the elevator to themselves, Zahra pushing the wheelchair out to the medical van, followed by Henri with the suitcase. He stood there waiting as she operated the hydraulic lift, taking the wheelchair inside the van, Lupu still in it.

She turned to him. 'You know, I always thought you were a bad old bastard, but you've been great.'

199

'I don't want to know, but I wish you well,' he said. 'Just do me a favour and leave Paris.'

He went back to the hotel and she drove away, stopping in a back street to call the Master. 'Trouble?' he asked.

'I'm afraid so.' She had a struggle to control her sobs, but he didn't comment, just allowed her to continue.

He was all sympathy when she'd finished. 'At least you've managed to get out of there safely. A pity Lupu mentioned the Master in his ramblings, but that can't be helped now. You have money in your account and your uncle will keep quiet for his own sake. You should be quite safe for a while in the barge, but I would advise you to move out of Paris soon and without Lupu.'

'I think you're right, Master.'

'I usually am. Take care.'

He thought about it for ten minutes or so. It was a mess, particularly the reference to her connection with him. Time to be proactive. He phoned Paris again and gave an anonymous voice an order.

When Zahra arrived at the *Rosamund*, it was early evening, dark and raining heavily. She turned to check Lupu in his wheelchair, but he slept in a drunken stupor now, so she left him there, boarded the barge, went into the galley to look for an umbrella, and found one in a corner.

An open bottle of Lupu's vermouth stood by the

sink, and she poured some into a glass and swallowed it down, feeling somehow at the final end of things, staring out of the galley window at the rain bouncing off the medical van. She froze as a policeman wearing a heavy-weather yellow oilskin uniform and riding a motorbike emerged from the alley opposite onto the quay. He pushed the bike up on its stand, dismounted, and proceeded to examine the vehicle with the kind of police torch that looked as if it doubled as a club.

She immediately panicked but pulled herself together, ran outside, and with her umbrella raised, approached him as he examined Lupu by torchlight, who still lolled in the wheelchair.

The policeman turned to Zahra, his eyes darkened by night bifocals under the peak of his helmet, the rest of his face covered by a weather guard. His voice was polite and neutral.

'What's the story here, madam?'

'He's a seriously sick man who insists on drinking when he shouldn't. He's just sleeping it off in the chair.'

'I'd like to check that, but the door appears to be locked.'

She said, 'It's controlled by the driver and only works when the engine is on.'

'I wonder if you could show me that,' he said. 'I'll hold your umbrella.'

'Of course,' she said, handed it to him, then climbed in behind the wheel and started the engine, which tumbled into life. She leaned out, the driver's door still ajar. 'There you are, Officer, the rear door is unlocked now. It locks again when the driver's door opens.'

'I'm very grateful, madam,' he said, and clubbed her with the torch, a savage blow across the side of the skull. She tilted to the right without a sound; he reached over, released the brake, slammed the door, and stood back as the van moved forward to the end of the quay, knocked down the guardrail, and went straight over into the Seine.

He moved to where the rail was damaged and shone his torch down into the water, where the van lay slightly tilted, the rear showing only briefly as little waves lapped. It was enough, nobody could have survived that, and he made a quick call to the Master as he walked back to his motorbike.

'Taken care of.'

'Are you certain?' the Master said.

'As the coffin lid closing,' the man in the police uniform told him, and rode away.

The sudden disappearance of Zahra and Lupu was noticed by a number of the members of staff, but was at first thought to be a case of guests who couldn't pay their bill doing a runner. But that made no sense at all, and when the hotel visited their security cameras, the game was up for Henri Laval. Normally, the police would have been called in, but the presence of Colonel Claude Duval in the hotel, because of Jake Cazalet's presence, brought in full DGSE powers, which superseded any police investigation. Added to that, when Duval was shown some of the security film he recognized Zahra at once and his nose twitched, for her relationship with Lupu was known to the DGSE. This was why he had Laval delivered to Cazalet's suite and in the presence of Sara Gideon and Dillon.

'Will this be entirely legal?' Sara inquired. 'What about due process and right to a lawyer and so on?'

'Sara, we of the French Secret Service believe in going in hard, and our Parliament totally supports us. I saw service in Algeria as a young man, and it had a great effect on me. To some I'm a dinosaur, but I get results, and I smell stinking fish here. I welcome you to join me as a courtesy. Former president Cazalet feels it would not be proper for him to join us and will stay in the other sitting room. I would also remind you that Laval is my prisoner and not yours.'

Dillon looked at Sara, who nodded, and he grinned at Duval. 'Agreed, so let's get on with it, you old devil.'

Duval nodded to Sonia, who had changed her waitress uniform for a black suit, and she ushered in her colleague from the airport and Henri Laval in handcuffs, who looked frightened to death.

Claude shook his head. 'What the hell have you been getting up to, Monsieur Laval?'

Henri seemed bereft of speech, his head shaking, and Duval carried on. 'Zahra le Ruez is a known consort of enemies of the State. We may not have Devil's Island to offer any more, but there are certain establishments, in Mali for instance, who could help us out with similar facilities.'

And Henri Laval broke, came apart at the seams, weeping wildly. 'No, I beg you, none of this is my fault. It is only because I was invited to return to the hotel to look after the Cazalet party's needs that I am here at all. To help junior staff under pressure, I check on the room-service needs of other suites and was shocked when Zahra opened the door of one of them to me.'

Sara cut in before Claude could speak. 'Why were you shocked?'

'I have a half-sister, Captain Gideon, that few people know about. Zahra is her daughter. She was an actress and then formed a relationship with a Chechen named Aleg Lupu.'

'A petty gangster turned jihadist for AQ in Syria,' Claude said. 'Recently wounded, we believe.'

'I know nothing of that, Colonel,' Laval pleaded. 'Only that they were staying here under false names and that it might be for the wrong reason and I told them they must go.'

'And what happened then?' Dillon put in.

'Lupu was drunk, crazy drunk, and he pulled out a silenced pistol and threatened me with it.'

'And what happened then?' Dillon went on.

'He said a strange thing to Zahra. He asked her what she thought the Master would say if he terminated her half-uncle.'

Sara laughed excitedly. 'The Master – so we know exactly who we're dealing with! What happened then, Henri?'

'He was so drunk, he lost his senses while still sitting in the wheelchair. I told her she'd have to leave, and I escorted them down in the elevator to a medical van she had waiting.'

Claude Duval said, 'And where did she go?'

'I told her she should leave Paris, hopefully without Lupu, so she just drove away, to her place, I supposed.'

'Which is?'

'A barge called *Rosamund*, moored to one of those quays close to Notre Dame. She's had it for years. It's in the phone book.' Henri Laval looked wretchedly tired. 'It's a mess, Colonel, isn't it?'

Claude patted his back. 'I believe you've told the truth this time, you stupid old fool. I'll see what I can do for you.' He nodded to Sonia and her friend. 'Take him into headquarters and book him.'

Henri departed between the two young officers and Claude moved away, talking into his mobile phone. As he finished, Jake Cazalet entered. 'That's a hell of a story. I got most of it. But tell me, Sean, what in hell was it all about? What were this Zahra and the boyfriend supposed to do?'

'That's pretty obvious, sir,' Sara said. 'I think the Master had given them instructions to shoot you.'

'And I agree,' Claude Duval said. 'I've just given orders for a team of my people to move in on this barge of Zahra le Ruez's. I'm going to join them there now, and if you and Sara would like to, that's fine.' He turned to Jake. 'It would be better if you stayed away.'

'I agree,' Cazalet told him, and returned to the other room.

Duval said, 'So, my dear friends, let's get down to the Seine.'

Things had moved fast on the quay, lights rigged to the *Rosamund*, illuminating the grisly scene. A river police special unit, working under DGSE supervision, had already recovered the medical van, there were two ambulances, an awning rigged between them against the relentless rain, both bodies recovered and lying on trestles beneath it, two police pathologists making a preliminary inspection. The party from the Ritz joined them, huddled under umbrellas.

'What have we got, Maurice?' Claude Duval demanded of the senior pathologist.

'Aleg Lupu, recently wounded in the thigh and still in the healing process. Death by drowning. Still in a wheelchair when recovered. The woman is Zahra le Ruez, also death by drowning,' Maurice said. 'But look at the side of her skull.'

Dillon and Sara moved in with Claude to take

a closer look. The bruising was very pronounced, the eyes half open.

'What do you make of that?' Claude asked.

'Probably clubbed in the side of the head, possibly instantly unconscious,' Maurice told him. 'Drowned afterwards.' He shrugged. 'The rear door of the van was locked.'

'So he couldn't have got out after the accident even if he was capable,' Sara put in.

'Exactly,' Maurice told her, 'except that this was no accident. The blow to the side of the woman's head speaks volumes. Somebody put it there and helped the van on its way over the edge of the quay into the Seine.' He turned to Claude. 'Do you agree, Colonel?'

'Believe me, the background of the case makes your theory highly likely. I'm invoking the anti-terrorism act on this one. Nothing released to public or press.'

Maurice looked interested. 'As important as that, then?'

'My friend, I think you'll find that it's more than likely that this one will be kept so quiet it's as if it didn't happen. I leave it in your capable hands.' He turned to Sara and Dillon. 'Let's return to the Ritz.'

An hour later, Roper and Ferguson were video-conferencing with Dillon, Sara, Jake Cazalet, and Duval.

'An extraordinary business,' Roper said.

'Oh, we agree on that,' Sara told him. 'But what happens now?'

'I think she means to me,' Jake Cazalet said. 'I know I was looked on as crazy by a number of people back home for wanting to come to Paris in the first place. I think we've all confirmed now that I'm still an Al Qaeda target.'

'I think we're all agreed on that,' Ferguson said. 'But what are your plans, Mr President?'

'Oh, I'm still coming to London. I'm not about to let those bastards stop me. I've only one stipulation, General.'

'And what would that be, sir?'

'That we forget I was once President of the United States. Stop calling me Mr President. Plain Mr Jake Cazalet will do. To particular friends, just Jake, and as far as I'm concerned, that applies to you, Charles.'

'I'll bear that in mind,' Ferguson hesitated, 'Jake.'

Cazalet turned to Claude. 'I'll leave in the morning.'

'Of course,' Duval said. 'But don't be surprised if I pop up in London.'

'One problem about the Dorchester,' Ferguson said. 'The Oliver Messel is apparently already in use, by an oil sheikh from the Gulf.'

'Ah, well, he must be a man of taste and discernment,' Cazalet said.

'Would a Park Suite interest you? They have a connecting door to a smaller suite, which would be useful from a security point of view. My people will take turns booked as staff. Captain Gideon is your secretary during the day and Dillon guarding the wall, as they say, by night.'

'Well, that's good to hear.' Cazalet turned to Dillon and Sara. 'So it's into battle, my friends, and let the Master do his worst.'

CHAPTER 9

In Washington, when Blake Johnson passed on the news to the Oval Office, the President was horrified.

'This is terrible,' he said. 'It means Cazalet is still a target. Damn it, Blake, the CIA told us Al Qaeda would fall back to lick their wounds. But here they are, just days later! Sometimes I wonder if anybody knows what they're doing around here.'

'The analysts might want to re-examine their assumptions.'

'Damn straight. Well, Jake sure as hell was a lucky bastard this time,' the President said. 'So what in the hell is he going to do now? Walk around London with a target on his back? There must be some way we can bring him home.' The President slammed his clenched fist on top of the desk. 'Why does he have to play the hero all the time?'

'Could be because that's what he is, Mr President. Decorated four times in Vietnam.'

'As if I didn't know that,' the President said. 'I don't suppose there's any way we can get London to give him a nudge?'

'No, the Prime Minister's even invited him to

spend a long weekend at his country place, Chequers. He's been a guest there before, but that was when he was President, of course.'

'Needless to say, I've never had that pleasure,' the President grumbled. 'But never mind that. If Cazalet's intent on continuing to put himself on display and take his chances, that's his choice. He'll have to take the consequences of things going disastrously wrong.'

'Oh, I doubt whether Charles Ferguson and his people would allow that to happen,' Blake said.

'Well, let's hope your faith is not misplaced,' the President said.

The next day, when Dillon and Sara were shown up, they found Cazalet ensconced on the fourth floor of the Dorchester, in a beautifully panelled suite with a wonderful master bedroom and clear views of Hyde Park stretching into the distance on the other side of Park Lane. He was enjoying a glass of champagne from a bottle somebody had thoughtfully left in an ice bucket on the dining table.

'How's it going?' Dillon said.

'Marvellous,' Cazalet told him. 'This will do me. Have a drink, both of you, I insist.' And he filled two glasses.

'No problems?' Sara asked.

'A good hotel concierge never forgets a face, but as we age, we distance ourselves from the young, who've probably never heard of Humphrey Bogart and *Casablanca*, never mind Jake Cazalet, who was President of the United States some years ago. You become someone they half recognize and wonder why. But never mind that. Let me show you in here.'

He opened a door leading into a smaller bedroom with bathroom, and a door on the other side that led into a similar room.

'That one really goes with another large suite, but they've locked it off so both of you could stay if necessary, a bedroom each.'

'Couldn't be better,' Dillon told him. 'And for security, we'll use the ballroom entrance to Park Lane, the rear lift.'

'Very convenient if you want to go for a run in Hyde Park.' Cazalet toasted them: 'Well, here's to us and damnation to the Master.' He emptied his glass. 'I wonder how long it will take him to discover where I am?'

'I wouldn't be surprised if he knows already,' Sara said.

Sara was right. In fact, he was already on the phone to Ali Herim.

'Where are you?'

'Running in the park with Khalid. As I told you, I get as bored with little to do as he does.'

'Then you'll be grateful to me for bringing a touch of colour into your drab lives. Cazalet has just booked into a fourth-floor suite at the Dorchester.'

'Good God,' Ali Herim said. 'So the attempt on his life in Paris failed.'

'I'm afraid so.' The Master gave him the room numbers. 'The two smaller rooms are self-contained, but linked to the main suite.'

'Presumably that's for security people?' Ali asked.

'I'd say so. Could be Dillon in one and Captain Gideon in another.'

'So what do you want us to do?' Ali demanded.

'First of all, when you were serving in the Secret Field Police in Iran, did you ever meet Colonel Declan Rashid face-to-face?'

'No,' Ali said firmly. 'I've discussed this with Khalid. We never even stood on a parade that the colonel was inspecting. Why is this important?'

'Because you're going to become fixtures at the Dorchester, and if Rashid comes to visit Cazalet there, I wouldn't want him to recognize you. If he'd met you during army days, you'd be of no use to me at all.'

'I can see that,' Ali said. 'So how do you want us to handle it?'

'Carry on at the Dorchester as you are now. You are Lance and Anthony Harvey, well-to-do young men with too much money, intent only on enjoying yourselves,' the Master said.

'It's more a pleasure than a duty to carry on like that,' Ali said. 'And then what?'

'That depends on the opposition,' the Master told him. 'But you'll have a significant part to play, never fear.'

He switched off, and Ali stood there in his track-suit thinking about it. Khalid had been throwing stones into the Thames as he waited. Here and there, people walked a dog, and on the other side of the park, a group of very young children played ball, supervised by two teachers.

'So what was that all about?' Khalid said.

'Cazalet's here and staying at the Dorchester.'

'So, the Master again?' Khalid nodded. 'Thank God for that. This should liven things up nicely.'

'Yes, but—' Ali made a sound of exasperation. 'I'm beginning to get brassed off with the whole business. Al Qaeda wants Cazalet dead. They tried in Nantucket, they tried in Paris. Both of them failed, and nobody told us why.' Ali shook his head. 'Too much of this is Ferguson on one side, the Master on the other, like actors behaving as the script tells them. It's like some extended game of chess that neither side wants to end.'

'Do you really believe that?' Khalid asked.

'Look at it this way,' Ali said. 'If the Master really wanted Cazalet dead, all he'd have to do is keep it simple.'

'And do what?'

'Send someone to his suite dressed as a waiter, a tray in his hand and a silenced Walther in his pocket. If someone else opens the door, apologize for the mistake and clear off. If it's Cazalet who obliges, give him a bullet between the eyes, shove him inside, and walk away.'

'Lots of things could go wrong with that,' Khalid told him.

'And lots could go right,' Ali said.

'I agree, but are you telling me that you'd be willing to do that?' Khalid persisted. 'Would you go upstairs to Cazalet's suite, dressed as a waiter, and shoot him if he answered the door?'

Ali was silent, deep in thought. 'No, I don't think I would,' he said finally. 'That's a problem, isn't it?'

His cousin put an arm about his shoulders. 'Which we've both shared ever since we changed sides and rescued Sara Gideon.'

'So what in hell are we going to do?'

'Right now? We'll keep quiet, coast along, and let's just see what happens during these next few days.' Khalid laughed coldly. 'He's a conniving bastard, the Master, but then so am I. Don't worry, I'll get us out of this mess when the right time comes.'

'But what about the Master?' Ali asked.

'Oh, I'll shoot the bastard if I have to,' Khalid said.

Three days a week, Terry Harker found time to visit the Russian Baths in Soho's Gate Street because he preferred the fierce heat of their steam rooms and an old-fashioned gym where he could pump iron. He was at ease in a terry-cloth robe, drinking a pint of Russian tea and reading the sports pages of the *Times,* when the Master found him on his mobile.

'Ah, Terry, there you are,' the Master said. 'I thought it was time we had a chat.'

A Cockney by birth and a hard and brutal boxer, Harker had been considerably affected by his years in the Grenadier Guards and was far from being a fool. His one weakness was the unfortunate fact that he genuinely loved Myra, in spite of her obvious faults. He was too intelligent to take issue with the Master on his own behalf, because there was no percentage in it. You didn't screw with Al Qaeda, it was as simple as that, even if Myra couldn't see it.

'What can I do for you?' he asked.

'I sent some material to you, details about Ferguson's people, some of whom will be familiar to you. The Salters, for example.'

'So you'd like them sorted, I suppose?' Terry said.

'Myra obviously would,' the Master told him. 'Revenge for her father.'

'She certainly wants that, don't kid yourself,' Terry told him.

'And expects you to do your bit, of course,' the Master said. 'How do you feel about that?'

'I like to keep her happy.'

'Well, in pursuance of that end, you can also please me considerably. Naturally, you'll receive appropriate remuneration. Does this interest you?'

'Of course it does,' Terry Harker said. 'Where exactly?'

'Cazalet's at the Dorchester. He is watched

over by Sean Dillon and Sara Gideon, twenty-four seven.'

'So how would one get at him?' Harker asked.

'For a man in his sixties, he's extremely fit. He likes to run, Terry, in the park.'

'Well, that doesn't sound so bad,' Terry told him. 'I can easily find a couple of people to put on a tracksuit. I could fix that up today. How far are they supposed to go? Do they just give him a battering, or do you want him dead?'

And the Master surprised him by saying, 'Let's hasten slowly on that. I'll let you know.'

'Well, it's your party,' Terry said. 'What else do you want me to take care of?'

'Well, the Salters for a start. You can leave them floating in the Thames as far as I'm concerned.'

Terry laughed. 'A lot of people have felt like that over the years, but the sods are still here. We'll see what we can do, is all I can promise. At best we can make life uncomfortable for them, which would please Myra. Cause trouble at the Dark Man or smash up this fancy restaurant by the river at Wapping, Harry's Place. We could frighten the hell out of all their society customers.'

'Then do it!' the Master said. 'I'll put twenty-five thousand pounds into your personal account this afternoon, just to help you with expenses. Don't mention it to Myra.'

Terry brightened considerably. 'Don't worry, I won't. Nice doing business with you. Anything else? What about the Gideon woman?'

'Well, she shot Fergus Tully in the face at Drumgoole,' the Master said. 'Which wouldn't exactly endear her to Myra. She's back at her grandfather's and has brought Tod Flynn's niece, Hannah, to live with her. I mentioned her in the stuff I sent you.'

'The girl who was crippled in a car bomb for which Tully and Bell were responsible, the one who plays the piano?' Terry shook his head. 'There's irony for you. Do you want anything done about Gideon?'

'Not at the moment. Just before she left to go to Drumgoole, some Army of God people had a go at her, or maybe the Brotherhood.'

'Did they, by God?' Terry said. 'What happened?'

The Master told him and Terry laughed his head off. 'That's the funniest thing I've heard in years. Are you sure it wasn't Dillon who intervened?'

'Absolutely, my sources are impeccable. In fact, they tell me that Ferguson and his people, plus Cazalet, are lunching at Highfield Court today, if that interests you.'

'Well, good luck to whoever your sources are, but not if they're that bastard Hamid Bey and those Army of God people and all the Brotherhood rubbish, and don't tell me I'm a racist. One of my great-grandfathers was a seaman from India who fetched up off a ship in the Pool of London and never went back. Anyway, I'll keep my eye on Highfield Court. I'd a sister called Hannah, so there's a coincidence.'

'I didn't know that.'

'Well, you wouldn't. When I was in Bosnia with the army, I got the news she'd been killed by a hit-and-run driver on the way home from school. Twelve years of age and guess what? She was learning the piano. Killed my mother. She never got over it.'

'What happened to the driver?' the Master asked.

'Not a thing. The police failed to trace whoever it was, my father did a runner, and I could do nothing. Busy saving Muslims from being massacred by Serbs in Bosnia.'

'I'm truly sorry, my friend,' the Master said.

'No, you're not,' Terry told him. 'And you're not my friend. Just make sure that twenty-five grand gets in my account this afternoon and I'll take care of what we've discussed,' and he switched off.

At Highfield Court, seated at the Schiedmayer, Hannah had spent the morning practising scales and working at exercises aimed at developing the dexterity in her hands and arms, but enough was enough. Thanks to her uncle Tod, she'd been raised to appreciate another kind of music, too, and she turned to it now, some classic Sinatra, then Cole Porter's 'From This Moment On'.

She gave it everything she had, filling the house with music, was aware of the sound of the Daimler arriving outside, and a moment later, Sadie showed Dillon and Ferguson into the room.

'Good heavens, she's bloody marvellous,' Ferguson whispered.

'Do you want to join me, Cousin?' she called to Dillon.

'Come off it, girl, barroom piano is what I do,' Dillon told her.

Cazalet and Sara entered at that moment, and Sara called, '*Great* barroom piano, Sean, so don't be a spoilsport and oblige the girl.'

Which Dillon did, crowding in beside her on the wide Victorian piano stool. As 'Night and Day' finished, they eased into 'As Time Goes By' and Sara joined them, singing it.

'What the hell is going on here,' Cazalet demanded. 'I've never heard anything like it. You'd think they were pros.'

'It gets like that sometimes round here,' Sadie remarked as she walked in with Nathan Gideon. 'This is your host, Mr Cazalet, and I'm your cook.' She shook hands. 'So if you're all ready, please adjourn to the dining room, where lunch awaits you.'

Leaving the Russian Baths and walking through Soho to where he'd left his Mini Cooper, Terry found himself still thinking about the conversation with the Master. The fact that Hannah Flynn now lived at Highfield Court had resurrected memories of the worst thing that ever happened to him, the untimely death of a sister he had truly loved. So, instead of driving back to Wapping and

Myra and the Sash, he changed direction and ended up at the top end of South Audley Street, sitting at a table outside a coffee shop, from which he got a clear view of Highfield Court in the small turning opposite.

Not long afterwards, Ferguson's Daimler coasted by, turned in at the gates, and he caught a glimpse of the general and Dillon getting out and going up the steps to the front door. The Alfa Romeo followed them, Sara Gideon at the wheel, Cazalet beside her.

Terry paid his bill, adjusted his Ray-Bans and crossed the road, and as he approached the house, he was aware of piano music, some of the best he'd heard in years. He paused on the corner by his Mini, opening the newspaper he was holding, pretending to consult it. After a while, the music stopped, so he returned to the café and sat down at the table again.

'Changed my mind,' he said when a waitress approached him. 'I think I'll have some lunch after all. The eggs Benedict look good to me, with an ice-cold lager to go with it, if you have such a thing.'

'Of course, sir,' she said, and went back inside. He opened his *Times* newspaper, sat back, and waited.

Lobster, cold cuts, salads, and Jersey Royal potatoes – Sadie had done a wonderful job, helped by Tony Doyle as waiter.

Ferguson said, 'Sadie, you've triumphed again, but we'll have to love you and leave you. We have to touch base with Roper and see what he's got planned for us. I assume you have no problem keeping the present system in place, with Staff Sergeant Doyle as a house guard?'

'Oh, I'd hate to be without the Royal Military Police at this stage, General,' she said.

There was laughter at that, and Sara said, 'I've decided to take Hannah with us to Holland Park, Sadie. I think it's time she met Roper.'

'You do as you please, Sara,' Sadie told her. 'I've got a house to run.' She nodded to Cazalet. 'A great pleasure to meet you, sir. Now, if you'll all excuse me . . .'

'And so must I,' Nathan Gideon announced. 'My sermon for the Sabbath awaits. The eternal task!'

Anonymous in his Ray-Bans, Terry Harker had kept his head down over the *Times*. About fifteen minutes after the cars had arrived, though, something curious had happened. A yellow van with 'Public Works' on the side had come and just . . . parked. Probably Hamid Bey out of control and sticking his nose in. He wondered if the Master knew about that, stood up, crossed over, and leaned down at the open window where two men wearing yellow oilskin jackets sat smoking.

'Who are you?' he said. 'Brotherhood or Army of God?'

Their faces said it all, and the bearded one scowled. 'I don't know what you're talking about.'

'Oh yes, you do.' Terry produced a flick knife and sprang the blade. 'Go back to Hamid Bey and tell him Highfield Court is off-limits. I'm going to keep checking. If I find you round here again, I'll cut your ear off.'

The looks of horror were enough, the one who was driving started the engine and drove away instantly. Terry returned to his table and sat down.

It was in a nice little enclave – a general store, the café, a hairdresser's, boutique, and a chemist's. An ageing man with a grey beard was trying to clean every window in sight, which explained the small van parked at the kerb with the legend 'Glassclear' painted on the side together with a telephone number.

Terry said to him, 'You're doing a good job there, Dad. On your own, are you?'

'At the moment, yes,' the man said in an Italian accent. 'I keep my fingers crossed that the bastard I employ will turn up tomorrow. Some of the properties around here are too big.'

'I can imagine.' Terry pointed across to Highfield Court. 'Take that, for instance. Lovely old place.'

'And I've been cleaning its windows for ten years. That belongs to Rabbi Nathan Gideon, but it's more than one man can handle. There's a lovely conservatory at one end, full of tropical plants, backing onto a music room. It's too much for me these days when I'm on my own. I'm getting too old.'

'Well, maybe your man will turn up tomorrow,' Terry said.

'I doubt it.'

'What's your name?'

'Roberto. Signori.'

'Well, I just might have a solution to your problem,' Terry said. 'I'm a journalist by profession. One of my most popular features started with me being a waiter for a short while, then writing about it. Next, I was a porter in a hospital, then a taxi driver.'

Roberto looked bewildered. 'Are you trying to say you would like to be a window cleaner? Why would anyone be interested in that?'

'You'd be surprised,' Terry said. 'You'd be doing me a favour.' He took a fifty-pound note out of his wallet and offered it. 'Of course, we'd also like a photo of you and me for the magazine, but we'll sort that out later. Do we have a deal?'

Roberto suddenly smiled and took the banknote. 'I think so, Signori. I shall be here at nine o'clock in the morning, when you can join me and we drive into the garden of the house together. They are particular about such things.'

'Roberto, old son, just call me Terence. I'm particular about everything, and I can't tell you how much I appreciate you allowing me to join you. Nine o'clock tomorrow morning. I'll be there.'

He was grinning when he paid his bill to the waitress and drove away, wondering what in the hell he was playing at. Not that it mattered, because for some crazy reason all he could hear was that wonderful music and he was more excited than he had been in years.

Sara and Dillon took their time getting to Holland Park, making for the Albert Hall first so that Hannah could have a look at the Royal College of Music. There was no sign of them when they reached the safe house, only Parker sitting behind the steering wheel and reading a book.

'Major Roper left word that he was blowing his cobwebs away on the firing range, Captain,' he told Sara. 'The others went off to join him.'

'Then so will we,' Sara told him.

The safe house boasted a particularly large garden for London, and the firing range was situated in a concrete bunker dating from the Second World War. A sloping tunnel took them down into a cold, gloomy room with targets of soldiers in uniform at the far end and brightly illuminated.

Roper, from his wheelchair, was emptying a silenced Beretta, the only sound one dull thud after another, and Cazalet and Ferguson watched. As the new arrivals advanced, he emptied the clip and pushed another one up the butt of the weapon.

'So you're the Hannah I've been hearing so much about,' he said as she limped toward him, stick in hand. He gestured towards the targets. 'What do you think?'

'Not bad,' she said.

'For a man in a wheelchair?'

'Who doesn't need to prove himself, Major.'

'There you go, Giles,' Sara Gideon said. 'You've met your match this time.'

'And something tells me you're very probably right,' he told her, and held out his hand to Hannah. 'I'm very pleased to meet you. I've got an idea that we're going to get along.'

Ferguson interrupted. 'Which is all very well, but you did suggest we had a go before discussing business.'

'Be my guests,' Roper said. 'Help yourselves to a weapon and get on with it. I think everyone here has been in an army of some description, so you should know what you're doing. As special guest, I suggest you go first, Jake.'

Cazalet helped himself to the Beretta. 'This will do me fine. Takes me straight back to Vietnam.' He took his time, going for heart shots and succeeding. Ferguson followed with a Smith & Wesson .38, no silencer possible, and the noise echoed around the bunker. Sara picked up a Glock, extended her arm, shot one of the targets in the heart, and put the weapon back on the table.

Roper glanced at Dillon. 'Sean?'

'Oh, what the hell.' Dillon drew the Colt .25 and fired very rapidly at the four remaining targets, catching three in the head but barely nicking the fourth. He cursed, ejected the clip, and replaced it with another.

Hannah limped to his side, reached, and took the Colt from him. 'I think you missed one, Cousin.' She shot the target between the eyes, then handed the Colt back to Dillon without a word.

There was an astonished silence, broken by Roper, who said, 'Well, that's a showstopper if ever I saw one.'

Later, the group met to discuss their situation. 'The President is not happy with you, I'm afraid, Jake. "Walking around London with a target on your back," I believe is what he said.'

'I suppose I'm sorry for him,' Cazalet said. 'A quick way for him to lose votes in the coming election would be me getting shot down in London by the Master's goons. It wouldn't be much as a vote-puller.'

Sara said, 'So can I ask, sir – why *are* you doing this?'

Ferguson was annoyed. 'Captain Gideon, you go too far.'

'No, I'll answer that. For any soldier, the war he's fighting is his own small part of the front, and beyond that is the bigger conflict he can't do much about. Al Qaeda is a large organization. You and I and your people haven't a hope in hell of defeating these people on the world stage. That's a matter for great nations. But for *this* little corner of Al Qaeda, this Master who tried to kill me twice – that we can do something about. I want

227

to find him and destroy him. What comes after is out of my hands.'

There was a slight pause, and Hannah said, 'I spoke to him.'

'What?' said Dillon. 'When was this?'

'A few days ago, before – before everything happened. My uncle Tod spoke to him on the phone, but it was on speaker and I heard everything they said. It wasn't anything you don't know. They were just discussing your visit to Drumgoole. But I just couldn't take it any more.'

'What did *you* say?' Cazalet asked.

'I shouted at him. Told him I knew an evil bastard when I heard one.'

'Did he reply?' Sara asked.

'He asked Uncle Tod if I was going to be a problem. Uncle Tod said no, but – oh, it was awful. He made me feel sick and frightened.'

The anger on Ferguson's face was plain to see. 'My dear girl, you are one of us now. There is no way this creature is going to get anywhere near you, I promise you.'

They all agreed, and then Roper said, 'All right, a piece of business. The Syria committee meetings in Paris may have been cancelled, but as it happens, the Hope Charity Foundation for orphans of the Syrian war had booked the ballroom at the Dorchester some time ago for a fundraising evening. It's now become something much bigger. The Prime Minister and various members of his Cabinet are going to attend, and the French

Foreign Minister is flying over. The PM would be grateful if you'd join him,' he said to Cazalet.

'We'll all go,' Ferguson put in. 'It'll be your introduction into London society, Hannah.'

'And God help you,' Dillon told her. 'Is it black tie?'

'We mustn't be too ostentatious, Dillon,' Ferguson said. 'After all, the emphasis *is* on charity. Do you feel up to it, Giles? You could take Colonel Rashid with you. He's desperate to get out of Rosedene, and it would please the French.'

'I think my chair might get swallowed up in the crowd,' Roper said.

'I'd be happy to help,' Hannah told him.

'That's kind of you,' he said. 'We'll see.'

Ferguson said to Cazalet, 'We'll make sure you're well-guarded. Dillon and Captain Gideon will be on duty.'

'Thank you, Charles,' Cazalet said. 'Now, can I interest anyone in a little supper at the hotel this evening? I'd welcome the company.'

'We'll sort something out,' Sara said. 'Leave it to me,' and they dispersed.

Terry, driving away from Highfield Court, had discovered several text messages on his phone, all from Myra, demanding to know where he was. Their tone ranged from petulance to rage, and for the first time he discovered he didn't like it. So, when he finally arrived at the Sash, he was angry more than anything else.

When he entered the pub, it was as dead as was to be expected at that time of day, only Eric, the head barman, checking wines.

'Is she in?' Terry asked.

'Ranting and raving like a loony,' Eric said. 'Biting everyone's head off. She's not pleased with you at all, so beware. I hope you haven't been doing anything naughty.'

'Get stuffed, Eric.'

'Not a chance.' Eric poured a large scotch and passed the glass across the bar. 'Get that down you, then go and face death bravely. Is there anything else I can do?'

'Yes, get hold of Guido Pirelli and Bruno Malone.'

'My God, who do you want killing?'

'That's my affair. Just do it.'

He left Eric, went upstairs two at a time and into his office, where he found Lucy, the accounts clerk, sporting a hunted look and a tear-stained face.

'Are you okay, girl?' he demanded, and the door to Myra's office swung open.

'You bastard,' she shouted. 'Where in the hell have you been? I checked the Russian Baths. You left hours ago.' Her face was swollen, make-up smeared. 'You've been with some woman, haven't you?'

She slapped him across the face, which he allowed, but when she tried to do it again, he blocked the blow and ran her back into her office and pushed her down into her chair.

'Pull yourself together. So you're grieving for your da, but something's going to be done about that. I haven't been tomming some tart, I've been talking to the Master. He calls me now, not you, so you better get used to it. Ferguson, Dillon and company, the Salters, will all be dealt with, only you've got to pull yourself together. What you need is a nice hot bath, get your hairdresser to call, so you can face the evening rush as only Myra Tully can. We mustn't let the punters down.'

She gazed at him in astonishment and then nodded. 'You're right, Terry, I've been very silly.'

He took her to the door. 'Off you go, girl, we'll have a lovely dinner later, but I've got important business to see to right now. You understand.'

'Of course, Terry. I'm so sorry.'

'You go and run your bath, and I'll have Eric bring you up a nice bottle of champagne.'

'You're so good to me, Terry. I don't deserve you.'

She went out through the office, and Lucy stared at him in amazement. 'Don't say a word,' he told her. 'She's a monster, that's the truth of it. We need a new regime round here and I'm it. If you need me, I'll be in my office.'

Myra undressed, put on a robe, sat down at her dressing table and ran a comb through her hair, her face like stone, thinking about Terry, the new model. *Face the evening as only Myra Tully can and don't let the punters down.* What a load of crap, which meant he was up to something and the sooner she found out what that was, the better.

Guido Pirelli and Bruno Malone looked relatively ordinary for contract killers. At the age of eighteen, they'd met as infantry recruits in the British Army, from which they'd been discharged five years later after time in Afghanistan. Employment in various so-called security firms abroad had followed, which gave them a reputation for succeeding when others failed. They never killed in England, however, for a practical reason. If you got caught, it was a life sentence for murder. But if you got caught for beating the hell out of somebody, and then you turned out to be a gallant soldier who'd suffered in Afghanistan, well, that was a different story. The 'gallant soldier' plea never failed to soften the heart of any British judge.

They sat and listened on one side of Terry's desk, while he explained from the other what he wanted and showed them pictures of Cazalet and Sara and Dillon.

'So you're quite clear,' Guido said. 'Your client doesn't want Cazalet dead?'

'I'll be honest with you, he's surprised me, but when I put it to him, he backed off, so for the moment, he seems to be happy with the idea of him getting a bloody good hiding. That's what made me think of you guys,' Terry said. 'So what do you think? Chances are he'll have a morning run tomorrow. I'm told he likes to leave by the ballroom entrance of the hotel into Park Lane and cross to Hyde Park from there. Are you up for it?'

Guido looked at Bruno. 'We're due in the Ukraine in two weeks, so it would give us something to do.'

'Spending-money job, really,' Bruno said. 'And after all, the big money's due for Ukraine.' He nodded to Terry. 'Ten grand, five thousand each, but cash.'

'Done,' Terry said. 'I've got that kind of money in the safe, so you can take it with you. Nice doing business with you.'

'One soldier to another,' Guido told him. 'Always makes a difference, old son,' and they exchanged handshakes.

Later that evening at the Dorchester, close to the bar at the ballroom end of the Promenade, Cazalet, Sara, and Dillon were seated at a banquette, sharing a bottle of champagne before going up to the Grill for dinner.

'How was Hannah?' Cazalet asked.

'She's got Tony Doyle and Sadie tonight, because my grandfather is making a speech at the Reform Club,' Sara told him. 'I didn't like to leave her. I'm beginning to feel she's the sister I never had, if you know what I mean.'

'She's a wonderful girl,' Cazalet said.

'Well, remember these hotel beds unscrew into two singles when they're needed,' Dillon said. 'That might be a good idea for the function tomorrow night.'

'That sounds an excellent idea to me,' Cazalet said.

From a few yards away, Ali and Khalid were watching them, drinking martini cocktails, twins in their navy blue blazers and white shirts of the finest Egyptian linen.

'My goodness, she's a handsome woman,' Khalid said, but before Ali could reply, his mobile trembled in his pocket.

The Master said, 'Where are you?'

'At the Dorchester watching Cazalet, Sara Gideon, and Dillon enjoying themselves.'

'Well, you'll be watching them even closer tomorrow night.'

'And why is that?' Ali asked.

'There's a big charity function in the ballroom there. The Prime Minister is coming, and a few cabinet members, plus the French Foreign Minister. He's asked Cazalet to join him, and I understand Ferguson and his people will be with him. So will you.'

'May I ask why?' Ali asked.

'The expression is "know thy enemy". Do I have to explain?'

'No, sir,' Ali told him.

'Good. I'll say good night.'

Khalid had been watching patiently. 'What did he want?' Ali told him and Khalid smiled. 'It's as good a way of spending an evening as any. Now, let's go and find a table for supper.'

At almost the same moment, Cazalet said to the others, 'Who's for dinner? I'm starving.'

Sara stood up, almost colliding with Khalid, and he eased back. 'I'm terribly sorry, ma'am, that was really rather stupid of me.'

'Not at all,' she said, smiling, and then frowned ever so slightly, as if puzzled.

Ali and Khalid walked away, and Dillon said, 'Are you all right? Is there a problem?'

'That young man,' she said.

Cazalet groaned. 'Quite the charmer, I'd say.'

'He called me ma'am,' Sara told him. 'It's a greeting my rank entitles me to, but how did he know I was an army officer?'

'Oh, he was probably just being polite, Sara,' Cazalet told her.

'I suppose,' she said, and sighed. 'I'm seeing plots everywhere.' She smiled. 'I'm sorry I can't go running with you tomorrow. That's out for me after I took that bullet in the leg at Abusan.'

'Well, you rode a horse at Drumgoole as well as any Grand National jockey I've ever seen,' Dillon told her. 'I've had words with the concierge, and somebody will pick you up at six and drive you up to the stables. Then you can come galloping down to the Park and meet Jake and me.'

'Sounds lovely.'

'I must say you've covered all the bases,' Cazalet said. 'Now, let's eat.'

CHAPTER 10

Six in the morning, traffic already flowing down Park Lane as a hotel car took Sara up towards Marble Arch and the stables. At the hotel, riding clothes had appeared from nowhere, including the ever-popular Australian drover's coat, which, from a sombre hint in the sky, seemed as if it might be needed. Sara was looking forward to it; her only regret was that Hannah wasn't with her, but perhaps something could be done about that on another morning.

It was about half past six when a porter let Cazalet and Dillon out of the ballroom entrance into Park Lane. They wore black anoraks, hooded and rain-proof, waited at the side of the pavement for a gap in the traffic, and then ran across to the other side, where there was a small gate in the ironwork fence.

Guido Pirelli and Bruno Malone had stayed back, blending where they could in the trees close to Broad Walk, where riders could circle around into Rotten Row and see the Household Cavalry at exercise if they were lucky, but not today, although there were plenty of tracksuited runners at various places in the distance.

Cazalet and Dillon paused on the edge of Broad Walk. 'She should be belting round here soon enough,' Dillon said. 'A cracking rider, believe me.'

Cazalet held out his hand. 'It's starting to rain, I thought it would. Let's cut through the trees, then run along the track in the direction she's coming from.'

'Okay, that sounds good to me,' Dillon said.

On the right of the track, the rain came slashing down, and Guido and Bruno came running out of the trees, slanting towards them.

'Could you help us?' Guido called. 'Does this take us to Rotten Row? We were told you can see the Cavalry exercising sometimes.'

Which could have been true enough, except for the fact that Bruno was holding a baseball bat against his right leg, hardly the usual equipment for somebody out for a morning run, and the fact that Dillon's inner voice, the product of years of hard living, had told him instantly that they were up to no good.

'We've got trouble,' he said.

'So it would appear,' Cazalet said. 'Increase the pace.'

Which they did, pulling ahead, and Guido produced a Walther, firing a single shot into the air. 'I'll cut you both down, I mean it.'

Dillon instantly produced his silenced Colt .25 and shot him. Guido stumbled and went flying, dropping the Walther. Bruno roared like an animal, moved in, the baseball bat raised ready to strike.

In the same moment, Sara arrived on the gallop, her mount barrelling into Bruno and bouncing him to one side, and he dropped the baseball bat and went down. He tried to pick it up again, and Cazalet raised a knee under his chin, sent him flat on his back, then picked up the baseball bat himself.

Sara had quieted her mare and sat there high in the saddle, looking down as Guido scrambled to his feet and stood there, clutching his right hand with his left, blood pumping through.

'How bad is it?' she demanded.

'Billy the Kid here shot me in the hand, ma'am, it went right through.'

There was that army thing again, like the night before. In a way, it irritated her, and she said, 'You've served in Afghanistan, haven't you? Which regiment?'

'Rifles, ma'am, Corporal Guido Pirelli, and my mate there is Private Bruno Malone. Helmand Province was our second home for nearly five years. Just like you, ma'am.'

'And what's that supposed to mean?'

'Well, I know all about you, killing all them Taliban at Abusan, getting the Military Cross and all.'

Bruno got up and went and slumped down on a park bench. 'I don't feel so good, that damn horse hit me like a tank.'

Sara ignored him and said to Guido, 'Your hand must be hurting.'

'Not yet, ma'am. It will later when the shock wears off, but I've been shot before.'

She used her teeth to pull off her right glove and tossed it to him. 'Put that on, it will help until you see a doctor. Search them both.'

Cazalet chose Bruno. Dillon took Guido, with no success except for the Walther, which Dillon found where Guido had dropped it.

'Just the weapon,' Dillon said. 'And a car ignition key and what looks like a key for a house.'

'Where's the house?' Sara demanded.

'Why should we tell you?' said Guido.

'Because I'll shoot your other hand if you don't!'

Guido hung his head and muttered, 'A flat by Cannon Wharf. And we've got a car parked in Upper Grosvenor Street. Nothing in it to trace us. We work clean.'

'I just bet you do,' Sara told him. 'Are those the instructions of the Master when you go on a job for him?'

Bruno looked puzzled. 'Who's this Master she's talking about, Guido?'

'Search me,' Guido said, and shrugged. 'I don't know anything about a Master.'

'Really?' Sara said. 'So who the hell were you attacking these gentlemen for?'

'Just tell her, for Christ's sake,' Bruno moaned. 'I think I'm going to be sick.'

Guido shrugged. 'We were doing a job for a friend. Terry Harker runs a pub in Wapping for a bird named Myra Tully. A real bitch. Told us he was acting for a client who wanted someone to give Mr Cazalet here a going-over.'

Cazalet said, 'Did he, now. Are you sure he didn't tell you to kill me?'

'Absolutely not, which our friend, Terry, couldn't understand. He emphasized we were to give you a thorough battering, but no more than that.'

Dillon shook his head. 'So crazy, it's got to be true. So what do we do with them, Sara?'

'Upper Grosvenor Street is only a little way up Park Lane. Run them to Rosedene to have Guido's wound treated – we can't have him go to A & E at an ordinary hospital, because that would involve the police – then, let them drive home themselves. But get their address and telephone number.' Sara glared down at them. 'You're a disgrace to the British Army. God knows how you survived Afghanistan. You just sit and behave yourselves until I confirm what's to happen to you.'

'We were due in the Ukraine in two weeks,' Guido said. 'Can't go now with this bloody hand.'

Sara shook her head, her mare standing. 'Oh, get them out of here, Sean, I'll see you at the hotel later.'

'I'll go with them,' Cazalet told her. 'I'd really like to.'

'Somebody at Rosedene will run you to the Dorchester, sir. A strange morning.'

'No, a memorable one,' Cazalet said, and they all dispersed.

* * *

There was a fountain on Lovers' Walk not too far from where the whole affair had taken place. From there the Master, dressed in raincoat and cap and clutching an unfurled umbrella, had witnessed everything that had taken place, had even achieved a closer inspection with a pair of sporting binoculars. Not that he could hear what they were saying, but then he didn't need to. As the old saying had it, every picture told a story. What idiots Pirelli and Malone had turned out to be. Something could be done about that, but what about Terry Harker, previously so reliable? Perhaps something was needed there also? There was much to be done, but he liked to keep busy, and as the rain increased with sudden force, he put up his umbrella and walked away.

At the Sash and in Myra's bed, Terry was awake early and lay there for an hour, ignoring her heavy breathing as he realized he hadn't the slightest idea what he was going to do when he got to Highfield Court except clean windows.

The whole thing had been a whim of the moment and sparked by the great music Hannah Flynn had played, which had brought memories of his sister to the surface. On the other hand, perhaps poor old Roberto's number-two guy wouldn't turn up, and a promise was a promise, as Terry's mum used to tell him when he was a kid. So he smiled, eased out of bed, grabbed for his dressing gown, and went down the hall to his own room.

241

Myra's eyes opened the minute he left, and as the door clicked behind him she lay there, frowning. She knew about Highfield Court, the Rabbi and Sara Gideon, the fact that she had brought Tod Flynn's niece back from Drumgoole with her, and that Tony Doyle was living in as house guard. All this had been confirmed by searching Terry's desk when he was out and discovering the information the Master had sent him.

Which meant she was angry at Terry for not having discussed these things with her, or letting her know where he was and why. She was aware that control was slipping away from her, her personality such that she was unable to deal with secrets in a rational manner, especially when it involved Terry. She just had to know.

To that end, she had checked the sat-nav on his Mini Cooper and had immediately discovered details of his trip to Highfield Court. Not a word about that, so why? It was as if she was being kept out of something, and she wasn't having that, so she got out of bed, went into the bathroom, and started to get ready for the fray.

Eric Logan drove up as Terry came out of the pub wearing jeans and anorak and a cloth cap. What didn't show was a two-shot derringer with hollow points, carried in a spring clip at the small of his back.

'You're out early,' Eric said. 'Where are you going?'

'Oh, I'll get a café breakfast somewhere, then Billingsgate for fish.'

'Don't forget some lobsters,' Eric said.

'Done. I'll see you later,' Terry said, got behind the wheel of the Cooper, and drove away.

Myra appeared not long after that, wearing an Oxford blue trouser suit, everything neat and tidy. 'Have you seen Terry?' she asked Eric.

'Sorry, Myra, you've just missed him. He was going to do the markets.' He smiled. 'You look good. All dressed up for Harrods, are we?'

'And others,' she said. 'I get sick of hanging around for taxis, Eric. Would you mind if I borrowed that old Ford of yours?'

'Whatever turns you on, Myra, be my guest.'

'You're a love,' she said, then jumped in and drove away.

The half-hour drive it took to get to Highfield Court calmed her down. She had no way of knowing if Terry would turn up here again. If he came, he came. She found a space in the line of parked cars, picked up a couple of magazines, plus a large coffee and a couple of croissants from the café, returned to the Ford, and waited.

In Highfield Court, Rabbi Gideon joined Sadie and Tony Doyle for breakfast. Shortly afterwards a car turned up to take the rabbi down to Brighton University for a day of seminars and an overnight stay as guest of honour at the faculty dinner. In the afternoon, Sara was to pick up Hannah and take her shopping for a suitable dress to wear at the Hope Charity function at the Dorchester, where she was to stay overnight, sharing Sara's room.

'It's all a bit unfair,' Hannah said to Sadie. 'You and Staff Sergeant Doyle seem to be missing all the fun.'

'Oh, I'm sure we'll get by,' Sadie said. 'There's always the television.'

Tony Doyle, who was clearing the table, said, 'Don't you worry about me, Hannah, I've got a new occupation. Sadie is teaching me Yiddish.'

'Is he any good?' Hannah asked.

'Let's say he's surprised me,' Sadie told her. 'But enough, it's time for your piano practice. As for you, Staff Sergeant, I've got a list as long as your arm of items we need from the supermarket.'

'Sooner rather than later, Mrs Cohen,' he said. 'It's best to get in that place early, and I'm not supposed to leave you for longer than half an hour.'

'Well, get started as soon as you like,' she said. 'And that applies to you as well, Hannah, off you go.'

Myra wore her Cartier sunglasses and kept well down behind the wheel of the Ford and almost missed the Cooper as it passed and pulled in beside Roberto's van, which was parked outside the general store. Terry, in his cap and anorak, and especially the Ray-Bans, looked more interesting than he should have as he joined Roberto in the van.

At that moment, the security gates of the house opened and Tony Doyle drove out, turned into Grosvenor Square, and vanished.

'Here we go, Signori,' Roberto said, and he drove across the road to the entrance, causing the gates to open again. A few moments only and they were into the drive, the gates closing behind them. Up at the front door, Sadie was cleaning glass panels with a chamois leather. 'Ah, it's you, Roberto. Who's your friend?'

'This is Terence,' Roberto told her. 'He's here to help me do the conservatory. It will look beautiful again.'

'Well, I look forward to that. I'll bring you some coffee and biscuits at eleven o'clock.'

After Hannah had practised for a while, Sadie came in with a mug of tea in each hand and offered her one.

'There you go, love, I know how you Irish love your tea. Dillon taught me that, though it's true of many Jewish people, particularly anyone with Russian ancestry.'

'But without milk.' Hannah laughed, and led the way out of the music room and into the tropical splendour of the conservatory.

There was a man outside, standing on the terrace, holding a hose, spraying the windows and moving along to the glass door that gave access to the gardens. He was looking at Hannah.

Sadie said, 'Roberto says he's here to help him today. His name's Terence.'

Hannah said nothing, just looked at him curiously, then when she'd finished her tea, went back to the conservatory and started to play an old jazz number, 'Fascinating Rhythm', very fast indeed, head down, her fingers dancing over the keys at a considerable speed. As she finished, there was applause. She looked up and saw that the glass door was open and Terry was standing inside, clapping.

'Bloody marvellous,' he said, a huge smile on his face. 'I've never heard the like. I used to have a sister named Hannah. She's dead now, but she was learning to play the piano.'

Sadie came into the music room behind Hannah. She was holding a sawn-off shotgun. 'We thought there was something odd about you as a window cleaner. I've just had a look at some photos we were given of people who are a danger to us.'

'Come off it, love, I don't know what you're talking about.' Terry was still smiling.

Sadie walked right past the Schiedmayer to confront him, and Hannah rose, lifted up the lid of the piano stool, reached inside, eased the Dickens box open, found the butt of the Colt .25 and took it out with her right hand.

Sadie was very close to him now. 'Terry Harker,' she said. 'That's your name, and I've just looked at three separate photos of you.'

He moved incredibly fast, brushing the shotgun to one side, his other hand grabbing and turning her against him, half choking her as she struggled, dropping the gun to the floor. His right hand produced the derringer and held it up so that Hannah could see.

'You won't be familiar with this, Hannah. It's a two-shot derringer, hollow-point cartridges. Could blow her head open.'

'Oh, dear, we can't have that,' she told him, and shot him, removing the lower half of his left ear. He cried out, pushing Sadie away, staggered back, clutching what was left of his ear, turned and lurched outside and down the steps, where he ran past Roberto and his van and disappeared into South Audley Street.

He'd managed to produce a handkerchief from his pocket, which he crushed against his ear as he ran towards the Cooper, got the door open and scrambled inside, driving off one-handed. Myra had seen all this, had been frozen in place by the shock of it, but when she saw Hannah and Sadie appear in the entrance to the house, realized that something catastrophic had taken place, started her car, and went after Terry.

Minutes later, Tony Doyle appeared in his army Land Rover, drove into the drive, smiling for the ladies. 'Well, here we are, the supplies got through. We can fort up for another week.' Sadie and Hannah looked at each other, and he frowned. 'What's up, has something happened?'

'Well, you could say that,' Sadie said. 'Hannah just shot Terry Harker, Myra Tully's boyfriend. He was threatening to kill me, and she saved my life. You'll want to get in touch with the general and see what he wants to do about it.'

Doyle turned to Hannah, feeling strangely helpless. 'Are you all right?'

'Of course I am, Tony,' Hannah said. 'He was a piece of shite who got what he deserved. Wouldn't have lasted more than half an hour on a wet Saturday night in Belfast City.' There was contempt in her voice. 'I don't know what you two want to do, but I'm going inside for another cup of tea,' and she went up the steps to the front door.

The private health clinic Terry used specialized in women's problems and plastic surgery, also anything that the London criminal fraternity came up with. Terry Harker had used their Dr Malik personally on a number of occasions, and had driven straight there.

Morphine had dulled his pain, but he was an angry man. 'What's the verdict, Doc?' he asked Malik.

'I don't think plastic surgery would do any good.'

'So I'll be left with half an ear?'

'Yes, but we'll have to see how it heals. It might not be as bad as you think.'

There was a disturbance outside, the door opened, and Myra came in and didn't help the situation by saying, 'My God, Terry, you look awful. I thought you'd be here.'

'Where the hell have you come from?' he demanded.

'I followed you, Terry, I was so worried.'

He glanced at Malik. 'Give us a minute, Doc.'

Malik departed, and Terry said, 'What do you mean, you followed me?'

'To Highfield Court. I just wanted to know what you were doing there. I was jealous.'

He made a quick adjustment to his story. 'You've got to understand. The Master wanted a close watch on the place because he wanted to know how the Flynn girl was getting on in there with the Gideons. I did a deal with their window cleaner to get me inside, but the housekeeper recognized me from some photos they have. The Flynn girl pulled a gun on me.'

'I know what I'd like to do to that little bitch.'

'Forget that. Ferguson won't want me in a police cell, he'll want me shooting my mouth off about the Master, which I'm not about to do. I'll have to drop out of sight for a while.'

'Will you go abroad?'

'That's what you can tell people if you're asked, but I've had a bolt-hole for a few years that no one else in the world knows about, so you go back to the Sash and forget about me for a while.'

'I don't know if I can do that,' she said.

'Do you want me to get nicked and end up in Belmarsh Prison with your husband?'

'Of course not.'

'Then leave now and keep your head down. If the going gets rough, turn to Eric.'

'The barman? Are you sure about that?'

'I haven't told you about him, because he prefers it that way. He was a sergeant in the Yorkshire Regiment in Afghanistan when I met him, in the BRF, the Brigade Reconnaissance Force, a special ops outfit of men from many regiments. According to a lot of people, they seemed to spend their time looking for death.'

'And you were one of them?' She was shocked.

'Never mind that,' he told her. 'He's got a brain, Eric, and he's topped more men than you've had hot dinners. They gave him a Queen's Gallantry Medal.'

'I don't know, bloody Afghanistan again. It seems to pop up everywhere. What's so special about it?'

'It's a very exclusive club, Myra, that you can't buy your way into, only experience. A season in hell that's touched the lives of all of its members from the Royal Family on.' He reached up, pulled her head down, and kissed her. 'Get the hell out of here, and if Ferguson or his people want you to talk, tell them to get stuffed and send for your lawyer.'

Ferguson called a council of war upon hearing of the incident, and they assembled at Highfield Court – Hannah and Cazalet, Roper and Dillon and the Salters, holding the meeting in the library. Tony Doyle, Hannah, and Sadie sat in.

'Let me say straight away that Staff Sergeant Doyle was not in any way at fault for leaving the house to go and shop for Sadie. It was within his remit,' Ferguson told them.

'I should think so,' Sadie said. 'The poor man has been stricken by guilt about the whole business.'

'Well, he doesn't need to be,' Dillon said. 'Sara and I questioned Roberto, the window cleaner, extremely closely. He's a simple man who fell for Harker's story. He shouldn't have taken the money, but he's no criminal.'

'I agree,' Ferguson said. 'Just as I do that although Captain Gideon broke standing orders by passing a Colt .25 with hollow points to a civilian, I thank God that she did.'

'And so say all of us,' Roper added cheerfully. 'Terry Harker has been a busy boy, not only this, but those two characters who ambushed you in the park,' he said to Cazalet. 'What's to be done with them?

'Well, if I'm allowed a view here,' Cazalet said, 'they aren't even worth throwing to the cops. It might make a colourful story for the press, but one I could do without.'

'I agree with you, sir,' Ferguson said. 'But we can't ignore Harker's activities.'

'I've checked him out,' said Roper. 'He has an excellent army record, served in special ops in Afghanistan. And interestingly, so did the head barman at the Sash, one Eric Logan. He even sports a Queen's Gallantry Medal.'

'What did he do to earn that?' Cazalet asked.

'He was guarding some civilians with kids when one of them discovered an explosive device. Logan ran off with it, threw it away just in time.'

'Splendid,' Ferguson said. 'Guaranteed to earn him a considerably lighter sentence from some benign old Tory judge the next time he's in court.'

'That's a bit cynical, General,' Hannah told him.

'I suppose it is, my dear,' he told her. 'It's the fault of the life I lead, which always disappoints. Anyway, I think someone needs to call in on Myra Tully at the Sash. I think that would be better coming from you, Harry.'

'My pleasure,' Salter said. 'I'll take Billy and Sean with me.'

Cannon Wharf was in an area of the Thames under development; two-thirds of the wharf itself was missing, leaving a jagged end pushing out over the river forty feet below. It was raining, an old man sitting under the kind of umbrella usually found on seaside beaches. A portable radio was offering him music, and he held a fishing rod out over a broken rail, though no line was suspended on it.

Guido Pirelli stared out at the man from the decaying house where he and Bruno lived for the moment. Bruno was making tea in the kitchen and passed him a cup.

'What the hell is he doing?' Guido asked. 'Sitting there for two hours. He must be crazy.'

'Well, living in a dump like this is enough to send anyone crazy,' Bruno said. 'We've got to find something better.'

'We will,' Bruno said, 'But we're in the hands of that Gideon woman. We can't just clear off, she'd have the police after us in no time.' He put down his cup, opened a cupboard, and took out a Waitrose shopping bag. 'Remember what's in here, ten thousand pounds in cash. Thank God Dillon and Cazalet didn't do a house search.'

'I don't blame them,' Bruno said. 'It stinks, this place. This is what they mean by a hovel. I can't take much more.'

'Okay, so why don't we take an evening off. Let's get a drink.'

'That's a great idea,' Bruno said. 'I'll get ready,' and he turned and ran upstairs.

Within ten minutes, they walked outside, an umbrella raised against the rain, laughing as they moved to their car. The old man turned and glanced at them, and Guido called, 'Caught anything yet?'

He got no response and moved around to the passenger door. 'You'll have to drive,' he told Bruno. 'My hand's killing me, and I need the other to carry the Waitrose bag. I'm not leaving that.'

'I'm a better driver than you anyway,' Bruno told him, got behind the wheel, and switched on, pushing his foot on the accelerator. The engine roared, the car seemed to leap forward, along the wharf past the fisherman, and Bruno stamped on the brake pedal and nothing happened at all. 'The brakes!' he shouted. 'Something's wrong!'

Guido reached to switch the engine off, but by then the car was moving too fast, flew over the broken edge of the wharf into space, tipped, and plunged down into the Thames forty feet below.

The fisherman sat there, stunned, then got to his feet and walked slowly to the end of the wharf, held on to a broken rail, and peered over. There was no sign of the car, but detritus had drifted up already, a couple of scarves, some loose cushions. And then a supermarket bag popped up, disgorging a great deal of what looked like paper, though he couldn't be sure, so he managed to find his mobile phone in his inside pocket and called for the River Police.

The moment Myra had left him, Terry had called Eric at the Sash and quickly told him what had happened.

'I don't know whether to laugh or cry,' Eric said. 'What a cock-up. What are you going to do? You could make a run for it. What have you heard from Guido and Bruno?'

'Not a thing, but I'm not going on the run, not to start with. I prefer to see how things turn out. I'll lose myself in the bolt-hole for a while. What condition is it in?'

'You're in luck – I hadn't checked it out for ages, but I looked in four weeks ago and was dismayed at what I found, so I've been cleaning the place up. You can move straight in. Do I tell Myra?'

'Like hell you do. You're the only other person in the world who knows my secret, so we keep it that way.'

'On my life, Terry, I've just crossed myself. I'll go now. Myra might arrive and want to know who's on the phone, but good luck with the bolt-hole.'

Terry lay there, thinking about it – it was an old Thames sailing barge named *Arabella*, and his great-grandfather, Benjamin Harker, had captained her for years. Now she was ending her days by St Jude's Dock, not too far from the Tower of London, a houseboat floating beside an old jetty, an electric cable and a water pipe connecting it with the shore. It was a haven from the outside world, and a private one. He couldn't wait to move in, so he got out of bed and had just finished dressing when his mobile sounded.

'Why, Terry,' the Master said. 'What a day this has been. All that nonsense of the morning in Hyde Park with those two clowns you provided. I thought they could only come to a bad end, and I'm not surprised to find they have. It seems they've driven straight off a wharf into the Thames, thus proving that as well as all their other flaws, whichever of them was at the wheel couldn't even drive properly.'

'You fucking bastard,' Terry said.

'Come now, Terry, what on earth were you playing at in Highfield Court?'

'I was trying to show that security there was capable of being breached,' Terry lied hoarsely. 'Who could have known that an eighteen-year-old girl would be so good with a pistol?'

'Where are you going now?'

'You know something,' Terry said. 'I'm not going to tell you, so you can stew on that,' and he clicked off.

Dr Malik walked in at that moment with a small parcel. 'I see you're ready to leave.' He offered the parcel. 'There are antibiotics in here, be sensible and take all of them. If you're still ahead of whatever game you're playing, see me in seven days. If you feel feverish at all, call me at once. No rush to pay me, I know you're good for it. One of the porters has cleaned the blood off your car seat.'

'You're a diamond,' Terry said, and left.

Earlier, when Myra had got back to the Sash, Eric was in the cellar, opening cases of wine that had just been delivered.

She called down to him, 'Can I have a word?'

He went up and found her seated on a bar stool. 'Eric, I need a really decent drink, because I've been having a terrible time. Could you manage one of those special Martini cocktails of yours?'

'Of course I can, anything for you, Myra. What's been going on, then?'

As he mixed, he listened to her version of events, which was a dramatic one to say the least.

256

When she was finished, he said, 'Bloody incredible, the whole thing. I was wondering why I hadn't heard anything from Terry. So he's cleared off, has he? France maybe?'

'No, all I can say is that he's going to ground. He wants me to take over, be strong and take charge of everything. He says if Ferguson and his people want to question me, I should tell them to get stuffed and call in my lawyers.'

'Well, I'd agree with him there, Myra. You've got to stand up tall in this life, that's what I say.'

'I'm glad you feel like that, because if I need help, he wants me to turn to you.'

Eric tried to look modest. 'Why, Myra, I'm touched, but any idea that I can stand in for Terry is a bit strong.'

'He thinks the world of you, Eric. I'd no idea you were such a hero in Afghanistan. They even gave you a medal.'

'I wouldn't make a big deal out of that, Myra. Lots of people got medals. It was that kind of war.'

'Never mind that. I've been thinking of Ferguson, but also the Salters. That idea I had of giving them some grief at the Dark Man or even Harry's Place? Terry seemed to agree with me. What about you?'

Eric was saved by the bell on that one, because just as he started to say, 'Well, Myra, the way I see it . . .' there was the sound of a vehicle arriving outside.

'Who have we got here?' he said, then Sean

Dillon and Harry and Billy Salter came down the entrance and approached the bar.

Myra exploded. 'What the hell do you bastards want in here? Go on, get out!'

'Why, Myra,' Harry Salter told her, 'I'm overwhelmed by the warmth of your greeting, and may I say you look even more ravishing when you're angry. And Eric Logan, as I live and breathe.'

Before she could answer, Eric said, 'Look, Mr Salter, you can see you're not welcome here. Unless you have a search warrant, I suggest you leave.'

'Can't do that, Eric,' Billy told him. 'I don't need one. I'm an officer of MI5 who has reason to believe that Terry Harker may be on these premises, an individual believed to have committed acts unlawful under a range of anti-terrorism laws.'

'Why, Billy,' Eric said. 'I'm impressed, but can you spell all that?'

Myra exploded. 'You've got a nerve, after what that little taig bitch did to my Terry. Shot him, she did. You should see his ear.'

Eric put a hand on her shoulder. 'Just cool it, girl, you're digging yourself in deep here.'

'I'd listen to him if I were you, Myra,' Dillon said. 'I can't say I care for him, but he means well.'

'And you're another taig bastard, Sean Dillon, just like that Flynn bitch. She deserved what she got.'

'Deserved getting crippled at fourteen, her parents killed by a Protestant bomb left in their

258

car by Frank Bell and your wonderful da?' Dillon turned to Eric. 'I'd like to get out of here before I do this creature an injury. Has Harker been here?'

Eric shook his head, his lies were perfect. 'No, but he phoned from Syon Clinic, where he got his ear patched up, and asked Myra to go bring him his passport. Said he was going to leave the country, France or Spain, as I understand it.' He turned to Myra as if apologizing. 'Sorry, love, it's better to tell the truth and get them off your back.'

For once, she had the wit to see what he was trying to do, managed to look troubled, sighed, and said, 'If you say so, Eric.'

Harry turned to his nephew. 'Are you satisfied?'

'Not really, but we can come back if we need to,' Billy said.

'I suppose so.' Harry looked around him. 'What a dump,' and he walked towards the entrance, Billy following.

Dillon ignored Myra but said to Eric, 'When I looked you up, it wasn't the medal you got that impressed me, it was what you did to earn it. I'd like to think what that said about you is true, so don't disappoint me. Leave this mess alone. I've seen the movie and it ends badly!'

He ran up the steps and out of the door, as she tossed her Martini glass after him and turned to Eric. 'If I had a gun in my hand, I'd shoot the bastard. Give me another drink.'

As he prepared it, her mobile sounded in her handbag and she pulled it out. 'Is that you, Terry?'

The Master said, 'I'm afraid not, although I spoke to him a short while ago.'

'The Master,' she whispered to Eric, and put it on speaker. 'What can I do for you?'

'I was wondering if Terry was there.'

'I'm afraid not. I saw him for a short while at the clinic where he was being treated for a gunshot wound to his ear. He told me he didn't expect any problems with the police, because Ferguson wouldn't want that.'

'Which is true. Where can I reach him?'

'I've no idea. He told me it was better if I didn't know. He did say France or Spain might be a possibility.'

'It seems to me that leaves you in a difficult situation, Myra.'

'Oh, I think I'm up to it,' she told him. 'I should have no difficulty running the club, especially with my bar manager assisting me. We've just had a visit, by the way, from the Salters and Sean Dillon.'

'They were looking for Terry, I suppose?'

'Yes. They made threats about anti-terrorism laws, and Harry Salter's nephew, Billy, turns out to work for MI5.'

'Yes, I was aware of that. It makes it more difficult to get at the Salters, in spite of their criminal background.'

'Well, it doesn't give me a problem,' Myra told him. 'I can put enough rough young men together any time I want who'd love to give the Salters' pub a real turning-over. Or worse. It wouldn't bother me in the slightest if the Dark Man sort of accidentally caught fire and burned to the ground.'

There was a slight pause, and then the Master said, 'That's really rather interesting. When could you do it?'

She looked inquiringly at Eric, who'd been listening, and he nodded. Myra said, 'Tonight.'

CHAPTER 11

I t was just after seven, people already flooding into the Dorchester for the fundraiser when Cazalet and Dillon peered in from the Promenade. They retreated to the bar and ordered Martinis as they waited for Sara and Hannah.

'It certainly looks as if everybody's going to be here,' Cazalet said.

Dillon's Codex sounded, and it was Roper, who said, 'Where are you?'

'Oh, at a bar as usual, waiting for the girls to join us,' Dillon said.

'I just wanted you to know that Declan will join you soon. Max Shelby's going to pick him up at Rosedene and drop him off. Howard Glynn has ordered him to join the crowd: Ferguson, the Prime Minister, the French Foreign Minister.'

'And Uncle Tom Cobley and all,' Dillon told him. 'We get the picture. I'll check in where necessary.'

'I'd advise it. Ferguson expects nothing less than perfection where the French are involved. A matter of national honour, I think.' Roper chuckled and switched off.

Cazalet was highly amused. 'A hard taskmaster, Charles Ferguson.'

'Most great men are,' Dillon told him.

'And the others?' Cazalet asked, 'Declan and this Max Shelby?'

'Well, buy me another Martini and I'll tell you.'

When Dillon was finished, Cazalet shook his head. 'An amazing story. An Iranian father and an Irish doctor for a mother.'

'A Bedouin father,' Dillon said. 'There's a difference. He has Irish nationality through his mother, so he's on our side now.'

'Thank God for that, but this Major Shelby? There's an unfortunate case. To lose his son and then his wife in such rotten circumstances.'

'Yes, but people like Max are the backbone of Army Intelligence, and these days, with so much terrorism, his language skills are essential. He and Sara were comrades in arms in Afghanistan. He's the superintendent of MI5's safe house here in London for the interrogation of suspects.'

'Who is this Howard Glynn?'

'Director General of MI5, who can't wait to meet you, like they all do, and it's Sir Charles.'

Cazalet said, 'Why do I get the impression that you're about to burst out laughing when you say something like that?'

'Because I am, but not at you. It's just that I'm bewitched at the sight of two incredibly handsome young ladies bearing down on us behind you.'

Cazalet swirled around to find Sara and Hannah approaching, wearing elegant black velvet evening suits, each with her walking stick, and looking more like twins than ever.

'Sensational,' he said to Dillon. 'Wouldn't you agree?'

'Absolutely,' Dillon told him. 'A champagne occasion, so let me do the honours,' and he turned to the bar to order. Sara said, 'Don't you think we'll be expected at the reception?'

Before Dillon could reply, his Codex rang again. Roper said, 'You're not having any good luck tonight, Sean. Guess who else is there? Hamid Bey with Sister Lily Shah. Needless to say, Ferguson is not pleased.'

He switched off, and Cazalet asked, 'Who the hell is Hamid Bey?'

Sara said, 'What you might term the opposition, sir.'

'So not on our side at all?'

'Not even a little bit,' Dillon told him, and the door opened and Max Shelby walked in from the ballroom.

'Sorry to spoil your fun, sir, but General Ferguson's looking concerned. Sir Howard Glynn is with him now, and they are expecting the PM and the French Foreign Minister at any moment. If you could follow me?'

'Of course.' Cazalet brushed past him.

Shelby stopped smiling. 'You've heard about Hamid Bey?'

Sara said, 'I'm afraid so, Max.'

'Can't keep the bastard out, you see, as he's bought his ticket. What a bloody world,' and he went out.

Before anyone could say anything, Declan peered in and Sara smiled and said, 'There you are. Colonel Declan Rashid, meet Hannah Flynn. You've heard enough about each other, so it's time you met. His mother was Irish, so that's one good thing.'

'Or everything,' Hannah said, and shook his hand.

Applause started to rise in the ballroom, and Dillon said, 'Sounds like the great and the good have arrived. Maybe it's time to be on the move.'

Behind them, people who had been seated around the Promenade bar were getting to their feet and crowding towards the ballroom entrance, most of them clutching entrance tickets. Among them were Ali and Khalid.

Declan had eased back, he and Dillon acting as buffers to Sara and Hannah, who were leaning on their walking sticks to one side of the double doors. As the pressure from those pushing forward increased, Ali and Khalid stemmed it.

Khalid gestured with his hand. 'Please, ma'am,' he said to Sara, and then the weight of the crowd pushed the two young men forward.

She turned to Declan. 'There he goes again. He called me "ma'am" last night when he excused himself in the bar. Only the military use "ma'am" these days.'

265

'Or the Royal Family,' Hannah said.

Declan seemed to be ignoring them, frowning slightly. 'What is it?' Sara demanded.

'I'm not sure. It was as if I knew them.'

'I doubt it, you must be at least twenty years older than they are. They're good public school products from their accents, although I should point out that when I was at Sandhurst, they weren't all children of privilege – there was a much wider variety than there used to be.'

'No, Sara, I know them from somewhere. I'll give it some thought.'

The ballroom was a scene of tremendous activity, waiters everywhere, passing through the crowd offering canapés and drinks. Important guests were standing in line to be introduced by Henry Frankel, the Cabinet Secretary, and his team to the PM and the French Foreign Minister and Cazalet, who, from the way people were pressing forward, was proving something of a draw.

Dillon lifted a couple of glasses of champagne from a passing tray and handed them to Sara and Hannah, while Declan procured two in the same way and passed one to Dillon, who emptied the glass, plunged into the crowd, and emerged with a wicker table and two chairs, which he placed by the wall and waved to the girls.

They came and sat down, and Sara said, 'So you're a miracle worker now?'

'It's been said before,' he said, and grinned.

Declan stood some little way off, scanning the room methodically for Ali and Khalid, enjoying no success at all, and there was something of an altercation taking place at the end of the presentation line. Hamid Bey was trying to force his presence, and Henry Frankel was just as forcefully keeping him out. Sister Lily Shah, in a blue uniform dress and a hood of the same colour, stood to one side looking miserable and uncomfortable.

Dillon forced his way through the crowd, by some miracle finding another wicker chair on the way, and took her by the arm, totally ignoring Henry Frankel and Hamid Bey.

'I really do feel that you need to sit down, so if you'll come this way, we'll find you some congenial company.'

Hamid Bey scowled ferociously, but Henry Frankel smiled wickedly, for he had known Dillon for many years. So – Hamid Bey was pushed rather forcefully out of the frame while Dillon led Lily Shah by the hand to Sara and Hannah. He put the chair down and eased her into it.

'Take your pick. One of them shot up and the other blown up, so with you having experienced the worst Lebanon had to offer, I'm sure you'll have a lot to talk about.'

He turned and walked away, Lily Shah watching him go with some astonishment. 'Is he always like that?'

'Only some of the time,' Sara Gideon said. 'We met at Rosedene, so you know who I am, but this is Hannah Flynn, Dillon's second cousin. Now, let's have another glass of champagne and you can tell us how things work at the Army of God dispensary,' and she waved to a passing waiter.

It wasn't surprising that Declan couldn't catch sight of Ali and Khalid. There were so many people crammed into that vast ballroom that it was virtually impossible to pick out individuals. Dillon got two more glasses and approached Hamid Bey, who was seated by a large potted palm, glaring malevolently at everyone in sight. Dillon, with his flair for languages, spoke good Arabic and cheerfully offered champagne to the imam.

'There you go, eat, drink, and be merry, for tomorrow we may die.'

Hamid Bey knocked the glass from his hand. 'May you burn in hell, apostate.'

'An interesting sentiment,' Dillon said. 'But I don't mind, as long as I meet you there.'

Hamid Bey plucked another glass from a passing waiter's tray and tossed the champagne in Dillon's face. People close to them saw what had happened and were shocked. Dillon's response was to lick his lips.

'Absolutely marvellous, old son, I enjoyed that.' He raised his glass. 'To our next merry meeting in hell.'

'My God,' Lily Shah said. 'Excuse me, ladies. I must go to the imam. His rages are ungovernable on occasion.'

'We understand,' Sara told her, and they watched her go, trying to take the imam's arm and getting pushed away, trailing after him when he turned and pushed through the crowd.

'Why couldn't you just shoot him?' Hannah asked.

'I was sorely tempted,' Dillon said, 'but that would deprive that nice lady of her supper, and I should point out that they are offering a superb buffet on the far side of the room. I suggest a visit may prove of benefit to all of us.'

'What about Declan?' Sara asked.

'You go and get a table. I'll see if he wants to join us.'

By chance, Declan had been phoned just a little earlier by Roper. The major had been feeling bored since not very much was going on, and he'd wondered how Declan was bearing up, considering he'd had two bullets pumped into him and was still in a post-operative stage.

'Anything of interest?' Roper asked.

'Those two men Sara is fascinated with, one addressed her as "ma'am", so she thinks he could be a soldier. I've heard them talk. English public school without a doubt.'

'So are you, clown. You went to St Paul's and sound like it, but you're half Bedouin, to be strictly accurate. Is there any chance these chaps could have been within your military experience?'

'I've a good memory for things like that. If they'd ever served with me, I'd know.'

'Okay, leave it with me. Perhaps Major Giles Roper's magic box will produce some trickery. Clear off and enjoy your supper, and I'll see what I can do.'

Dillon, who had been waiting patiently, said, 'All finished now, can we go to eat?'

'Of course. I'm leaving it in Roper's hands. If anyone can solve my problem, it's he, so lead on. I'm quite hungry.'

About an hour and a half earlier, it had started to rain, a particularly high tide stirring the Thames, a five-knot current running, and the fresh river smell mingled with the rain to give a sharp edge to things.

The Dark Man at Wapping had been Harry Salter's first property and was still his favourite place in the world, in spite of the millions he had made since he'd turned from a life of crime, after making the discovery that using the same talents could make him a fortune from legitimate business as well.

He still took a lot of pride in the pub, but that early in the evening business was quiet and likely to stay that way in view of the weather. Joe Baxter and Sam Hall were having a beer at the bar, Dora the barmaid reading a newspaper, Harry drinking scotch at the table of his personal booth, Billy enjoying a nice cup of tea because he'd only drunk alcohol once in his life and at the age of fifteen. That once had been enough.

'I don't think they'll turn out tonight, Harry,' he said to his uncle.

Harry looked up from the sports page. 'Who are we talking about?'

'Well, the punters for a start. It's hardly an evening for a night out at dear old Wapping, the way the weather is shaping up. I'd say the same will apply for the Sash. Myra Tully won't know what she's going to do next with Terry Harker out of the equation. He's going nowhere, that bastard. He'll be lifted before he knows what's hit him.'

'Could be,' Harry said. 'He's too well known. Have you heard from Hasim?'

'No, but I will. He's never failed to call in yet.'

Harry nodded. 'A good kid.'

Hasim was a mixture of East End Cockney and Jamaican and devoted to the Salters, and he'd been inserted into the staff of the Sash as a potboy, a particularly lowly job that involved sweeping the floors, cleaning toilets, and most things in between. His instructions were to keep his head down and listen to every conversation that he could, and he'd proved more than useful.

Harry poured himself another scotch and said, 'I like that kid.'

'So do I,' Billy said. 'He was doing well with his boxing at Jacko's Health Club, but I had to pull him out of that. It would have been a dead give-away if he'd been recognized by someone from the Sash.'

Sam Hall and Joe Baxter had been listening in,

and Sam said, 'He's a brave kid, because if that Tully bitch found out what he was doing, he'd be chopped liver, and she'd take real pleasure in doing it herself.'

'Well, I wouldn't disagree,' Harry said. 'She's a bleeding nutter, just like her old da.'

'So do you think we should pull the kid out of there?' Billy asked.

The front door of the pub swung open with a crash, a sudden blast of wind sweeping in, rain before it, followed by Hasim, who was soaked to the skin. He lurched towards Harry's booth and fell into a chair.

'Sorry, Mr Salter,' he gasped. 'I need to catch my breath. I've run all the way from the Sash.'

Dora shouted, 'Gawd help us, look at the state of him.' She disappeared into the back of the bar, reappeared with a bath towel, and came around and enveloped him. 'Poor soul, he'll catch his death.'

'What's happened, son?' Harry demanded.

'Well, it's been a hell of a day, what with you and Billy and Mr Dillon paying a visit earlier. Myra Tully's a raving lunatic, if you ask me. She was going on about what she intended to do to you all.'

'And Eric?' Billy said. 'The head barman. How was he taking all this?'

'There's been no sign of Mr Harker, so from what I've heard, it's Eric this and Eric that, and he seems to be going along with it.'

'Going along with what?' Harry asked.

'She wants to burn you out. I've heard her say

that more than once. I'm just the sweeper in the background, and I think she forgets I'm there.' He shook his head. 'In fact, I think they all do. She told Eric that the time has come to sort you out and destroy the Dark Man once and for all by burning it down.'

'And how would they do that?' Harry asked.

'Approach from the river using the old motor launch, the *Tara*, Eric Logan, and three or four of their gang.'

'And Eric's going along with this nonsense?' Harry asked.

'She's so crazy, she says she intends to take part herself. Walking around with a pistol in her hand, mouthing off.' Hasim shrugged. 'Eric seems sort of overwhelmed.'

'But he intends to do it?'

'Well, that was the impression I got when I managed to sneak off. I figured if I grabbed a vehicle from the car park, I'd alert them, so I took to the towpath and ran all the way.'

There was a brief silence, and Dora said, 'Well, I never.'

Billy slapped Hasim on the back. 'Good lad. You've made your bones today. Take him to my bedroom, Dora, fast as you like. Dry him off and find him fresh clothes, boots. I want him down here in fifteen minutes. Now, go.'

Which Hasim and Dora did, both bewildered. Harry said, 'What are you going to do?'

'I'm going to go downriver to the Sash in the

inflatable. I've shown Hasim how to handle it in the past, so now that pays off. I'm just going to change into my wet suit.' He smiled coldly. 'You haven't forgotten that, thanks to Dillon, I'm a master diver?'

'And what's that got to do with the price of eggs?' his uncle demanded.

'Oh, I'm sure I'll manage to find something nasty to do to that motor launch,' and Billy hurried behind the bar and went upstairs.

Early-evening shadows were falling as Hasim stood at the wheel of the large inflatable, one very similar to those used by the River Police. He was rather enjoying himself.

'What happens when we get there?'

'We'll see,' Billy told him. 'The one thing you couldn't tell me was when they intended to strike, so we could be hanging around for a while. It's all in the lap of the gods, Hasim. The older you get, the more you realize that.'

'Anything you say, boss.'

Billy checked his watch and noted it was just after seven. They'd be starting to crowd into the ballroom now at the Dorchester. He had a sudden impulse to phone Roper, but decided not to. No point until he had some good news.

'So what do we do when we actually see them coming?' Hasim asked.

'I'm going to be waiting for them in the engine room.'

'What are you going to do there?'

'Open the seacocks. The water pours in, the *Tara* sinks. It's very simple. Even better if it takes its passengers with it, particularly when they're as unpleasant as Myra Tully.'

'Merciful Allah,' Hasim said. 'And you would be willing to do this?'

'I don't see why not. If she boards the *Tara*, that means she intends to burn the Dark Man to the ground and everyone in it. The Scriptures say an eye for an eye, and I'm sure the Koran says something similar.'

Hasim couldn't think of a suitable reply, and in any case, they were approaching their destination, and Billy found some binoculars in a side pocket and focused on the Sash.

The rain provided a grey curtain, vehicles in the car park perfectly visible, but not for long before darkness would descend. A number of boats were tied up along the old-fashioned towpath, but there was no sign of anyone around.

He said to Hasim, 'That's the *Tara* with the scarlet-and-cream wheelhouse. Just drop me at the end of the towpath, then drift out and switch off among those smaller vessels. I'm going to explore the *Tara*. If I'm still on board and they arrive, you must follow when they take off. Is that understood?'

'Yes,' Hasim said. 'Though it sounds a little bit crazy to me.'

'I have my mobile and you have yours. We can keep in touch, so just do as I say.'

The inflatable edged in, Billy took a last look up at the Sash through the binoculars, and he saw Myra and Eric emerge from the entrance followed by three men.

'They're coming,' Billy said. 'I'm out of it, so you do as I've told you.'

He jumped to the towpath, moved quickly to the *Tara*, boarded, and behind him Hasim took the inflatable away.

There was an instant smell of petrol when Billy stepped over the rail. Preparations had already been made and there was a row of jerry cans at one end of the deck. He slid down into the saloon. There was no smell of petrol there and everything seemed normal, so he went back on deck, crouching. The party from the Sash were closer now and there was raucous laughter, more than hinting that drink had been taken, but he moved to the front of the wheelhouse, opened the hatch to the engine room, and dropped inside.

He could hear everything, Myra laughing drunkenly. 'We'll have another little drink and then depart to give that bastard Harry Salter the surprise of his life.'

Eric sounded far from happy. 'Come on, Myra, enough is enough.'

'Don't you try and tell me what to do, Eric Logan,' she said. 'You can take your sodding medal and go and jump in the Thames with it. There's only one captain on this ship. Now, let's get moving or I'll take over the wheel myself. I'll be with my friends when you want me.'

Peering out of the engine-room hatchway, Billy could see the back of her disappearing down to the saloon, heard Eric's footsteps as he ascended to the wheelhouse to switch on the engine, which coughed into life. He reached out of the partially raised hatch and shot the bolt of the companionway door leading to the saloon below. Then he dropped down beside the engine again and peered out of a small port window.

Above him, Eric Logan had phoned Terry Harker in desperation and found him resting in bed at the bolt-hole.

'I'm right up the creek, Terry,' Eric said. 'And there isn't a thing I can do about it.'

'Well, tell me, for God's sake.'

Which Eric did. 'Down below with those bastards. God knows what's going on.'

'Damn you, Eric, you know exactly what's going on. She's getting laid. Who in the hell came up with the idea of having a go at the Salters?'

'The Master got in touch with me. He was all for it, and Myra spoke to him. Told him she'd love to burn the Dark Man down. What do I do?'

'I'm the last man to ask at the moment, Eric. I'm lying here crippled, in hiding from everybody. Why can't you turn the *Tara* around and sail back?'

'Because she won't have it. I've never seen her so drunk.'

'Then she can go to hell her own way,' Terry

said. 'I'm in no condition to do anything about it. You'll have to handle this, old son.'

It was really getting dark now, lights flickering everywhere, Hasim in the inflatable some way back.

Billy called him and got a reply at once. Hasim said, 'I was getting worried. What's happening?'

'Myra's drunk out of her mind and down below with entirely the wrong kind of people.'

'And Eric?'

'I'll have to have words. Be ready.'

He knelt down and unscrewed the seacocks one after another, then went up the ladder and hauled himself out on deck, to find a furious banging on the companionway door and Myra shouting, 'What's going on? Get this bloody door open.'

The *Tara* was suddenly sluggish with the weight of the water pouring into her, the deck tilting and Billy slipping back against the rail. At the same moment, Eric slid down the rails from the wheelhouse and gaped in astonishment.

'Where the hell did you come from?' In the same moment, he pulled a Browning out of the pocket of the sailor's pea jacket he was wearing and shot Billy at close quarters, bouncing him against the rail. Billy reached for the silenced Colt .25 he habitually wore in a rear belt clip and shot him between the eyes, driving him back over the rail into the Thames. Thanks to the bulletproof vest he'd been wearing himself, he was only struggling for breath, but knee-deep in water, the *Tara* down by the head. Just in time, Hasim roared up to the rescue. Billy fell into the inflatable and they fled as the *Tara* disappeared.

Hasim cried, 'Are you okay? What happened. Did you let them out?'

'I didn't get a chance. Eric pulled a gun on me and knocked me over. Lucky I'm wearing a vest, but I had to return fire to stop him from doing it again. By that time, it was too late to get the door to the saloon open.'

'I wonder where Eric will wash up.'

'Maybe nowhere. More than half of the bodies that go in are never seen again. The Thames is a tidal river, and on occasion, fierce currents can wash any corpse straight out to sea.'

'So what do you think will happen?' Hasim asked.

'To me and you? Nothing. The kind of people who are involved in an affair like this don't complain, Hasim, not to the authorities and certainly not to the police. Myra Tully was spawned by as evil a family as any in the criminal under-world. Her husband is doing fifteen years in Belmarsh Prison. The only word from Scotland Yard will be good riddance. Now let's get back to the Dark Man.'

'Which will be a distinct pleasure for me after my time at the Sash,' Hasim told him.

'Well, there you are, then,' Billy said. 'Take us home.'

★ ★ ★

Back at the pub, Billy showered and changed, noting the severe bruising he'd received from the pistol shot, then he phoned Roper. 'You can tell Ferguson from me that Myra Tully and Eric Logan no longer present a problem.'

'Well, that *is* interesting,' Roper said. 'Tell me,' which Billy did, and when he was finished, Roper grunted approval. 'An unpleasant human being. I can't see that she'll be mourned by anyone.'

'Terry Harker, perhaps?' Billy said.

'He'll be too busy keeping his head down. No, I can't see a problem there. This was a good one, Billy, but you're rapidly running out of your nine lives, so take care.'

'Don't I always?' Billy said. 'I'll let Dillon know.'

The events of Billy's early evening on the river reached Dillon as he was enjoying supper at the fundraiser in the company of Sara, Hannah, and Declan Rashid.

When it was finished, Dillon said, 'What do you think?'

Declan said, 'Of Billy? Well, he obviously doesn't take prisoners.'

Dillon said, 'He was a gangster from an early age, but then, he would be, with Harry as his uncle. I remember when Blake Johnson was being held by thugs in a remote country house in Devon. I was going to surprise the villains by parachuting from a small plane. Billy insisted on going with me – even though he'd never jumped before or had any training.'

Sara said, 'His hobby is moral philosophy, which, wait for it, he was introduced to by Dillon.' She turned to Dillon. 'What was your impression when you first met him, Sean?'

'That he was like someone out of one of those French gangster movies with Alain Delon. In fact, ask him what he is and he might shock you by saying he's a gangster.'

'Well, some people would say that as an agent of MI5, that's what he is,' Sara pointed out. She turned to Hannah. 'What do you think?'

'That he's brave and good with women and was probably an altar boy when he was young. As for him locking the door on that boat so that Myra Tully drowned in the saloon, kicking and screaming? I'll tell you what I think. I think she was a complete bitch who deserved everything she got.' The orchestra suddenly erupted into one of Cole Porter's finest, 'Night and Day.' 'Ah, real music,' she said, and turned to Sara. 'Shall we go and sit closer? At least we can enjoy listening.'

'What a good idea,' Sara said.

As Dillon and Declan followed, the colonel's mobile sounded and it was Roper. 'I think I may have solved your problem.'

'How?' Declan asked.

'You said you would have remembered those chaps if you'd soldiered with them.'

'Definitely, and I haven't.'

'But what was the most recent appointment you received from the Minister of War in Tehran?'

'Well, I was promoted to second-in-command of the Secret Field Police in the rank of full colonel. But I never inspected them. Everything happened in such a rush.'

'There are one hundred and fifty officers, mainly young, in that unit. Weren't you given a file listing them, and their records, by the War Minister?'

'My God, what a fool I am,' Declan said. 'I had to catch an embassy plane to Beirut. Everything happened so fast, but I do recall now a ministry secure file of all officers in the SFP, plus photos.'

'I have obtained access to that information, and if you go and sit down in some quiet corner with your Codex, you can browse the photos and see where it gets you.'

Declan returned to the Promenade bar, which was comparatively quiet, ordered a Martini cocktail, and started examining the photos. He found his quarry within fifteen minutes, standing in line, crisply uniformed, soldiers at their best, and called Roper at once.

'I've got them. Captains Ali Herim and Khalid Abed. They're unmistakable.'

'Just hang on and I'll process them at once,' Roper told him.

Declan swallowed his Martini, ordered another, and sat there on the bar stool, emotions mixed. The implication here was that they were up to no good, the enemy, but it certainly didn't sit comfortably with him. People in the West had forgotten that before the Gulf War, Iran had fought Saddam Hussein for eight rather savage years.

The door swung open behind him, and Sara and Hannah entered, followed by Dillon. 'So there you are,' Sara said. 'We were wondering what happened to you.'

'I've been dealing with Roper. He's discovered who the mysterious young men are who keep calling you ma'am, Sara. It seems they're officers in my old unit. I'm waiting to hear what else Roper digs up.'

Roper came back to him. 'They have excellent army records, these boys. They are cousins. Ali Herim is posing as one Lance Harvey, Khalid Abed as his brother, Anthony. Would you believe they went to Winchester and a year at Sandhurst?'

'I've learned to believe anything you tell me now, Giles,' Declan said. 'But that isn't the point. What are they doing here?'

'Spies,' Roper told him. 'They're classic. But listen, how's this for a wild supposition? Sara Gideon was attacked by Brotherhood members not long ago at Highfield House, right? And two complete strangers intervened wearing ski masks, and beat hell out of them.'

'Cockney hard boys interfering,' Declan said. 'That was the suggestion.'

'Which didn't make sense,' Roper told him. 'But

what does is two young toughs with special forces training.'

'You mean—? But why would they do that?' Declan asked.

'Maybe because they went to Winchester and have better manners,' Sara said. 'It would certainly answer a lot of questions for me.'

'Well, you've got their photos on Declan's mobile and you girls have met them face-to-face. I suggest you people leave the crowd and see what you can find, while I notify Ferguson about what's going on.'

'Which he won't like one little bit,' Dillon said. 'What a night. First we had Billy drowning people in the Thames, now spies at the Dorchester. Where will it end?'

'Just shut up, Sean, and let's get on with it.' And she led the way out.

Terry Harker had found an old terry-cloth dressing gown from his boxing days but was still cold, lying on the bed in the bolt-hole, listening to the rain pounding down outside.

When his mobile sounded, he answered instantly, and the Master said, 'How are you feeling?'

'I've been shot, you idiot, how do you expect me to feel?'

'Even worse when I tell you what's happened to your friends Eric, Myra, and the little task force whose intention was to burn the Dark Man to the ground.'

'Okay, so tell me the worst. What went wrong?'

'Wrong for your friends, you mean? Happy to oblige. Billy Salter boarded the *Tara*, and when he found Myra considerably worse for wear and with three roughnecks for company, he locked them in the saloon and opened the seacocks.'

Terry was aware of sweat rolling down his face in spite of the cold and said hoarsely, 'What happened to Myra, did Eric manage to save her?'

'He did get a shot off, which didn't do the slightest good, as Billy was wearing a vest. Billy responded by shooting him between the eyes and just managed to transfer boats as the *Tara* went down.'

'Bastard,' Terry roared. 'I'll get Billy Salter for what he's done to Myra, and maybe I'll get you.'

'Stop making stupid threats, Terry. We'll get the lot of them, I promise you,' the Master said, and switched off.

CHAPTER 12

The ballroom seemed more crowded than ever, particularly the dance floor, and it was obvious that a good time was being had by all. Dillon and Declan, Sara and Hannah, paused after coming in from the Promenade bar and Roper spoke to Dillon.

'Where are you?' Roper asked. Dillon told him, and Roper said, 'Wait there. Ferguson wants a word. He's not exactly happy.'

Dillon had just started telling the others when Ferguson pushed his way through the crowd, followed by Henry Frankel, who was smiling cheerfully as usual.

'Ah, there you are,' Frankel said. 'Isn't this fun? I've heard all about young Billy Salter's exploits and now this. I haven't had such a good time in years.'

'Do shut up, Henry,' Ferguson said grimly. 'There's nothing funny about it,' and he addressed the group. 'I've had a quick word with Jake Cazalet, so he knows what's going on. He's proved very popular tonight, thank God, so he's helping the PM by keeping the French Foreign Minister happy, plus Sir Howard Glynn and assorted hangers-on.'

'So what do you want us to do?' Sara asked.

'Find them, Captain,' Ferguson said. 'These two, Herim and Khalid. Find them now.' He turned to Frankel, face grim. 'Have you anything worthwhile to say, Henry?'

'Yes, Charles, come back and sit down before you have a stroke.' He took Ferguson's arm and winked at Dillon. 'Good luck, you lot,' and he led Ferguson away.

There was still a sizeable crowd over by the buffet. Ali and Khalid had managed to get a table early in the evening and had hung on to it. The view of the ballroom was good, and a couple of very large potted palms gave a certain cover. Ali waited there for Khalid to return, eyes scanning the crowd.

He had felt uncomfortable on first meeting Sara Gideon, and even more so in the Promenade bar earlier. When she'd looked at him, he'd sensed a query and couldn't understand why. The sight of Declan Rashid in the flesh hadn't worried him, though, because he knew for a fact that they'd never had occasion to meet during their army service.

There was a disturbance a few yards away, Hamid Bey arguing with a young waiter at the buffet, Lily Shah trying to placate him. He gave her an elbow that sent her staggering, and Ali jumped to his feet and caught her as Khalid appeared, carrying Krug in a bucket and two glasses.

'Get up, woman,' Hamid Bey said harshly in Arabic, and Ali answered him in the same language.

'She is not your dog, so give her the respect the Koran expects you to offer her as a woman.' He shook his head. 'There is only one dog here.' He turned to Lily. 'Are you all right?'

'I was an army nurse for seven years. I carry a Colt in my purse. I'm fine.' She turned to the imam. 'We parked in Henry Street. I'm going now.'

'No, you aren't,' he told her.

'You can get a cab when you're ready,' she replied.

She made straight for the door that a waiter had used and was gone. Hamid Bey glared at Ali and Khalid and went after her.

The cork had already been thumbed out of the bottle of Krug, and Khalid filled two glasses. 'There you are, Cousin. What a bastard that man was.'

'And did you notice they'd parked in Henry Street?' Ali asked. 'That's where we left our car.'

He raised his glass and saw Hannah standing nearby, leaning on her walking stick, remembered she'd arrived with Sara Gideon and knew they were in trouble.

But he played out his role. 'We have a little lost lamb here, Tony,' and he smiled at Hannah. 'Can we help?'

'Only if you're Captains Ali Herim and Khalid Abed of the SFP. And I have to tell you, I've seen your photos, so there's no point in denying it. You're lovely chaps and your performance is first-rate. You should have been actors.'

Khalid smiled engagingly. 'That's been said before. I realize who you are. The pianist.'

'Who was blown up with your mother and father,' Ali said. 'Which explains your walking stick.'

Khalid topped up his glass of Krug, offered it to her, and Hannah took it automatically. 'Nice to chat, but we'll have to love you and leave you.'

'Don't try to follow us,' Ali said. 'It's not worth the struggle with the walking stick.'

'Ah, gentlemen to the end.'

'We try, I suppose,' Khalid said. 'Life really is a bitch sometimes, but then you found that out rather early.' He nodded to Ali, and then they rushed the door at the end of the bar and were gone.

Hannah sat down at the empty table, drank the Krug, and called Sara, who answered at once. 'Where are you?'

'Sitting by the bar at the end of the buffet. I found them, and to be frank, they're rather nice.'

She quickly covered the business with Hamid Bey and Lily Shah, the confrontation with Ali and Khalid. 'Just one thing. When Lily walked out on the imam, she told them they were parked in Henry Street. Does that ring any bells with you?'

'I know it well. It's a short walk to the hotel. A quiet street with good parking, close to South Audley Street. That's why people use it.'

'Ali Herim heard that and mentioned that he and Khalid Abed had also parked there.'

'Say no more,' Sara told her. 'Dillon's got his old Mini parked out front. Join us as quickly as you can.'

Ali was already on the phone to the Master as they negotiated the maze of corridors on the ground floor.

'The roof's fallen in,' he said crisply, and explained what had happened, including the clash with Hamid Bey and Lily.

'I'm wondering whether they will still be in Henry Street when you get there,' the Master said.

'We'll have to go and see,' Ali told him. 'No choice. What happens next, that's the thing. It's all unravelling. It won't take Roper long to work out where we've been living. He probably knows now.'

'Yes, I'd avoid the place in Pimlico. If you've obeyed orders, you'll have backup passports on your person?'

'We have,' Ali said.

'Excellent. Just find your car and get out of there. Find a modest hotel for the night, and I'll be in touch with a new plan of action for you.'

'And the Minister of War in Tehran?'

'You don't go anywhere near him. Roper has

probably penetrated his systems. Just get to Henry Street, recover your car, and drive carefully away.'

He switched off, and a few moments later, Ali and Khalid had opened a service door and peered out into Park Lane. Taxis were pulling in, people already leaving the function, and it was raining heavily. Ali closed the service door again.

'We'll get soaked. See if there's anything that'll help around here.' And there was. A storeroom with a number of yellow oilskins and a large Dorchester umbrella.

'We can share it,' Ali said, and they put on the oilskins, stepped out into Park Lane, then opened the umbrella and walked briskly away.

'English rain,' Ali said. 'There's nothing like it.'

'I remember the military history course making a point about that when we did our Sandhurst year,' Khalid reminded him. 'How the Romans never ceased complaining about the weather in Britain during four hundred years of occupation.'

'They invented socks because of it,' Ali told him. 'Mind you, this is exceptional.'

'No, it's not. Remember Syria last November, when we weren't supposed to be there anyway? I thought the great flood had returned. You know, Noah from the Bible?'

Ali nodded. 'I admit that was bad, especially as they were shooting at us so much.'

'Yes, it didn't help.' Khalid nodded. 'But I've

been thinking. What did the Master mean by a modest hotel? Where would we find such a place?'

'I haven't the slightest idea, but does it give you a problem?'

'Yes, it does, because it seems to me that if you're rich, which we are, the obvious place to hide is in a rich man's hotel.'

Ali laughed out loud. 'And where's your logic for that?'

'Because it would be the last place anyone would look for men on the run.'

Ali was amazed. 'My dearest cousin, you're going to come to a bad end one day, but not because you aren't clever. Ah, here we are at Henry Street.'

They started along the pavement, well-lit by streetlamps, and there were many vehicles parked, not only automobiles. Their blue Mini Cooper was some distance away, and as they walked towards it, they came to a large van of a type much used by hospitals. The insignia on the side said 'Pound Street Dispensary'.

They paused, and Khalid said, 'It must be Lily Shah.'

They crowded together, peering inside, and found her leaning back behind the driving wheel, eyes closed. Ali tapped on the window, her eyes opened, obviously alarmed, and then she recognized them, opened the door, and stepped out.

'It's you,' she said, and shook her head. 'I dozed off.'

'And Hamid Bey?' Ali asked. 'What happened to him?'

'He didn't turn up. He must have got a taxi after all. I've humiliated him. He won't forgive me for doing that.'

Ali said, 'Excuse me, but you're holding your purse in one hand and the silenced Colt .25 in the other.'

She glanced down, surprised for just a moment. 'Yes, sitting there, giving him a chance to turn up, I held the gun in my lap, I suppose because it made me feel safe. And then I dozed off.'

A car's engine roared into life higher up the street. No lights went on, the driver's window was down, a shadowy figure within, aiming a silenced weapon that coughed deeply as one round after another fired.

And it was Lily Shah who returned fire first, in a reflex, since she was already holding her weapon, dull sounds that hardly disturbed the peace of the street. She cried out, lurching against Ali, a bullet going through her left arm, and as he held her close, leaning over her, he was shot in the back. Khalid joined in, jumping into the street, pulling out his Walther, hitting the vehicle through the rear window as it sped away.

A few moments later, Dillon's Mini came around the corner, Declan beside him, the girls in the back, and they were shocked to find the damage. Dillon was out in seconds.

He stood there, soaking in the rain. 'Damn this

downpour. People started to leave early. Parking was chaotic.'

Khalid said, 'Never mind, Mr Dillon, I'm sure you know who we are. My friend has been shot in the back, the lady in the arm.'

'By whom?' Sara asked.

'At this stage of the game, I can only guess, but I believe we've been ambushed by a man known to you as the Master.'

Dillon was already on the phone to Roper. 'Rosedene. These people have suffered serious damage. Sister Lily Shah was driving a large van – we'll use that to get the wounded to you as fast as possible, but we'll all come.'

So Ali and Lily were taken away by Dillon, with Sara tending them in the back of the van. Declan drove the Mini Cooper, and Khalid drove Dillon's Mini with Hannah, whose new evening suit was so soaked it was obviously ruined. The exchange of silenced pistols had been quiet enough, only the sound of vehicles being something to apologize for.

As Hannah was getting in the Mini with Khalid, a door opened and a burly man appeared on the front step. 'Is that it?' he called. 'Can we have some peace?'

'Peace, is it?' Hannah said. 'We don't do that these days, mister. You'll get plenty when you're dead, though,' and Khalid drove her away, laughing helplessly.

★   ★   ★

It was providential that Professor Charles Bellamy had had occasion to call in late at Rosedene to check the progress of a few patients before going home. The prospect of two people suffering from gunshot wounds, one of them critically, changed the last part of that plan. Maggie Duncan had to recall staff at every level to present him with two surgical teams capable of working at such a sustained level, and that was not easy.

'No rest for the wicked tonight, Professor,' she said as they prepared to start.

'No rest for anyone, I'm afraid, including you, Matron,' he said formally. 'I'm relying on you to assist.'

Declan, Sara, and Hannah sat with Dillon in the hospitality room, along with Khalid. After a while, Parker wheeled Roper in, followed by Henry Frankel and Ferguson.

'It looks like we're all here,' Ferguson said. 'So thank you, Parker, for putting in twenty hours today. Get to the kitchen for some supper and they'll also have a bed for you.'

'Thank you, General,' Parker said, and went out.

'There will be beds for everyone,' Ferguson continued. 'Colonel Rashid, as the walking wounded, I suggest you leave us now. Also you, young lady,' he said to Hannah. 'Captain Gideon, Dillon, and Major Roper will stay with the prisoner.'

Declan and Hannah left, she with obvious reluctance, and Ferguson said, 'Let's get on with

295

it, Major Roper. I suspect we'd all like to get to bed. I certainly would.'

'I share the sentiment, General.' Roper turned to Khalid. 'I know all about you. Winchester, Sandhurst, an officer and a gentleman. You speak English, French, Farsi, and Arabic. Correct?'

'Yes, Major.'

'Your army record has been exemplary. I doubt whether the British High Command could fault it, so what the hell are you and your comrade, now fighting for his life on the operating table, doing involving yourselves with Al Qaeda and the cult of the Master?'

Ferguson broke in. 'I've already spoken to Professor Bellamy, and I must tell you, it will be a very close-run thing with your friend. The heart was touched at one side. It will take all his skill.'

Khalid said, 'Thank you, General. Ali and I are cousins, posted to London, as you know, as Captain Lance Harvey and his brother Tony. About four weeks ago, this one called the Master phoned our Minister of War, told him Colonel Declan Rashid was a traitor, and that you and your people were enemies of Iran. So the minister told us to find out all we could about you.'

'Do you approve of Al Qaeda?'

'No, I don't, and neither does the Minister of War. He was simply being expedient. In Iran, we prefer to rule our own country and not be ruled by someone else. I think you make a mistake in allowing too much power to those who think otherwise.'

'Such as?' Sara asked.

'It's happening around you. The Army of God, the Brotherhood.'

'And you don't approve of them, either?'

'I wouldn't approve of people who behave like that in my own country, so why would I approve of such people here?'

'Which is why when you saw Captain Gideon being attacked at her own home about three weeks ago, you put on ski masks and went to the rescue. You'd been keeping watch on her house anyway, I presume,' Roper said, smiling.

'Can I ask why you did that?' Sara said.

'One soldier to another, you know how it is, Captain. We admired you, and we didn't like them.'

Ferguson said, 'As good a reason as I've ever heard. Are you happy, Henry?'

'Absolutely,' the Cabinet Secretary said. 'Everything a soldier should be.'

'I suspect that's the Sandhurst training,' Ferguson suggested.

'I don't care what it is,' Frankel told him. 'Just make sure he stays on our side. I don't know about the rest of you, but I'm going to bed and I'll see you at breakfast.'

And with that, they adjourned.

It was providential that the Master had been paying close attention to the events at the

Dorchester when he received Ali's phone call. On the other hand, desperate situations brought out the best in him.

He'd arrived at Henry Street and seen Lily Shah standing beside her van, then climbing in as he passed. With no sign of the Iranians, he'd parked on the other side, where he'd sat, lights out, nursing a Glock pistol, window down and his collar up against the rain.

It had all happened so fast, starting with the Iranians coming around the corner. His attack was absolutely necessary, though the fact that Lily Shah had returned fire was a shock. That she'd been hit, although still standing, was obvious, as was the fact that Ali Herim had gone down. But Khalid had damaged the Master's car, his rear window gone, and he needed to get rid of it fast, which he did, dumping it in a dark lane off South Audley Street and walking back to the general area of the Dorchester, where he might mingle with respectable people if he had to walk home.

A problem now, the Iranians. The Minister of War would be furious at such a turn of events. Even if Ali Kerim died, it wouldn't help the situation, since Khalid Abed was fighting fit. It would have suited everyone, politics being the dirty game it was, if they'd both ended up dead in the gutter, but they hadn't.

On the other hand, nobody at the Ministry of Defence would want them touched with any kind of publicity. They would never have to stand up in court or anything like that. Those days were gone. And Charles Ferguson was the original conniving bastard and would be ecstatic if he could recruit them. He smiled. If the CIA didn't beat him to the punch, that is.

He walked through Shepherd Market, where he knew there was a late-night coffee shop, and found it almost empty. So he sat in a corner, enjoying two espressos, and analysed his present situation. His bosses on the Council had to be kept sweet, and Ferguson's people were still a problem. The fact that Cazalet was now in London and a possible target was to his credit, so what wasn't?

The answer was easy. Hamid Bey. The Master had warned him against attending the Hope Charity Foundation evening because his erratic behavior made him out of place, but he'd still gone.

'You know what, Hamid,' he said softly. 'I'm going to have to do something about you.'

He dropped some money on the table, left and hailed a taxi, telling the driver to take him to Pound Street.

It was late, but he knew where Hamid Bey's personal vehicle, an estate, was parked, in a dimly lit garage below the apartment that went with his job. He raised the bonnet of the engine and reached in to make adjustments to the flow of braking fluid. It was always difficult to get it just right. Satisfied, he closed the bonnet and walked away, calling Hamid Bey, who didn't answer for a while, and when he did, sounded cautious.

'Who is it?'

'The Master, and you must listen, my friend.'

'What is it?'

'Lily Shah accompanied you to the Dorchester this evening, correct?'

'Yes, she did.'

'The two of you parked a Pound Street van in Henry Street not far from the hotel. Apparently, when Lily returned to reclaim it, she was shot in the arm, and it seems one of my two Iranians, who'd also been at the fundraiser, was shot in the back.'

Hamid Bey said, 'Is Lily all right? What's happening?'

'The wounded are being cared for by Professor Charles Bellamy at Rosedene.'

'A great surgeon,' Hamid Bey said. 'And a fine hospital. They'll probably try to poach Lily.'

'Do you think she should be somewhere else?'

'She's a Christian, but she is very popular here.'

'That is beside the point,' said the Master. 'Lily's mother was a Jew. The fact that her father was Christian doesn't matter. Her mother was Jewish, and that means Lily is. It's a fact of life that can't be altered. I don't think we can trust her any longer.'

He switched off, leaving Hamid Bey profoundly depressed. He spent the night badly, barely slept at all, and was on the phone to Rosedene at eight o'clock the following morning.

Maggie Duncan took the call she had been expecting, for Ferguson had warned her it would come and that Hamid Bey, based on past experience, was likely to be awkward. As it turned out, the reverse was true.

He arrived with flowers from a garden centre and wearing a grey flannel suit. Maggie Duncan gave him Yemeni coffee in the hospitality room, and information, amazed at how civil he was being, warning him that in spite of the bullet passing straight through Lily's left arm, the bone had been chipped, a serious complication that was likely to take time and a considerable amount of therapy to put right.

They studiously avoided discussing the reasons for what had happened, and when he hoped that the other victim was doing well, she shrugged and said his problem was rather more serious. Then she led him to a pleasant room where Lily, pale and ill-looking, her left arm heavily bandaged and supported, smiled weakly at him. Maggie said twenty minutes and left them to it.

Lily seemed tired. 'You look completely different. Have you somewhere to go?'

'I did have, but now I am here,' he said. 'To apologize for my behaviour over many months. I don't know why, but suddenly I feel completely different. Perhaps the terrible shock of what happened to you and that young man.' He shrugged.

'He is far, far worse than me, imam. It's a mercy that we are in the hands of these people here, and Professor Bellamy.' Her eyes filled with tears. 'People can be so wonderful, and just at the right time. You have come to say something to me, I think?'

'It is not an easy thing to do. Over the time we've known each other, I have behaved badly. You see, you had a husband when you came to Pound Street, and I loved you from the moment I saw you. But this was wrong, especially for a religious leader, so I became what I became. When your husband went to Gaza and was killed, I thought it was a reminder from heaven that I had been wrong. But now I feel quite different.'

'And why would that be?'

'The Master spoke to me last night and told me your mother was a Jew.'

'Why would he do that?'

'I think it gave him pleasure to try to hurt me, expecting that as a Muslim, I would turn away.'

'And what *did* it do to you?'

'Made me want to comfort you and tell you it didn't matter.' She nodded, as if considering the point. 'You're tired, so I'll go now. If you need me, you know where I am. There is no obligation.'

He turned just as Maggie Duncan was opening the door, and she ushered him out. 'She seems to be crying?'

He smiled gravely. 'I hope for the right reason, Matron. If I may, I'll keep in touch.'

'Of course.'

He left, and she returned to Lily. 'All right, my dear?'

'Absolutely. I just got the greatest surprise of my life, but I'll sleep again now, I think, and speak later.'

Hamid Bey was surprisingly calm as he drove away. It was the strangest feeling that everything had changed, and as he put his foot down and the car increased speed, he smiled, thinking of the Master. He'd only meant harm by telling Hamid that Lily was Jewish, but he had opened up a new pathway for him instead, and hopefully for her also.

There were roadworks at the bottom of the hill that he'd had to negotiate on the way up, but now the car started to shake going into the bend. He stamped on the brakes and nothing happened, nothing at all. He scraped around by some miracle and found a five-ton concrete truck slewed across the road, workers scrambling out of trenches, and then there was only the truck as he swept on like a bullet, and then there was nothing.

Giles Roper picked up a police report of the accident and called Maggie Duncan at once.

'You were expecting Hamid Bey, Matron?'

'Yes, he's been and gone.'

'Further than you think. Killed in a car crash not much more than a mile or two from you.'

'That's dreadful,' she said, and groaned. 'How am I going to tell Lily Shah about this?'

'How is she?'

'Very poorly.'

'I should have thought he was the last person she needed to see.'

'No, he was completely different. No robes, business suit, quiet and well-mannered. A new model in every way. To be honest, having experienced him as he was before, it was very strange to see him like that.'

'And Lily?'

'She'd cried a little when they spoke, but they parted on good terms. She's sleeping quite deeply now. God knows how I'm going to break the news to her.'

'And how many times have you had to say that over the years? Take care.'

In the penthouse apartment on the huge top floor of the Edwardian house in Mayfair, the Master sat at the desk in his velvet dressing gown, drinking coffee and listening to the transmitter pouring out information, useful or otherwise, compiled continuously by the Grand Council. It was morning and he was just risen, having followed his usual practice of walking home instead of using a taxi, for security was his personal obsession.

He had just heard the news of Hamid Bey's

death, which he had not intended. His exploit with the imam's car had been meant to teach the man a lesson, not kill him. A nuisance, since it would be necessary to find someone to fill his place. The Grand Council would feel considerably put out, but that would be easy enough to handle. He could always blame Ferguson's people.

He poured more coffee, then moved to the window and peered out. He loved this part of Mayfair, the rooftops, the echo of Big Ben in the distance, even the damn rain washing the streets below and the promise of more. He thought of Lily. She was not in good condition, but she would survive. Ali Herim was something else again and very possibly would die. But that was all right. He was a soldier and had taken a soldier's risks. But they all were when you considered it. Ferguson, Cazalet, Sara Gideon, even Dillon, to give him his due, though his army had been the IRA.

People like the Salters were different, of course, cheap gangsters when you thought of it. Just look at what Billy Salter had done to the *Tara*, and it suddenly struck him that he hadn't checked to see if Terry Harker was still surviving.

The *Arabella* in St Jude's Dock was a miserable place to be, swamped in mist and heavy rain. The only good thing about it was that the electric cable and water pipe connection to the shore supply were still holding up, so there was a certain amount of heat to make the all-pervading damp bearable, especially with a blanket over your shoulders, which Terry had.

He was past being unshaven, a beard sprouting, and he'd removed the dressing from his ear, which was better than he had feared. There was powdered milk, frozen meals to microwave, tinned food, and booze. Plenty of that, and he was pouring hot water into a large whiskey when the phone buzzed.

He hesitated, then found the Master when he answered. 'How are you bearing up?'

'How the hell do you think I am?' Terry asked. 'It's like living in a swamp. How are things doing at the Sash?'

'I haven't the slightest idea. For God's sake, Terry, it was only two days ago that *Tara* went plunging to the bottom, and God knows where she is now. This bad weather coupled with exceptional currents can bounce wrecks all the way down to the Goodwin Sands and the sea.'

'Is that supposed to make me feel better?' Terry drank some of his whiskey. 'When you think what Billy Salter did.' He shook his head. 'And I thought I'd seen some bad times in the army, but never mind that. What *is* going to happen to the Sash? Who's running the place, paying the staff, ordering the supplies, replacing the booze?'

'Breathe deeply and start getting your head straight,' the Master told him. 'So much has happened in a short time. The Sash has stopped dead for a while. It can wait.'

'What for? A few more people to get knocked off?' Terry demanded.

'If that's what it takes, yes. You know how these Sicilian mafiosi have it. All your doubts will be resolved.'

'I'm not sure about that any more,' Terry said.

'You've nowhere to go. *I'm* all you've got. So shut up, and wait. I'll be in touch.'

CHAPTER 13

So much had happened that Ferguson decided it was time to call a meeting. Cazalet had insisted on staying involved and arrived with Sara and Hannah. Billy and Harry Salter were there, Declan with Khalid Abed, and Ferguson was with Henry Frankel, who was representing the Prime Minister.

Ferguson said, 'I'd like to start by expressing our appreciation to Jake Cazalet for insisting on being here.'

'It's where I should be,' Cazalet said. 'I was there at the beginning, so I certainly have every intention of being here at the end.'

Ferguson said, 'This affair is only a few weeks old, but the carnage has been terrific. Those two Chechen assassins at Nantucket, Bell and Tully at Drumgoole, although we still have no idea who shot Dr Ali Saif outside the gate here. He's been close to death, but rallying.'

Roper said, 'He still finds speech very difficult, so if his response is poor when you try to communicate, do the best you can.'

'We'll take that on board,' Ferguson said. 'Then

we have Terry Harker, wounded and on the run, thanks to Hannah being as expert with a pistol as she is at playing a piano.'

Harry cut in, 'Have we any information on where he is?'

'Not at the moment,' Roper said. 'But it's only a matter of time.'

Ferguson carried on. 'Then we have the people on the *Tara*. Congratulations to Billy for that operation, at considerable personal risk, and I've no complaints about the way he had to do it.'

Sara said, 'So what about the shooting last night?'

'It appears likely that the Master struck personally, his intention being to dispose of Captains Abed and Herim. I'm going to allow Colonel Rashid to explain that situation to you.'

Declan did, finishing by saying, 'I think we all see that these two young officers had little choice in what they did. Captain Ali Herim is hanging on to life by a thread. Whether he lives or dies – the two of them are on our side now.'

'Well, I'll second that,' Harry said.

Ferguson turned to Roper. 'Anything to add?'

'Just to confirm – when the boys told the Master they'd been rumbled and were making a run for it, there's no doubt he was the one who ambushed them, because they had to be shut up. Lily took him on and he'd no hesitation in shooting her, which shows what a ruthless bastard he is, considering that she was obviously the woman he used on Nantucket.'

'So what will he do now?' Cazalet said.

Roper said, 'My opinion? It has to be something spectacular. The Grand Council has to be so displeased with him that he's hanging by a thread. Whatever it is has got to be fast.'

'So will we,' Ferguson said. 'So I suggest we adjourn for lunch and put our thinking caps on. Anything you can come up with will be welcome. Speak to Roper or me or shout it aloud.'

Ferguson's Codex sounded, he listened, got up and walked away to his office, and Cazalet took the seat he'd vacated beside Roper. 'Could we talk?'

'Of course, Mr President.' Roper had used the title automatically and didn't know why, except that there was something very serious about Cazalet at that moment.

'Years ago, my first presidential term took place while the war between the IRA and the British Army was at its worst, blood on the streets. British Intelligence had an agreement to keep us fully informed of the most delicate intelligence, but it turned out that it was being passed on by someone on the White House staff to various Irish sources linked to terrorism.' He turned to Roper. 'It was slightly before your time, Major. You were busy defusing complicated bombs.'

'Indeed I was, sir.'

'Well, we couldn't accept that, and then we came across a special computer program called

Synod. The CIA had used it in the Cold War, and it had enjoyed considerable success in catching Russian spies.'

'Would have been a bit before my time. Do you recall how it worked, sir?' Roper asked.

'It was like an early version of Echelon. Millions of conversations passed through word recognition. You'd insert a name and the computer tagged it for you, then it took you back, so that you could listen to the relevant conversations. We caught the villain of the piece, a White House senior staffer no one would have suspected.'

Sara said, 'So maybe we could do the same with the Master's mobile phones that have passed through our hands. You've still got the one the Master gave Tod Flynn, I hope?' she asked Dillon.

'Not that I got anywhere with it, but yes, I have,' he told her. 'And I'd presume Lily Shah has one, if she really was the lady sympathetic to their cause that the Master mentioned.'

'Of course,' Roper said. 'She's bound to have, surely.'

Cazalet said to Roper, 'Interesting, isn't it, but I suppose yanking old hardware like that back into service is pretty well impossible?'

'Actually, no. In fact, it's got me so intrigued, I can't wait to try it. So if you don't mind, I'm going to get to work. I'd appreciate you letting me have that mobile phone, Sean.'

'It's upstairs in my room,' Dillon told him. 'I'll get it for you.'

He was back quickly, gave it to Roper, then joined the others. Of Ferguson there was no sign.

'He's been gone long enough,' Dillon said. 'I wonder if there's something wrong,' and at that moment, Ferguson hurried in and called to Maggie Hall, 'Coffee, and strong as you like. I can do with it.'

'Trouble?' Dillon asked.

'You could say. Sir Howard Glynn turned up at Rosedene with Max Shelby. They hadn't appreciated how serious Ali Herim's gunshot wound was, and Glynn was very interested, having served as an army surgeon when he was in uniform, so he got deep in conversation with Bellamy. Then there was quite a fuss.'

'What happened?' Dillon asked.

'Ali Saif had some sort of convulsive fit, couldn't speak because of choking, and his struggles caused him to yank out some of his lines.'

'And Lily?' Sara asked.

'Woke up, having problems with her mobile. According to Maggie Duncan, she thought it was the Master and said it wouldn't speak to her. Obviously, she was delirious.'

Hannah made a face and whispered to Sara, 'I'd say Roper might like to have a listen to that phone. Perhaps we should go and get it for him.'

'I'm up for it if you want to take a run to Rosedene,' Dillon said. 'I'll just tell Roper we're going and we'll get out of here.'

'And I'll see if he's getting anywhere with Synod,' Cazalet told them, and led the way out.

At Rosedene they found Maggie Duncan holding the fort. She said, 'Bellamy's at Great Ormond Street. Heart operation on a child, no avoiding that, but Dr Saif has settled down now. Sir Howard and Max Shelby were shocked at his condition. He seemed to be choking at one stage.'

'We understand he had a fit,' Sara said.

'Well, Dr Saif being MI5 now, their concern is personal. He's terribly badly off and getting through to him is difficult. He has that . . . hunted look that you sometimes see in hospitals, as if the individual wonders what's going to happen next. I'll take you in.'

Ali Saif was lying there, festooned with lines that monitored his vital organs, the low hum of machines that were essential to keeping him alive. Suddenly, his eyes opened. He stared at them, and then panic set in and he seemed to shrink, pulling out the line to his saline bags. Maggie, backed by a young nurse standing at her elbow, had to rush to save him. As they struggled to hold him so they could insert his line again, Dillon stepped forward instinctively to help, trying to hold him still.

Saif's eyes widened as if recognizing him for the first time, and he gripped Dillon's tie. 'Sean?' he asked hoarsely, hesitated as if not sure, then spoke in Arabic very fast.

A third nurse had appeared, a hypodermic ready. Maggie said, 'Is something going on here, Sean?'

'Yes, I think so, but give him rest for the moment. I'll take care of things.'

The needle went in, the result was incredibly quick, Dillon easing his tie free, and between them, he was dropped back against the pillow, every line in his body thoroughly checked. Maggie nodded to her two nurses, who left.

Sara's face was blank, frozen, without expression. Hannah looked from one to another. 'Is there the slightest chance that one of you could please explain what's been going on here? I can speak Irish, Cousin, and so can you, but what was he using when he talked to you?'

'Arabic,' he said. 'Sara can tell you what he said, and rather better than I can. I'm choking on it at the moment.'

There was a terrible silence. 'Perhaps I should leave?' Maggie Duncan said.

'You're as much entitled to be here as I am, after all the years you've given to our damn trade. Sara, explain to Hannah, if you don't mind.'

'Ali Saif was speaking Arabic, and what he said to Sean was: Beware the Devil who comes to you disguised as your best friend,' Sara said. 'But you are my best friend and the major is the Devil.'

Maggie said, 'The major? You don't mean – Shelby? Max Shelby?' No tears, her face was if carved from stone, but Maggie Duncan's eyes were wild. 'Oh, dear God, what would make anyone say such a thing?'

Sara put an arm around her. 'There's always a reason, Maggie, even though it's a bad one to other people.' She kissed her on the forehead. 'Not a word to Bellamy, and certainly not to Sir Howard Glynn. This is for bigger people than us to decide on. Keep a close eye on Saif and Lily, though I doubt they'll be in any danger now.'

'As you say, Captain.'

'Good, then we'll go back to Holland Park with the news.'

Maggie nodded. 'God help me, but I want so much to find there's an explanation.'

'Well, hang on to that thought if it makes you feel better,' Dillon told her. 'As we say in County Down, pigs might fly, but I doubt it.' When they were at the car, he said, 'Would you mind driving, Sara, and you sit with her, Hannah? I'm going to call Roper and tell him what's happened.'

'You mean prepare him for the worst,' Hannah said. It would be something of a shock to hear that your enemy turned out to be somebody you'd always thought was on your side.

'The world we live in can be a strange place sometimes. Ask Declan Rashid about it. On our last big case involving Al Qaeda, the Master turned out to be not only an important Iranian general, he was Declan Rashid's commanding officer.'

'That must have given Declan a problem,' Hannah said as they drove away.

'It certainly did, which is why he's where he is today.'

Dillon cut in. 'I'm calling Roper now.'

He was answered at once. Dillon said, 'What would you say if I told you I know who the Master is?'

'If you tell me Major Max Shelby, I'd say Snap!' Roper said. 'Because that was what Synod tells me. He answered the Flynn mobile you'd provided, Sean, and cut it on the instant. When he heard my voice, I suspect. But he'd been caught by the link, and he can't get away from that.'

'His address?'

'Top floor of an old Edwardian town house in a quiet part of Mayfair, not far from the Connaught Hotel.'

'Does he know that he's blown?' Sara cut in.

'All I can say is that we haven't approached him in any way. It's an extremely tricky situation.'

'A policy decision which obviously can't continue. Take Rosedene, for example. Maggie Duncan's already aware of the possibility. How does she handle the situation if he contacts her to enquire how Lily Shah and Ali Herim are doing, and Dr Ali Saif? It's got to be sorted, and quickly.'

'It will be, and at the highest level, Sean.' Roper said. 'Ferguson has reported to Downing Street and taken Cazalet with him. If he hadn't mentioned Synod, we'd still be in the dark.'

'So it's all hands to the pumps, is it?' Dillon said. 'Well, he could do worse than draft in a man like Cazalet.'

'Exactly,' Roper said. 'I can't get over the fact that such important answers came from a system supposedly way out of date.'

'Or listening to the ravings of a very sick man which turned out to be true,' Dillon said. 'We'll see soon.'

Max Shelby's day had been a disaster. First, Sir Howard Glynn's chauffeur had been violently sick while waiting to take him to Rosedene to visit Lily and Captain Ali Herim, so Shelby had had to replace him. And it had been a grave error on his part to look in on Ali Saif in the first place. Shelby had tried to assassinate him outside Holland Park because he'd been aware for some time of Saif's suspicions of him. Rosedene had been the wrong place to close in on Saif, with Lily Shah wandering around like a frightened ghost. Saif's fear of him didn't help either.

Worst of all, and very clumsy, to try and finish Saif off by pulling out the lines necessary to keep him alive had got him nowhere except to fuel suspicion from Maggie Duncan. That had been confirmed when he had phoned her, asking to be put through to Lily, and had been refused and asked not to phone again.

That, coupled with a dearth of telephone calls, spoke for itself. It was time to go, but where? He was giving everyone a terrible problem. His great-great-grandfather who'd built the house, a survivor of war in Afghanistan and a major general, would have had an easy answer to fall back on. A large brandy and a pistol to blow out your brains, but that would have been a betrayal of not only his son but his wife. Al Qaeda and the Grand Council would not be pleased, but he didn't give a damn about them when it came right down to it. They'd looked on him as a prize of war, if you like. A seriously disturbed individual who'd lost his son, and because of that, his wife, and wanted to make someone pay.

In the Prime Minister's office, the PM, Cazalet, and Henry Frankel were deep in discussion when there was a tap at the door. Frankel opened it, and Ferguson entered. 'Any news?' the PM asked.

'He's been seen coming out of the Connaught Hotel. That's very close to his house in Mayfair. If he's going home, I'll know very soon.'

'And then you'll speak to him?' the Prime Minister asked.

'Yes, I think so.' He turned to Cazalet. 'What do you think?'

'Well, I can see you favour the friendly approach.'

'We'd much rather this whole unfortunate business wasn't happening at all,' Ferguson said. 'I'd prefer a chance to make it look like that. The British press would make a meal of it, and as for television . . .' He shrugged.

'One thing I learned was never to jump to conclusions,' said Cazalet. 'We all wish it never happened, so go easy. Negotiate, that's what I learned as a junior officer in Vietnam dealing with the enemy, and as President of the United States years later.'

'I'll bear that in mind,' Ferguson said, and took out his Codex.

'Well, you do that,' Frankel said. 'And don't forget he shot two men and a woman who are patients in Rosedene because of his itchy trigger finger.'

'Yes, all very unfortunate, Henry,' Ferguson said, 'but they're not dead yet. Now, kindly shut up while I make this call.' He got an instant response and said, 'That you, Max? So you're at home now?'

'I should have thought that was obvious, Charles. I'm surprised you didn't have me lifted. You'd enough people on the job.'

'Don't be silly,' Ferguson said. 'It'd be a stupid thing to grab you publicly. A police car might drive past at the wrong moment and wonder what was going on. Where would we be then?'

'I wonder why I didn't think of that,' Shelby said. 'What happens now?'

'We need to talk.'

'What about?'

'Well, there's the fact that you've been going around shooting people. We can't have that.'

Shelby laughed. 'You old hypocrite. You've been doing that for years. Anyway, I don't want to talk to you any more. I'll have words with Sara Gideon and Dillon at my house. It's the pride and joy of my great-great-grandfather, the general. He called it Kabul Place, so that he'd never forget how long it had taken him to get out of that city alive. It had another makeover in Edwardian times, and I've improved it with modern security equipment. You'd be wasting your time trying to break in, even if you used the SAS.'

'Max, why on earth would we do that? We just want to sort this unfortunate business out.'

'Sara and Dillon, that's all, and I'll see them in the entry porch. Four o'clock and on the dot. If they're not there, I'll shut up shop. Give the PM my regards. Tell him I voted for him last time and have never regretted it. President Cazalet, you're a credit to your country. That's it, gentlemen, curtain to applause.' And he switched off.

Henry Frankel said, 'If you ask me, I think he's on something.'

'Never mind, we've got him,' Ferguson said. 'I trust you're all right with that, Prime Minister. I'm returning to Holland Park to brief the troops. I'm sure you'd like to join me,' he said to Cazalet, 'and you'll be very welcome as well, Henry, as long as you'll promise to keep your trap shut.'

In the computer room, Roper played a recording of the phone conversation, which was listened to again by Henry Frankel and Cazalet, while the Salters, Sara, Dillon, and Hannah tried to make sense of it for the first time.

When it finished, Frankel said, 'I stand by what I said. He must be on some drug. How can he keep himself so calm and controlled after all that he's done?'

Hannah said, 'Maybe it goes something like this. His son died horribly in the Afghan War, his mother as a consequence of that. Frankly, I'm surprised he hasn't taken an overdose and finished things.'

'The voice of youth,' Frankel said.

'Not exactly,' Hannah told him. 'The fruits of bitter experience, of being blown up by a bomb in your car that took your mother and father, crippled you and left you going out of your mind, until some wonderful therapists and psychiatrists took you by the hand and said not that way, this way, and restored you to sanity.'

Henry Frankel was horrified, as they all sat taking in what had been said, and Hannah looked about her and stood up. 'I've shocked you, I'm afraid, but it's important to realize that the man who has betrayed his friends and shot people is not the same man he once was. That's the real tragedy here. I'm in my room, if anyone wants me.'

She turned and walked out, her stick tapping, and Sara stood up and went after her.

★   ★   ★

321

Henry Frankel departed, very subdued, and Harry Salter moved to say goodbye to Roper. 'Any developments with the Sash?'

'Closed up tight,' Roper said. 'The few members of staff left, laid off. It seems Myra Tully was way in over her head with loans. The bank's slapped a bankruptcy order on the business.'

'And what about the *Tara*?'

'Missing from its moorings. Reported to the River Police by the bank as possibly stolen. They tell me it happens all the time.'

'Nothing seems to be safe these days,' Harry said. 'Come on, Billy,' and they left.

The rain continued heavy and persistent all day, and there was more than a hint of fog as Parker drove the splendid old Daimler that was Ferguson's special pride down towards Mayfair. Ferguson and Cazalet, Sara and Dillon, sat in the back.

'Not much sign of MI5 today,' Cazalet said. 'That surprises me.'

'An operation like this is by Prime Minister's Warrant, and usually we don't need anyone else – except when we do, and that's today. As a professional courtesy, Sir Howard Glynn has placed a substantial number of his people around Kabul Place.'

'I suppose that's very kind of him.' Cazalet turned to Sara. 'Wouldn't you agree, Captain? It certainly makes sense to me.'

'The only thing about that, sir, is that it will

make such good sense to Max that he'll probably do something that's not expected. I've soldiered with him in the badlands of Helmand Province, and he survived twelve years out there.'

'I'm well aware of that,' Ferguson said. 'So it's up to you to ferret out what he might be considering.'

'Which is exactly what we're going to do.' Dillon said, gazing out. 'This rain takes me back to Belfast at its worst, when you felt the Troubles were going to last forever.'

'I thought they did, Sean,' Sara said, as the Daimler drew up to the imposing pile that was Kabul Place.

Parker was opening the door for her before the others had time to unscramble themselves. She was out ahead of Dillon, and as he found her, Ferguson pulled the door closed behind them and the Daimler left.

Dillon watched it disappear into the rain as Sara opened a small umbrella she had been carrying. He looked up at the house and there was nothing Afghan about it, tall at five storeys including the roof area.

'I presume you've been here more than once in the past.'

'Never.' She shook her head. 'It was a known thing that Max and his wife didn't entertain. I met him at first, before I met you, because we soldiered together with the Intelligence Corps. He was my mentor when it came to Pashto.'

'Did you know his wife?'

'Absolutely. A gentle soul who endured bad health for years. She went totally to pieces when their son was killed in Helmand. She simply couldn't cope.'

A voice rang out. 'All right, when you've finished talking about me, get up here before you're washed away,' Max Shelby called.

The garage area was around the back, as was most of the garden, which was small, but picturesque at the front, a path leading to broad steps mounting to a large conservatory porch, Victorian style, metalwork bars, the front door behind it leading into the darkness of a hall. Max Shelby sat staring out through the bars, and was sitting by a wicker table, an open bottle of Chianti and a glass standing on it, a Glock pistol close to his hand.

'Why the pistol, Max?' Dillon asked. 'I thought we were friends.'

'I don't have any of those any more, and that includes you, Sara. The Glock is to show whoever is watching us through binoculars that I mean business. These things pump out seventeen rounds, as both of you know.' He raised his glass of wine. 'I'm happy with this, but if you'll sit down at the table I've laid for you, there's a thermos of tea, another of coffee, and an open bottle of Irish whiskey, knowing you both have a taste for it.'

There was a garden table laid out just beside the open door to the porch, two chairs beside it, rain drifting in, as Sara poured coffee and spoke for the first time.

'I thought I knew you, Max, and I find I didn't.' She wrapped her hands around the mug. 'It's not quite the worst thing to happen in my life, but it comes close. The first was hearing that my parents on holiday in Jerusalem had been killed by a Hamas bus bomb.'

'God help me, but I'm sorry for your hurt, girl,' he said. 'It was not intended.'

'You could have fooled me,' Dillon said. 'There are two men and a woman up there at Rosedene now with your bullets in them. Was that not intended? What about Lily Shah, a kind and decent woman hard-used by life, conned into believing your lies?'

Sara broke in, her voice urgent and angry. 'Just tell us, Max, what was so important that it justified the terrible things you've done.'

'Well, we could start with the stupid politicians who bungled operations over a twelve-year period in Afghanistan. Who took no notice of the fact that the Russian campaign there was a total disaster, with thousands dead. Even Alexander the Great couldn't get out of the country fast enough. I wanted revenge for the obscenity of my butchered son's body parts hanging from a thorn tree outside some wretched village in Helmand, and for my wife, reduced by all this to a walking corpse, reduced to cramming pills down her throat to end her torment. Does any of this mean a thing to you?'

'Dreadful, all of it.' Sara shook her head. 'But revenge is not going to get us anywhere.'

'Oh, yes it is. As we leave Helmand Province, the Taliban are moving back in, so can Washington or London tell us what it was all about? As for my link with Al Qaeda, they knew how it was with me. That I didn't give a stuff about Osama bin Laden, but I've been beyond price to them. An insider in the Security Service who isn't even a Muslim. A bit like Philby during the Cold War, working for the Security Service on one hand and the KGB on the other.'

'There can only be one end to this. You realize that, don't you?'

'Oh, the executioners will be out,' Max Shelby said. 'They'll all prefer me dead. I've only one thing to say, and that's catch me if you can. It would be much better if you go now.'

Sara said, 'When I was a very young officer in Bosnia, shocked by all those bodies, you told me that honour was everything to a soldier, because without it you were just a butcher.'

'As the times change, all men change with them. That was then, this is now.'

'I wish I'd cheated on the terms of this meeting, because I honoured it and didn't put a pistol in my pocket. If I had, I'd have shot you dead by now.'

'If you could,' he said calmly.

Dillon said, 'I shouldn't have listened to her when she persuaded me to leave my pistol at home.'

Sara had reached the road, and the Daimler moved in to get her. Max said, 'Well, what's to stop me from emptying this Glock into you right now?'

'Your plan, Max. You were always the clever bastard, so there's method to your madness, and to shoot me dead right now would ruin it, whatever it is.'

Max had stopped smiling. 'Shut your mouth and get out of here, otherwise I might change my mind and pull the trigger.'

'On a quiet street in Mayfair? That would be a stupid thing to do, and you were never that. On the other hand, it would indicate to most people that you really have gone mad.'

Max stood there rigid, the Glock raised in his right hand, a fixed look on his face, and then he smiled. 'Why, Dillon, you almost had me,' and his smile had a certain triumph in it. 'Go on, clear off.' He turned away, slamming the door on the other side of the bars, and Dillon moved back, scanning the façade of Kabul Place, then swung to meet the Daimler, which pulled in to pick him up.

Sara said, 'What was that all about?'

'Oh, I didn't like how he'd been with you, so I was bracing him.'

'What's that supposed to mean?' she said.

Cazalet smiled. 'Means trying to pick a fight.'

'It almost worked,' Dillon said. 'I invited him to shoot me, trashed him, and for an instant there I thought he might pull the trigger, but that would have ruined his plan.'

'Just get your breath for a minute,' Sara said. 'What plan?'

'I haven't the slightest idea, but I'm certain he's got one. Sorry, Sara, you'd have to have been there to realize it.'

'I get the impression you really think he's crazy,' Cazalet said.

'All the wicked and evil things he's experienced are true enough,' Dillon said. 'The barbarity of what happened to his son, the mental destruction of his wife, are true enough, but they're turning him inward, and it's been very destructive to his personality. He's not the old Max any more, but he still has some control. He demonstrated that by not shooting me when I taunted him.'

Ferguson said, 'I won't have this. The MI5 agents about Kabul Place are to invade the house when it gets dark. A power failure will then shut off any fancy security systems, so access should be no problem.'

'What if he puts up armed resistance?' Dillon asked.

'I'd rather have him in one piece,' Ferguson said. 'But if it has to be that way, so be it.'

'So much tidier,' Sara said as the Daimler swept in to the front entrance of the Dorchester.

'Don't be bitter, Captain Gideon,' said Ferguson as Parker braked to a halt. 'I'm hoping this is going to work.'

★   ★   ★

Of course Max Shelby had a plan, a product of the boyish games of childhood. The general opinion of Kabul Place was that it was Victorian but refurbished in Edwardian times. Living at home and attending St Paul's School as a day boy, Kabul Place had been better than a storybook. His father away in the army, his mother indulgent, he roamed at will in the darkness below, a halogen lamp held high, prising open closed-up entrances and frequently following the sound of water to strange places.

Few people realized that the London Underground was riddled with tunnels that ran for miles all over the city – Norman and Tudor sewers, a network of smaller rivers leading to the Thames that the Georgians and, later, the Victorians, in their wisdom, covered over. It had remained his hobby, places where you only needed a sledgehammer to smash through crumbling Victorian bricks to create a point of entry that could be easily camouflaged.

So in his present situation, he'd expected the kind of attack that Ferguson had described, not just because it was obvious, but because it was the only way that would make sense to his enemy, but he'd no intention of waiting for them.

He had made preparations for this situation a long time before and went up in the lift to the penthouse, where he had left a yellow waterproof overall of the type used by sewage workers, changed into it quickly, plus rubber boots and a safety helmet with a strong spotlight fixed to it to guide the way.

He had informed Al Qaeda's Grand Council of the situation, the green light on his transceiver pinged softly, he pressed the button, and the voice said, 'Situation understood, your action approved now and in the future. Any help needed will be available.'

He closed the transceiver's neat case and put it into a large military duffel bag. Just as he'd thought. They'd hang on to him while there was still a game to be played, which meant he was still in business. From his desk drawer he took a silenced Glock and slipped it into his right pocket, then took out a Walther PPK and put it in his left.

There were two pineapple grenades at the back of the drawer. He examined them in turn, frowning, then remembered taking them from the body of an Afridi he'd killed. He shrugged, dropped them into the duffel, then reached for a smaller bag that he'd packed quickly. Lightweight black suit, shirt, shoes, a toilet bag, his credit card, a thousand in cash, passport, and army identity papers. He closed it, dropped it into the larger duffel, which he zipped. He looked out to the streets below, found them dark enough to send him hurrying to the lift with the duffel, descending all the way to the cellars, where he turned on the lights, hurried through three corridors, one of which ended with a large wooden chair against the wall, an old-fashioned halogen light hanging from a hook. He switched on his helmet light, and as he did the same with the halogen, the power cut off.

There were already sounds of movement upstairs, so he swung back the chair, threw the duffel inside, and followed it, taking the halogen light with him and pulling the chair back into place. There were shouts in the distance, boots pounding, but they were already fading as Max Shelby hurried from one tunnel to another, the duffel hanging from its strap on his left shoulder.

The combination of his helmet light and the halogen lamp illuminated the tunnels as never before, and on occasion he was ankle-deep, and at one point to his knees. The constant rain of the last few days, of course – but it didn't matter because he had no intention of following the maze of tunnels to the Thames itself, a mile or more away. He had another destination in mind, and then everything changed as he stepped out of a side tunnel and found a mirror image of himself standing foot-deep in water, staring at him, a net in one hand and a rake in the other.

'Who the hell are you?' the man demanded belligerently.

'Never mind who I am,' Max said. 'What are you up to? Scavenging? Or are you looking for bodies?'

'You can talk. I'd like to see what you've got in that duffel.'

'Feel free.' Max reached in, took out a pineapple grenade, removed the pin with his teeth, lobbed it at him, and ducked back into the side tunnel. The roar echoed, drowning whatever cries there were.

As things calmed, he stepped out to examine the carnage. The other man had obviously been killed instantly. His own action had been on impulse, so that he was not even sure what it was supposed to have achieved. Perhaps he *was* mad now, and this would be the final proof to Ferguson and the rest.

The face he looked down on was unrecognizable, the yellow uniform exactly like his own but ripped to bloodstained tatters. He felt inside the torn jacket, found a cheap wallet containing a name, a hostel address, and thirty pounds in cash.

A life to no purpose, or perhaps some purpose? There was a question here. Say a truly desperate man who had suffered more than most in his private life, a man once highly respected but now harried by authority, faced only public shame of the worst sort and decided to stop running and end it all?

It could work if he was careful. He could keep the Glock, which was an illegal weapon. The Walther had been issued and was traceable, so it went into a pocket of the dead man's uniform, together with Max's passport, army identity papers, all soaked in bloodstained water, as were the items in the small bag.

He'd been running through those tunnels, dogs on his heels in a way, and the point had come where he'd had enough. Why he'd chosen such a dreadful way to do it could only be explained by a soldier who would have known it would bring death on the instant. The other grenade discovered in the duffel would be recognized as Russian, a relic of the Soviet war in Afghanistan. With luck it would all make sense, for a while at least, together with the halogen light that he bounced off the wall, smashing it.

Which left him the transceiver in its leather case, shockproof, impervious. He started to run now, holding it in his left hand, aware of sounds in the distance, finally passing across a concrete slope that resembled a waterfall because of recent rain. The tunnel there was smaller, rougher, an area discovered in his youth. He finally reached the crude steps, a grilled gate where he had to crouch and apply force to open it, and emerged into the darkness of an overgrown garden in one of the lanes at the back of Shepherd Market.

Another relic from boyhood, one of his favourites, the modest building had once been the stable for the cobbled street, converted into a garage with a flat above it. A dead end, a tiny garden, nobody to wonder who he was, so he had been able to come and go for years, no obvious connection with Kabul Place, even during army time and MI5. After all, if there was one thing the Security Services had taught him, it was how simply one could change. Dye job for the hair, and there was plenty of that in the bathroom, false moustache, tinted glasses, and a tweed cap. He certainly had no intention of sitting around, and, after all, cab drivers came in all shapes and sizes, and it was an old London black cab he'd kept in the garage for years, so useful for parking and the police just waved you on most of the time.

The kitchen needed tidying, but there was plenty of canned food in the cupboards and the freezer full of useful items. He went up to the modest bedroom, reported to the transceiver that he was still alive, and went into the bathroom for a shower, whistling. Tomorrow was another day.

'They say it's pretty foul, Charles,' Sir Howard Glynn told Ferguson. 'You and your people have a right to see him, I suppose. And I have to because I was his boss. Professor George Langley, whom you know well enough, is doing the autopsy at Church Street Mortuary, which is where the body is now. I'm going straight there – if you and those involved want to see him, you can join me.'

'I'll certainly be there. Don't know about the others. May I bring Cazalet?'

'Why not? I'll see you then.'

Ferguson sat there thinking about it, then called Roper and filled him in. 'I feel I have to go, but I'll leave it to you to speak to the others, if you don't mind. Would you consider going?'

'Absolutely not,' Roper told him. 'I'm old-fashioned, and I've seen too many good men dead in my time to have any kind of sympathy with a traitor, whatever his excuses.'

Ferguson sighed deeply. 'It's a point of view, Major, and you're entitled to it if anybody is. I'll leave it to you.'

Sara went, of course, and Dillon only because she did, and Ferguson and Cazalet and Sir Howard and three MI5 people who looked troubled. Billy Salter arrived late and joined Sara and Dillon as they were all just going in to hear what Professor Langley had to say.

The room was lined with white tiles, fluorescent lighting bouncing off them harshly, low buzzing noises in the background. What was left of the body lay naked on a steel operating table and looked appalling, and two of the MI5 people gagged, turned, and hurried out. Sara held a silk scarf to her mouth, Dillon took her other hand.

Ferguson said, 'Professor, will you please confirm what you have told me on the telephone?'

'Certainly,' Langley said. 'As you can see from the state of the corpse, the body has been damaged extensively by the explosion of a pineapple fragmentation grenade.'

'So death would have been instantaneous?' Ferguson said.

'I can guarantee that. Also terribly damaging, as you see.'

335

'Is there anything else of particular interest here?'

'Well, there were many things we could not check because of the destruction, but we were able to confirm his blood type with samples from the cadaver. Interesting, that.'

'Why would that be?' Dillon asked.

'Because Major Shelby's blood type was relatively rare, B positive, and so is the body's. That occurs in only eight per cent of the UK population. It was noted in his army records, but confirmed again from a sample taken from the corpse. Normally, some DNA checks would be made, but in this case it would lead nowhere. His wife was cremated a few weeks ago, his son butchered by the Taliban in Afghanistan. In such tragic circumstances, best to bring matters to a close.'

Sara turned to Dillon, who had an arm around her shoulders. 'So that's it, Sean?'

'Exactly,' Ferguson said. 'With everything coming to a head, he decided to put an end to it all. By Prime Minister's Warrant, I now invoke the Official Secrets Act. He will give a Closed Court Order. No jury necessary, and an instant cremation order will be issued in view of the state of the remains.'

He shook Langley's hand. 'Many thanks, George. Rotten business, but there you are.'

'Thank God it's over,' Sir Howard said on the way out.

'I agree, and a blessing that there's not even a hint in the press,' Ferguson said. 'Henry Frankel is waiting with bated breath at Number Ten to hear that the matter is resolved.'

'And Rosedene?' Sara asked.

'Things are looking much better for Ali Saif, and Ali Kerim seems to have turned a corner. Khalid Abed guards them fiercely. As for Lily Shah, Maggie Duncan wants her on staff.'

'That's wonderful,' Sara said.

'Yes, I thought that,' Ferguson smiled. 'Shall we meet at the Dorchester later for a nightcap?'

Dillon laughed. 'It's one o'clock in the morning, and MI5 invaded Kabul Place early last night. What's happened since, his death, the pressure of officialdom to get the whole business finished at every level, has been incredible.'

'I'm beginning to feel as if it never happened,' Sara said.

'Which is exactly the way Downing Street wants it treated, God help me,' Ferguson told her. 'It'd be a lot better for all of us if we could see it that way. I must go now, because I really am expected by the PM.'

He got into the Daimler, Parker drove him away, and Billy grinned. 'Well, that's me finished, the simple foot soldier who gets things done, waving off the great and the good.'

'And where would we be without you?' Sara said, and kissed him on the cheek. 'It's the sort of thing Shakespeare would have written about.'

'Well, I don't know about that.' He smiled. 'It would have made a great script, but God knows who they'd get to play Max,' and he walked off into the rain to find his car.

Cazalet said, 'As I'm still in London, you two are still responsible for my security, which means you have the availability of those two extra bedrooms in my suite, so I have a suggestion. To hell with the time. Let's go and sample the best twenty-four-hour room service in London.'

Dillon said to Sara, 'He's got a point. I don't remember having dinner.'

Sara's smile was small but there. 'Come to think of it, neither do I, and it would give us the chance to say goodbye properly.'

'Excellent,' Cazalet said. 'So lend me that rather small umbrella and I'll go out in this glorious London rain and hail a cab.'

CHAPTER 14

The following morning, having spent the night in his wheelchair in the computer room as usual, Roper came awake to a solid, driving performance of 'From This Moment On', followed the sound, and found himself in the dining room with Hannah seated at the piano, wearing her dressing gown.

'What a great way to wake anybody up,' he said.

'I couldn't agree more.'

'Have you eaten?'

'No, but I've placed my order.'

The kitchen door swung open to admit Maggie Hall with a tray. 'Full Irish breakfast. That means it's soda bread, and not easy to come by in Holland Park.'

'I know what it means,' Roper said. 'And I'd still prefer a bacon sandwich and a mug of tea.'

With no comment, she returned to the kitchen, and Hannah got up from the piano and joined him. 'It was all happening last night, then?' she said as she started to eat. 'Were you surprised?'

'About Max? The Troubles cured me of being surprised at anything in this life ever again. What happened in Ulster damaged you and me. Afghanistan and the same for him. He wanted somebody to pay.'

'But life doesn't work like that, does it?' Hannah said.

'You heard the recording of what he said to Sara and Dillon about how his son had died, his wife. Nothing could pay for that. Did you speak to Sara?'

'Yes, she told me about all the horrid stuff, the autopsy, viewing the body, and so on. So that's it, then? It's all over?'

'Legally dead, cremated. Anyway, real life begins again. What are you going to do?'

'Sara was saying how Cazalet feels he's got to return to Washington to show his face after all that's happened. He said there was a danger that he'd be summoned to return under Presidential Warrant if he didn't make a move, but I'm sure he was joking.'

'And what about you?' Roper asked.

'Sara wants me back at the house, to sit down at that Schiedmayer and get really serious again. Her grandfather thinks I should, and Sadie is threatening to come and get me.' Hannah laughed. 'I bet she would if she had to, but very soon I'll be a student at the Royal College of Music. Four wonderful years waiting.'

'Which you richly deserve,' he said. 'Just as long as you don't forget us. So get back to the piano and play me out. I've got to return to my screens.'

★   ★   ★

Max Shelby had slept well and had awoken to the green light on his transceiver pinging softly. He pressed the button as usual, and as the voice spoke, he listened intently. He never failed to be amazed at how up-to-date they were with their information. He was not only legally dead, but cremated, everything having obviously been rushed through. Cazalet intended to return to Washington, was still booked at the hotel for another three nights, but unless there was a real chance at the target, he was to leave it alone and it was an order. Now he was dead, he was too valuable to risk.

Now, that he didn't care for, and he put together a breakfast, feeling thoroughly angry. This was not to his liking at all, to be manipulated by someone sitting at a desk, sifting through the information pouring in, selecting what he considered suitable targets.

Well, it was not the way the old Max Shelby had operated and certainly wouldn't suit the new version. He'd have to show them, and he finished his coffee, went upstairs and checked his wardrobe, selecting a slightly old-fashioned country suit in brown Harris tweed, brown shoes, a pale blue shirt and a military-looking tie, as befitting an older man.

He found his make up box in the bathroom cabinet, selected a grey mustache, touched it with glue, and fixed it in place. There happened to be an old pair of horn-rimmed spectacles in the box, which completed the picture as he ran a comb through his hair, leaving him looking like a retired bank manager and very respectable.

His appearance made him feel happy and confident, but to do what? The transceiver was quiet and not transmitting, his Glock lay on the table beside it, and he unloaded it and carefully reloaded it, an old habit, slipped it in a waist holster on his left side. The constant rain of the past week rattled against the window with renewed force.

Which made him think of Terry Harker, nursing half an ear in his bolt-hole, as he liked to call it, the old *Arabella*, Rotting away, cold and damp, he'd probably gone out on deck to be shocked by the total desolation of the place, boats of all kinds, decaying everywhere. St Jude's Dock, and it amused Max to recall that St Jude was the patron saint of lost causes. Terry Harker could have made a better choice, but then what could you expect of a man who'd made a fool of himself over a creature like Myra Tully? And an impulse came to him, a wild and crazy impulse. He knew he shouldn't – but, come on, whom was Harker going to tell?

His supposition had been even worse, for Terry was shivering with fever in spite of a heavy boxer's tracksuit, plus several blankets. He *had* gone up on deck to check the weather, and received a soaking while discovering that there appeared to be a problem with the electric cable connecting his boat to the jetty, which, although intermittent, was showing signs of failing completely. That would make it impossible for him to continue in his present situation.

He rolled over, reaching for a bottle of brandy that stood on the bedside table beside a Browning Hi Power pistol, a relic of his army days. He managed to unscrew the cap, swallowed some down, and his mobile sounded. He screwed the cap back on, although knocking the Browning to the floor, then answered.

'Who is it?' he croaked.

'Why, Terry,' Max Shelby said. 'You sound terrible. Is everything okay? I thought it was time I checked how you were doing. I don't expect this weather is helping you. How's the ear coming along, better?'

'No, it isn't. I think I may need more antibiotics and I have a fever, so I don't need you pretending to be so bright and cheerful, as if we were friends. What do you want?'

'I'm concerned about you, and I do happen to *be* bright and cheerful, because, in a way, it's as if I've been reborn.'

Terry said, 'What in the hell are you talking about?'

'The word is that I'm really Major Max Shelby of MI5 who has taken to working for Al Qaeda because the money is better.'

Terry said, 'What a load of rubbish. Go on, clear off.'

'Now you do disappoint me,' Max said. 'When

I told you about the sinking of the *Tara*, you said you'd get Billy Salter and maybe me, because of what happened to Myra.'

'So I will,' Terry said.

'You're not even in the same league as Billy. He was screwing Myra and you were too stupid to see that. I've visited your bolt-hole when you were out, but next time I'll drop in to see how your face looks these days. I know the address, the old *Arabella* at St Jude's Dock. Myra gave it to me after going through your drawers. You couldn't even trust her.'

'You bastard! What makes you think I won't tell everybody who you really are, Major?'

'Oh, please, Terry, who are you going to tell? No one will believe you! And anyway, my boy – you're dying! Such a shame!'

He laughed and was gone.

Terry Harker had never known such anger, not even in the boxing ring at the height of his power, and it was a killing rage directed completely at Billy Salter, a need to destroy him face-to-face, punch him into the ground in the way that had taken him to a championship of the British Army. On the other hand, if he couldn't see him, he could hear his voice, and he knew the phone number of the Dark Man well enough. So, fortified with more brandy, he made the call to Billy Salter.

* * *

344

Sam Hall had driven Harry to the City to meet the accountant, Joe Baxter was helping Dora sort out the wine in the still room, and Hasim was floor-polishing with a machine. Billy was in oilskins, sitting in Harry's booth enjoying coffee and reading the *Times*, just in from checking the boats in the rain when his phone rang.

Terry Harker's voice was hoarse and rough as he said, 'Is that you, Billy?'

'It certainly is, but I haven't got the slightest idea who you are. You sound as if you're at death's door, old son.'

'I'm not your old son, not after what you did to Myra and Eric.'

'And what would that be?' Billy asked. 'I mean, where's this story coming from?'

'The Master, you shite.' The drink was getting to Terry now. 'He's been on the phone and told me he feels reborn because he's Major Max Shelby who's taken to working for Al Qaeda. Says the money's better.'

'Terry, if that's you, somebody's having you on, and where are you calling from?'

'I'm not falling for that, no cops,' Terry said.

'Okay, how about it couldn't have been Max Shelby, because he was cremated last night.'

'You've got it wrong. He told me he was being paid more money by Al Qaeda than MI5, and that next time he'd drop in to see me instead of phoning. He knows my address.'

'Oh, that's good,' Billy said quickly. 'And where would that be?'

And it worked, for poor drunken Terry answered at once. '*Arabella*, moored at the jetty in St Jude's Dock.'

'Well, that's nice to know, so this is what I want you to do. Have a nice cup of tea, lie down and wait, and I'll arrange for Max Shelby to come round to see you.'

'All right,' Terry said. 'But no cops.'

'Now, would I do that to you?' Billy asked. 'I'll see you soon.'

Billy said to Dora, 'I'm going out, love, something needs seeing over at the Sash. I'll take Hasim. We'll go in the inflatable.'

'Like a monsoon out there, Billy. Is that wise?' she said.

'Things to be done, Dora, and I'd like the lad to get as much experience in that boat as possible.'

'Same as the River Police use,' Hasim told her. 'Could have a career in that.'

Dora patted his face. 'You're too nice to be a policeman, but if you have to go, wear those waterproof tunics with the hoods. You'll be catching your deaths from a cold if you don't.'

Billy led his way to his office at the end of the bar, opened a cupboard, and took out a couple of bulletproof vests, tossing one to Hasim.

'These things are made of nylon and titanium.

They'll stop any kind of bullet you're likely to encounter, and at point-blank range. Wear it next to your skin underneath the tunic.'

'Are we likely to be doing some shooting?' Hasim asked.

'I might have to, but your vest is only a precaution where there is a possibility of stray rounds flying around. That is not likely to happen to you, because you'll be staying with the boat while I'm gone. So let's get to it.'

That the whole business had really got to Terry Harker had given Max Shelby enormous satisfaction, but that could only come from seeing his prey face-to-face, being able to judge their pain – and for that he'd have to go out.

So he found an old trench coat, tweed cap and scarf, and a conventional umbrella, opened the garage and took off in the black cab, not to telephone this time, for it was no longer enough. Only the reality of Terry Harker and the *Arabella*, tied to the jetty at St Jude's Dock, could be that.

At the Dark Man, Hasim had gone ahead to the boat, and Dora came in as Billy finished getting ready. She found him loading his favorite Colt .25, the silenced version.

'Hollow point?' she asked.

'You should know, Dora.'

'Something serious. Forgive me being nosy, but it's how I feel.'

Billy smiled. 'Ain't life strange? You never thought you'd end up playing grandmother to a homeless Muslim boy, did you?'

'Muslim Cockney,' she corrected him, 'and if you want to know, I love him, and when I see you fitting that weapon into its belt holster, I worry, just like I've done for you over the years, and it could be starting all over with Hasim.'

'Being with MI5 makes me respectable now. Hasim's like a kid brother who's got to learn to handle himself in a dangerous world. That's where I come in.' He kissed her on the forehead. 'Don't worry, Dora, I've got it in hand,' and he was gone.

Hasim was enjoying being in charge of the inflatable, had taken it away from its moorings with a certain dash and didn't mind the rain at all.

'So you know where you're going?' Billy said.

'Of course I do. Those new Thames charts you got are clear and easy, and we'll be there in twenty minutes. The one I'm using is under the canopy, well marked, by the binoculars.'

Which Billy quickly found as they turned into the shore, the whole place looking thoroughly miserable, a slight mist, the decaying warehouses in the rain, the crumbling boats, and using the magnification he managed to identify the target.

'There you are, the *Arabella*,' he told Hasim. 'Kill the engine, let her drift in among those boats, though half of them appear to be sinking. I'll go up those stone steps, keep my head down, and see if anyone's at home.'

'Is there likely to be trouble?' Hasim asked.

'The guy involved was in a bad way when he phoned me. He has a fever and he's been drinking too much, but he's my problem, not yours.' He passed him the binoculars. 'Just keep your eyes open, but you must stay down here. That's an order.'

'Whatever you say,' Hasim told him reluctantly.

Billy mounted the stone steps and paused on the blind side of the wheelhouse. From the sound of Terry coughing his heart out up in the cabin, he was in an even worse state than he had been earlier.

Changing the situation on impulse, he phoned Roper and got an instant reply. 'I thought you'd fallen out of the loop,' Roper said. 'I phoned the Dark Man; Harry was out and Dora sounded unhappy. Where are you?'

'I'll tell you if you'll listen. A dreadful bloody place called St Jude's Dock. I spoke earlier to a very sick Terry Harker, who is holed up here. He phoned to tell me he intended to kill me for what I'd done to Myra and said that the Master had been in touch, claiming to still be Max Shelby. Hasim's standing off in the inflatable, and I'm visiting the cabin to see how Terry's getting on.'

'For heaven's sake, you must let *me* get things moving. Why are you doing this?'

349

'Because it's there, isn't that what they say? I'll just go down and sort out Terry. Weapons being a specialty of his, I think it would be wise of you to let Mr Teague know that he and his disposal team could be needed.'

'Just think about it again,' Roper pleaded as Billy opened a decaying mahogany door of the old houseboat and went below.

'Who is it?' Terry cried. 'Stay where you are.'

He was crouching on the narrow bed in the corner in his tracksuit, blankets all over the place, his face wild. The Browning in his right hand constantly shook.

Billy stayed very calm, standing on the bottom step, clutching the steel pole that supported the steps. The smell of brandy was very obvious, and Terry reached for an open bottle that stood on the bedside table. He held it to his mouth and tossed it away.

'Empty,' he said, and suddenly frowned. 'Billy Salter, you bastard. So you've finally made it? But not on your own, I won't believe that.'

'It's the truth,' Billy said, turning slightly, still clutching the pole in his left hand, but hoping for a chance to grab for his Colt with the right.

'Stand still, damn you,' Terry told him, and everything happened at once.

There was the sound of a vehicle driving up outside and braking. A minute only and the door to the deck opened. Hasim peered in and was immediately pushed headlong down the steps, to be grabbed by Billy, and they fell heavily to the floor together.

Terry Harker shouted up at Max Shelby, framed in the deck doorway. 'Who the hell are you?'

All that got him was a bullet between the eyes that drove him backwards onto the bed.

Hasim seemed dazed from his fall, but Billy managed to pull him up protectingly, only to receive two shots in the back from Max that drove him across the cabin to fall on his face.

There was silence after the wildness, Hasim sobbing a little as he tried to get up, gasping for breath, and Max moved in to kick. 'Cry-baby,' he said contemptuously.

'No, brave boy,' Billy Salter replied, crouched in the corner behind, and he fired four of the dreaded hollow-point cartridges into the rear of Max's skull, exploding it like a watermelon.

Hasim stared at him in awe. 'I thought you were dead.'

'I told you there's nothing like a nylon-and-titanium bulletproof vest for protection, even when a weapon is fired at you at point-blank range.'

'So why wasn't this man wearing one?'

'I recognized him. His moustache is false.' Billy peeled it off and removed the glasses. 'He works for MI5, but forgot that I do. His two bullets in my back were a waste of time. Mine worked because I shot him in the head. But what's your story?'

'I was worried when I heard some of the things you said to Major Roper, and when you went below and the shouting started, I just had to come and see if there was anything I could do. Then the black cab turned up, and when the driver asked what was going on, I begged him for help. When he got out of the cab, he grabbed me and then shoved me down here. Why was he such a bad bastard?'

'Believe it or not, but he had his problems. It would take time to explain, and from the sound of it I think the cavalry's arriving, so let's steal Terry's umbrella and go up on deck to receive them.'

They stood on the jetty, sheltering from the rain under the old umbrella, and a very large black van coasted in silently and five men in black overalls got out. Their leader was a tall and rather distinguished-looking man with silver hair.

'This is what we call the Disposal Team,' Billy said softly to Hasim. 'They'll see to the bodies and clean up. You won't know they've been here.'

'So they're undertakers?' Hasim asked.

'Our own *private* undertakers. Ferguson decided too many real bad guys, terrorists and such, were getting away with their misdeeds, and the courts didn't seem to be able to do much.'

'So how do you handle it?'

'Summary justice.'

Hasim frowned. 'And what's that?'

'Without the usual legal procedures, just like what's happened here. We take care of the rough stuff, and our friends who've just arrived handle what comes after. Those two corpses will be twelve pounds of grey ash in about two hours from now. They'll be cremated.'

'Is that legal?' Hasim asked.

'It is to Ferguson. Let's say it saves a lot of court time and leave it at that,' Billy told him, and held out his hand to the men approaching. 'Mr Teague, how are you?'

'Good, William,' Teague replied. 'Your uncle Harry is well, I trust?'

'He always is,' Billy said as Teague's people joined him with two stretchers, body bags, and cleaning materials. 'You've two down in the cabin. Terry Harker, a well-known villain in the East End, and Major Max Shelby, whom I believe you knew.'

Teague frowned. 'Yes, but there was not much left to recognize of the face of the man we cremated last night. Excuse me for a moment.'

He went below and was back instantly. 'This one *is* Major Max Shelby without a doubt. Your bullets, if they were yours, have wreaked most of their damage to the back of the skull. There's enough of the face for me to confirm his identity. So who was the doppelgänger we sent to the ovens last night?'

'I haven't the slightest idea.'

Hasim said, 'That black cab that he turned up

in is years old. I'm interested in cars, and a thing like that would carry its registration booklet on board, other stuff like insurance, and definitely an address. That was the law then.'

Teague actually smiled. 'Young man, I think you've got something here. We'll impound the vehicle, take it with us, and explore it thoroughly at the workshops. It may offer a solution to the mystery of what Max Shelby was up to in more ways than one.'

Two men with a body bag on a stretcher emerged from the *Arabella* behind them, followed by a second, and they moved quickly to the black van and loaded the stretchers inside. All four men returned at once with brushes and buckets.

'You've got half an hour to normalize things as much as possible, and then I want out of here.' They trooped below, he turned to speak to Billy and Hasim again, and a van moved onto the jetty and came towards them. 'I do believe that's our friends from Holland Park.'

Sara was at the wheel, Dillon beside her, getting out as she braked to a halt. 'Mr Teague, good to see you, and you, Hasim.'

'And good to see you, Mr Dillon. What a morning we've had,' Hasim said.

'Well, you can tell Major Roper all about it. He's in the back,' Sara told him, and switched on the hydraulic system that opened the rear door and lowered Roper in his wheelchair to the ground.

'What's been happening, Billy?' he demanded.

'It's complicated, but what you should know is the Master turned up here in the flesh, Max Shelby as I live and breathe, and Mr Teague will confirm that for you.'

Roper turned inquiringly to Teague, who said, 'It's true, I'm afraid, so who we cremated last night is a conundrum, especially as they had the same highly unusual blood group, but that could just have been by chance, Major.'

'A blood group found in only eight percent of the UK population? Hardly likely,' Roper said.

'So is winning millions on the National Lottery, but somebody does and frequently,' Billy said. 'Mr Teague is going to pursue enquiries that could give you some answers. You may tell Ferguson on my behalf that Terry Harker is dead, shot between the eyes by Max Shelby in a lively fracas here. Where is he, by the way?'

'Cocktail party at Downing Street to say goodbye to Cazalet and the French Foreign Minister,' Sara said. 'Boring stuff with a bunch of politicians.'

'Well, Hasim and I had an interesting time, which involved him being thrown down the cabin steps by Max, who shot me in the back twice, forgetting I was wearing the usual bulletproof vest recommended by MI5. I, of course, made sure of him, blasting four hollow-point cartridges into the back of his skull. So – I'm keeping in practice. I did kill someone today.'

Dillon's face stayed calm, but Sara looked troubled. Roper said, 'Ferguson will need to see you, Billy.'

'What for, another dose of the great and the good waiting graciously to thank the simple foot soldier who's got things right again? Well, I've had it. I need a rest from all that. I'm going to take it, and you can tell the great man I've no idea when I'll be back or if I ever will. Come on, Hasim, let's get out of this disgusting place.'

He was down the stone steps and into the inflatable and casting off by the time Hasim caught up with him and said, 'Where now?'

'Home, I suppose.' Billy Salter turned his face up to the rain, eyes wide open.

'Are you okay?' Hasim asked, troubled.

'Just allowing the rain to wash away my sins,' said Billy.

'And do you think that might help?'

'Not with the load I have to carry, but let's get moving, I've had enough of this place.'

As they roared away, Sara said, 'Does he mean it?'

'For now he does.' Roper shrugged. 'But he'll be back.'

'How can we be certain of that?' she asked.

'Because he has nowhere else to go,' Dillon told her. 'So let's get out of here before you ask me if that also applies to us.'